THE
MAGICIAN'S
WORKSHOP

Also by Christopher Hansen and J.R. Fehr
A Pirate's Guide t' th' Grammar of Story: A Creative Writing Curriculum
www.piratesguidestory.com

The Magician's Workshop, Volume Two
www.oceea.com

Also by J.R. Fehr
Skyblind
www.jrfehr.com

THE
MAGICIAN'S
WORKSHOP

VOLUME ONE

Christopher Hansen and J.R. Fehr

Wondertale

The Magician's Workshop, Volume One
Copyright © 2017 by Christopher R. Hansen and J.R. Fehr
MW logo copyright © 2016 by Christopher R. Hansen
Cover copyright © 2017 by Christopher R. Hansen

Published by Wondertale, California, USA
www.thewondertale.com
www.oceea.com

ISBN-10: 1-945353-01-5
ISBN-13: 978-1-945353-01-7

MW logo design by Sej Baur
Book design by Jennifer Hansen
Dedication page design by Everett Ranni
"Spiral Jetty" cover image by Greg Rakozy
Copy editing by Leigh Ann Robinson

Back cover quote attributions are as follows. Crimson: Namrata Ganti, *redpillows* (book review blog). Yellow: Anonymous Amazon Customer. Red: Charlie Mulligan, Jr. High Schoolteacher. Blue: Georgia, *Chill And Read Book Reviews*. Green: Mari, Goodreads Reviewer. Indigo: Richard Fehr, J.R. Fehr's dad. (He's biased, of course, but he's always wanted to be quoted on a book cover, so we decided to make that dream a reality.) Orange: Dii, *Tome Tender Book Blog*. Violet: Claire Lee, *A Thousand Lives* (blog). You may have noticed that Cyan wasn't quoted. This is because Cyan doesn't like to draw attention to itself. It is, nonetheless, responsible for the synopsis.

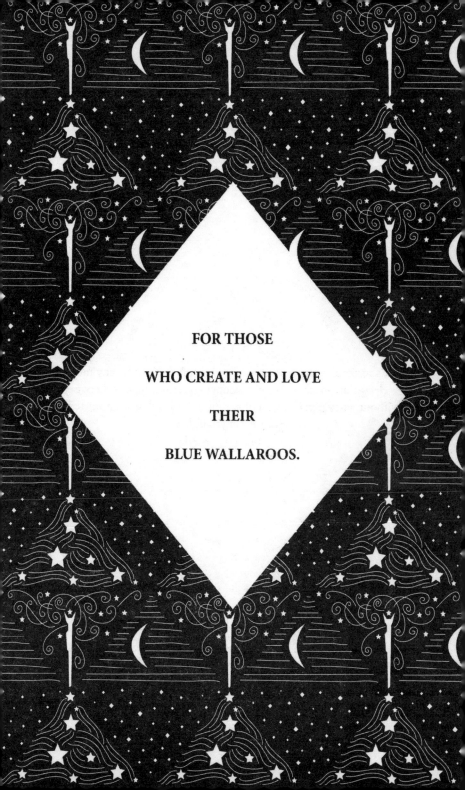

FOR THOSE

WHO CREATE AND LOVE

THEIR

BLUE WALLAROOS.

Table of Contents

The Islands of O'Ceea

First
Watch

Region 1

Cloudy Peaks

Four Kings

Region 2

Golden Vale

Swinging
Vines

Summer Breeze

The
Magician's
Workshop

Region 3

Crystal Lake

Sunny Rock

Region 4

Oak Falls

Region 5

The Former
Region 6

Welcome to O'Ceea

Hello and welcome to *The Magician's Workshop*!

When we first started dreaming about this story, we expected to write a tale that would fit snugly inside a single book. But the characters wow-dazzled us, and we found ourselves writing stacks of pages about them. It was great fun, and in the end we wound up with what we considered to be a fantastic problem: the story had become too long for one book!

We decided to solve this problem by dividing the story into a series of volumes. The individual books are labeled Volume One, Volume Two, and so on, to emphasize the fact that these are not stand alone stories. Instead, *The Magician's Workshop* is a single story told through the point of view of multiple main characters.

Think of it as one grand, epic tale, where the narrative merely takes a brief pause at the end of one volume before continuing on in the next.

You should also know that Volume One and Two are meant to be read together. We encourage you to read them both, one right after the other.

Now, on to the story!

-The Authors

The Magician's Call
~Layauna~

Projections have the power to alter reality for good or for evil.
—Author Unknown

"Layauna is-a Wind! Stop slouching by the window and come warm up by the fire," Mother shouted to her from the other side of the house.

"It's just a projection, Mom," Layauna replied. "It's not going to keep me warm."

"Young lady, that's not the point. This is a family day."

"Yeah, yeah," Layauna mumbled, "but I'm cold."

She pulled herself away from the window and shuffled into the projection room. Her mother and little brother, Sorgan, lay sprawled out next to the flickering fire that Sorgan had projected in the center of the room. Her grandfather was currently in the middle of a serious discussion with one of his servants a few feet away, so Layauna sat down next to her mother and said under her breath, "Why can't I just go out and play with my friends?"

"We've been through this already, Layauna."

"I like being outside."

"You'll get soaking wet. You just said you're cold."

"Aw, please," Layauna begged. "You know I don't mind real rain."

"No," her mother answered. "Today is special."

"Yeah! Grandfather's here!" Sorgan exclaimed loud enough for all to hear. "I never want to leave when Grandfather comes to visit."

Layauna gave her little brother a nasty glare and thought, *Come on, Sorgan. You hate this as much as I do.*

She liked her grandfather for the most part, but it was always difficult when he visited. Whenever he was around, her mom kept pushing "family time." She claimed it was a bonding experience for everyone, but Layauna saw right through her mom's tricks. It wasn't about bonding; it was about showing off.

"Most people would do almost anything to spend a single moment with our Grandfather," Sorgan continued. "Isn't that right, Mom?"

"That's exactly right," her mother answered. "All of us—including you, Layauna—should be exceptionally thankful each and every time he comes to see us."

Layauna looked over her shoulder and caught sight of her grandfather's knowing eye. *Oh, he heard that. Thanks a lot, Mom.*

Her grandfather concluded the conversation with his servant and sent the man out the front door and on his way. He then came over and sat down right beside Layauna. More now than before, she wanted to run outside.

"It's time for everyone to take their medicine," her mother said in a cheerful tone, then reached for a tray that contained a few pieces of namra. Layauna groaned inwardly. Namra was a disgusting violet root—coarse and hard to chew—that tasted like pure concentrated bitterness.

Sorgan snatched a piece and immediately began to wiggle his nose and scrunch his face to make what she assumed was some type of flavor projection. Why her brother insisted on making dumb faces in order to make projections was beyond her.

"Layauna, you too," Mother instructed as she passed the tray over.

"No, thank you."

"Don't start this again, you know it's good for you," Mother commanded. "Your grandfather has always . . ."

". . . eaten a root every day," Layauna said, finishing her mom's sentence, "and he was a great magician in the Workshop. I know."

Layauna glanced at her grandfather, Eyan is-a Bolt, the famous Yellow magician, formerly of the Third Magnitude. Even though he was now retired, he was still well-known throughout every single island on O'Ceea. Her brother was right when he said that most people would be in ecstasy to be this close to him. *Yet all I want to do is get away. What's wrong with me?*

She tried to look at his face, but couldn't bring herself to see the disappointed look in his eye that she knew must be there. *He knows I want to leave.* Instead, she set her focus on the collar that he wore around his neck.

The Yellow-infused piece of fabric was covered with the various markings that he had earned throughout his illustrious career. Although all of the credentials buttoned on it were important, it was the two pieces of platinum thread that really mattered. They were woven across the top and bottom of his collar and connected together in the center to form the symbol of the Magician's Workshop. This proclaimed to all who saw him that he had been one of the Eight: the most powerful, successful, famous, and influential—as well as richest—people in all the islands.

But to Layauna he was just her grandfather, and she wasn't so impressed. In fact, the sight of his priceless collar made her sad. It used to captivate her; she remembered how she had delighted in its swirling, exuberant light when she was a child. But looking at it now, she realized that his Yellow did not feel warm or comforting as it once had.

"Child," her grandfather said after a moment. "Namra roots are renowned for enhancing one's focus and control. A little something you could use more of, wouldn't you agree?"

"Yes, Grandfather." Layauna bit her lower lip. *But whenever I eat it I taste every bit of its disgustingness.* She wanted to explain herself, but she decided it would be best to keep her thoughts inside.

Everyone on the Island of the Oak Falls projected delicious flavors onto their namra root just before they ate it. Her brother usually made his taste like strawberries. She knew she should too. But the last time she had tried to project a delectable flavor onto her piece of the noxious root, the flavor that came out from her was even more revolting than that of the namra on its own. The taste of it had made her vomit.

The memory of what had happened that day came flooding back to her in an instant. She vividly recalled the horror of watching everything inside her stomach spew out all over their table at Nosy's, the fancy restaurant that they had always gone to on Ancestors Day to share a meal together. Even though she had spent the rest of the day crying and saying she was sorry, Grandfather never took them to that restaurant again. *That was our last family meal with all of us together. I ruined everything.*

She wanted to explain to her grandfather that, not long after this, she had decided to stop making flavor projections. She wanted to tell everyone that she had tasted every bitter bit of her daily dose of namra since then. But she didn't. *That happened ages ago, and everyone is still teasing me about it. I'm thirteen now! I deserve to be treated like a grown up.*

Instead of saying any of this, she asked, "Could you maybe place one of your flavor projections on my piece? I bet it would taste better than anything I could make."

While her flavor projections tasted vile, her grandfather's were incredible. Everyone knew Magician Eyan was a master of taste and smell. But, after he had retired from the Workshop, he rarely shared them with anyone. Layauna could only remember him creating something expressly for her three times in her entire life. One was a chocolate banana pudding for her tenth birthday party, another was an apple made to taste like he had drizzled it with pure caramel, and the third was a cup of water he had turned into a berry-flavored liquid that was so good it brought her to tears.

More than anything, she craved to taste one of his projected flavors on her piece of namra. *Imagine how yummy it would be then!*

But from the disapproving look on her grandfather's face, she knew before he spoke that he wouldn't do it for her. "No," he answered firmly.

Layauna lowered her head and stared at the floor.

She would have stayed like that, but the sudden sensation of a firm finger tapping her on the forehead forced her to look up. As she did, she caught the grim stare of her mother from across the fire.

"Don't you dare embarrass me in front of your grandfather any more than you already have," her mother projected her voice privately into Layauna's ears.

Father never forced me to eat it, she thought to herself. *But Father isn't here anymore.* Layauna knew this was a fight she could not win. She selected the smallest piece from the tray and disposed it into her mouth. As usual, the taste was foul.

"I made mine taste like blueberries this time!" Sorgan announced. Layauna knew he was itching for a compliment from their grandfather, but the old man remained silent.

"Nice." Layauna tried her best to sound polite while also trying not to gag from the taste of the root. *This is going to be a long day.*

"What do you think of my fire, Grandfather?" Sorgan asked.

Grandfather's eyes turned glassy for a moment as he said, "Very impressive."

Sorgan flashed his mischievous smile. "What about you, Layauna? Do you like it? Grandfather does."

"Uh—yeah, sure. It's fine, I guess," Layauna replied distantly.

"Oh really? So you don't think it's too . . . SCARY!?" All of a sudden, Sorgan lifted up his right eyebrow, wiggled his nose, and puckered his lips. The fire flared up and the flames took on the appearance of an open mouth with sharp fangs. The fire-face leapt out and snapped at Layauna with a loud hiss.

"Ahhhh!" She screamed and scrambled backwards away from the fire.

"Ha ha ha!" Sorgan bent over laughing.

"Sorgan!" their mother scolded. "That was not very polite! Normal fires only, please."

"Aw, but Mom!"

"Sorgan." Mother narrowed her eyes.

"Yes, ma'am," Sorgan said, and then he rubbed his face with his two hands, causing the fire to shrink back to its original form.

Now on the floor, Layauna struggled to slow her breathing as she dug her nails into the wooden floorboards.

"That was a pretty scary monster," Grandfather said after a moment. "You might have a knack for horror, my boy."

"You think?" Sorgan beamed.

"Oh yes," Grandfather agreed. "Look at how you scared your sister."

All eyes turned to her.

"That's easy." Sorgan shrugged. "She's a baby."

Layauna responded by creating the sound of a growling, wild beast and projected it into her brother's ears.

"Mom! She's doing it again!" Sorgan whimpered as he covered his ears with his hands. *Who's the baby now?!*

"Children! Enough!" their mother snapped.

Layauna pulled her knees up to her chest and hid her face. *I wonder if there are any other families as rotten as mine.*

"The Workshop has a serious need for magicians with a knack for horror," Grandfather continued his train of thought.

Grandfather was looking at Layauna when he spoke, but it was Sorgan who answered, "Do you think I could really become one?"

"You need to be a mage first. But, if you do have a Color, there is a good chance. Every Bolt has the potential to be a great magician," Grandfather affirmed.

But we're not Bolts.

"That's right," Mother agreed. "That's why we dedicate time every day to practice making projections. Hey, how about we all play the story game?"

"Really? With Grandfather?" Sorgan chirped.

Layauna groaned. The only thing she hated more than forced family time was playing the story game. "Could I go to my room, please? I don't feel very well."

"No," Mother chided, "this is a precious moment with your grandfather. It's every child's dream to create projections with a magician of the Third Magnitude. Who wants to begin?"

"I'll start," Grandfather announced. He stood up and paced around the room. "Once, long ago, in the Old World, there was a brave knight named Exander is-a Bolt." As he spoke, the image of a small knight materialized in the space above the fire. The knight wore gold armor with a violet lightning bolt on the front, and he held a long sword that shimmered with the light of Sorgan's fire. The knight was masterful in detail and looked in every way like a real person.

"My turn, my turn!" Sorgan jumped up. ". . . And the knight was going to a massive, dark tower!" He pushed his index finger into his nostril and dug around, causing a dark, spiraling tower to appear in front of the knight.

". . . Inside the tower," Mother added, "was a lonely but uncommonly beautiful princess."

A delicate little princess appeared in the window of the tower. Layauna rolled her eyes when she saw how much the grainy, ill-defined princess looked like her mother.

"Help! Help! I'm all alone!" the princess cried in a tiny voice.

The knight heard the cry, looked in the direction of the far-off tower, and grinned from ear to ear. All the eyes of the family turned to Layauna.

"Come on, it's your turn," Sorgan prodded.

"I don't want to play."

"You have to play, dear," her mother insisted. "Those are the rules."

"Please," Layauna pleaded, "I really don't want to . . . can't I just watch?"

Her mother gave that stern look again.

"Fine!" Layauna grumbled. *If Grandfather wasn't around, Mother wouldn't force us to do this! Why did he have to visit today?*

Layauna felt herself getting angry, so she shut her eyes and tried to relax. *It's okay. It's not a big deal. Just picture something nice that will make Mother and Grandfather happy.*

She imagined a horse, thinking the knight could use it to travel to the tower. She saw it in her mind: pure white, with a beautiful black mane. She imagined it prancing through the forest with elegance and grace, gentle enough for a child to ride.

But, sure enough, when she opened her eyes, what she saw was not a beautiful white horse. It was a black, two-headed hell-dog with patches of fiery red hair and sharp, cruel fangs.

Layauna gasped. *That came out of me?*

The hellish creature charged at the knight, growling and snapping, and the two projections began to battle each other.

"Oh!" Grandfather gave a yelp of genuine surprise. "I raised the . . . I mean, the knight raised the Sword of Justice and—" But before her grandfather could finish speaking, Layauna's hell-dog leapt through the air, caught the knight in its jaws, and bit his head off.

"Oh dear," her mother whispered, and the little princess in the tower began to glower at Layauna.

What did I just do? Layauna slid away from the fire-lit projections, but the hell-dog noticed and turned its vicious face toward her, licked its lips, and advanced on her, growing larger with each step. She spun away from the beast and began to cry when she saw it open its mouths and bare its sharp, bloody teeth.

Just ignore it, she told herself, *and it'll go away.* The hell-dog, which was now a full-sized beast, was only a few inches away from her. It put one mouth to her neck and the other to her face. Its chilling breath pierced her to the core.

It's not working. I have to leave! Layauna spun and sprinted through the long hallways and spacious rooms of her large house in a desperate attempt to get outside.

Because the monster that came out of her was only a projection, she knew it couldn't hurt her—at least not in any physical way. However, the fear she felt was real enough to cause her to run for her life, as if an actual beast with razor-sharp teeth and claws were chasing her.

Stupid projections! Stupid projections!

She burst through the enormous front door, crossed their luxurious green lawn, and then rushed into the neighboring forest. The blinding rain drenched her as she ran—fast and hard—but she wasn't fast enough. The hell-dog was right on her heels.

"Get away!" she screamed at the top of her lungs.

"Disappear!" she commanded as she waved her arms. As stupid as her brother looked when he scrunched up his face to make a projection, at least his projections stopped when his face went back to normal.

"Enough! No more!" she ordered and clapped her hands. But the hell-dog didn't vanish. Instead, a barrage of tiny indigo bats shot out of Layauna and swarmed it. The two heads of the monster snapped at the bats as they swooped in.

She hadn't intended to do that, and the shock of it caused her to lose her balance as she suddenly tripped on a root and fell face first into the brush. She rolled over onto her back and looked up into the sky as more and more bats poured out of her, filling the forest. *What's happening?!*

Layauna scrambled to her feet and swatted at the bats, but they kept streaming out of her body. So she took flight once again, weaving through the trees until at last she stumbled out of the forest and onto the beach.

"Be defeated!" she screamed at her horrible projections, but still they didn't disappear. Instead, a second hell-dog appeared next to her. This one faced the first hell-dog, and the two growled and bared their teeth at each other. Then, without warning, they leapt up and engaged in a vicious battle while the swarm of bats swooped down and attacked them both.

"Get out of me! GET OUT!" The more she screamed, the more bats, hell-dogs, and other monstrous creatures burrowed their way out of her skin to join in the battle.

"No!" she cried as she dropped to her knees and covered her head with her arms. She could no longer see the monsters, but she could hear them hissing, snarling, and roaring as they devoured one another in a bloody, chaotic battle.

Creating a scary projection when she meant to create something normal was not a new experience for Layauna, but these were different; they were more ruthless, brutal, and vicious than anything she'd projected before.

It's getting worse, she realized, and she screamed "No more, no more!" over and over until her voice gave out. "Please, no more," she wheezed one final time.

And then, with no air left, she collapsed on the sand.

*　　　*　　　*

Layauna awoke to the soothing sound of ocean waves. It took her a moment to remember how she'd ended up on the beach, but as soon as she did, she jolted up and jerked her head in every direction, searching for the monsters.

They're gone. She relaxed when she realized it was true. The beach was empty, and there was no lingering evidence of the horrific attack.

"Well done! That was quite the spectacle!" Grandfather's voice took her by surprise.

Where'd he come from? Layauna spun around and spotted him leaning on a tree while chewing a piece of namra.

"Don't be afraid. I dissolved the monsters for you."

"Thanks," she breathed with a sigh of relief. "I don't . . . I have no idea where they all came from."

"From you," he said in a matter-of-fact way. "Come over here. I want you to taste something."

Layauna rose up from the sand and took a few apprehensive steps toward him. As she approached, he held out a piece of fresh namra. *Huh?* She was more confused than disgusted at the sight of the root. "I ate some earlier," she said.

"Yes, I know, but I want you to taste a portion of mine."

Her view of the namra root completely flipped. Certain it would have one of her grandfather's flavors projected onto it, she wanted to taste it more than anything in all of O'Ceea. "Really? Are you sure? I know you don't share your flavor projections much anymore."

"I'm sure. Taste it."

Layauna took it eagerly and plopped it into her mouth, expecting the most delectable sensations. Instead, it was far more bitter than a normal piece of namra—the worst she'd ever tasted in her entire life. The urge to gag was strong but she forced herself to hold it in. She turned her horrified eyes to her smiling grandfather and felt the weight of his betrayal. *Why would he lie to me?*

"Keep it in, if you can," her grandfather commanded.

"But . . ."

"I know it's horrible," he said.

Layauna didn't understand. "Why do you look so happy?"

"I'm chewing on the same root you are. I buy my namra from a farmer who grows it in a way that intensifies the natural bitterness. I keep a piece in my mouth most of the day."

That's disgusting! "Why would you do that?"

"Because I've discovered that bitterness makes a person's projections more powerful. And you, sweet granddaughter of mine, have powerful projections."

"I do?"

"Yes. Your two-headed hell-dog tore the head off my knight. I didn't put a lot of Power into it, but your projection easily overpowered mine."

"Really?" Layauna could hardly believe what he was saying. No one had ever told her anything like this before.

"You saw it for yourself. You are far more powerful than you realize. It was quite a challenge for even me to extinguish all the dogs and bats that came out of you," Grandfather continued. "That's why you couldn't dissolve them yourself."

Layauna wrapped her arms around herself, grabbed her shoulders tight, and said, "I hate them."

"No, no. They'll be your glory. Your projections are just more powerful than you are right now; that's common for those who have been eating pure namra root for a long time. You haven't been projecting flavors to mask the bitterness, have you?"

He knows? She felt her heart skip a beat. "I . . . no . . . I haven't. Not since that horrible meal four years ago when . . ." She couldn't bring herself to say the last part out loud.

She didn't need to finish the sentence, though. The look of compassion on her grandfather's face indicated that he knew exactly what she was thinking.

"You know what bitterness is, don't you?" he asked.

His question was confusing, but she sensed he was speaking about something more than namra root. *Father left the week after that meal.* "Um, I guess so. I don't understand . . . what's happening? Why do all of these monsters come out of me?"

"Dearling, you have more Power than anyone on this island. In fact, you are more powerful than some magicians of the First Magnitude."

"I am?"

"Yes, and you are still a child. Your skill with Power—and Kingdom and Glory—will grow stronger with time and training. You can swallow the namra root now," he said, and she happily obeyed. "Now, I think it is time for us to go."

Oh. It is getting late, she realized all at once. *We should get home. I'm certain Mom's flooded with worry about us being out in the rain all this time.* She shivered as she felt the dampness on her skin and hair. "Let's hurry back. I'm cold," she said as she stepped onto the path that led to her house.

"No, this way." Grandfather motioned to the path that led to Aesal, the island's port town. "There is much to do if we're going to have you ready."

"Ready?" asked Layauna as she followed her grandfather. "Ready for what?"

"For this," he said as he took a guava out of his pocket. He clicked his tongue back and forth and handed it to her. "Try this. It will clear any lingering bitterness from your mouth."

She was hesitant to try something again, but she trusted that her grandfather wouldn't trick her a second time. She bit into the fruit.

The guava was the most luscious thing she had ever tasted and, true to Grandfather's word, it cleared all the bitterness of the namra root from her mouth. *This is so good!* She ate it slowly, careful to enjoy every bite, allowing the sweet juices to drip over her lips and linger on her tongue.

By the time they arrived at the port where her grandfather's luxury yacht was docked, she'd consumed every last bit of the fruit. Layauna saw the boat at a distance as they approached the port and noticed that her grandfather's many servants were relaxing on board. As soon as they saw him approach, however, the boat became a flurry of activity.

"Get ready to set sail," he ordered when they arrived.

"Yes, Magician Eyan," a servant replied.

I wonder why he's in such a hurry to leave. Mother will be disappointed.

"Bring me a voice cube," Grandfather shouted to another servant.

The servant arrived with a little yellow cube. Layauna watched with wonder as her grandfather held the cube to his mouth and projected his voice into it. "My daughter, do not panic. Layauna is with me, and all is well," he said. He handed the cube back to his servant. "Make sure my daughter gets this."

"Of course," the servant said with a bow, and he took off running.

"That guava was the best thing I've ever tasted," Layauna reiterated, hoping he would give her another one.

"It's the best-tasting projection I've ever discovered. But, believe it or not, there's something else I've tasted that's far better than even that."

Layauna's eyes grew wide with wonder. "I can't imagine anything tasting better."

"You won't have to imagine it. Now that I know how much Power you have, I'm certain you will taste it," Grandfather said as he stepped onto the boat. "But it's not something you taste with your tongue; it's what you taste when you become a magician and are allowed to sit under the Master in the Workshop."

"The Workshop? I don't understand."

"Come. You have a lot to learn before you will be able to control your projections. It's time we go." Grandfather held out his hand for Layauna to join him on his yacht.

"Wait—you want me to go with you? Now? What about Mother? And Sorgan? They'll wonder where we went."

"You don't have to concern yourself about your mother anymore. You have a great life ahead of you—you're a Bolt. There is Color in you, I know it. The life that awaits you is far better than anything in your wildest dreams."

"I still don't understand."

Grandfather reached out, grasped Layauna's hand, and tugged her up onto the boat. "Don't you see, Dearling? You're about to become an extraordinary magician."

The Finger of Fire
~Kai~

Rain fell and filled O'Ceea 'til islands were all that remained of a land which once was whole.

> —Mage Palacious is-a Star, from the poem *The World Beneath the Sea*

Kai is-a Shield woke that morning full of energy. *This is going to be a great day!* He knew it. School was over, and he was on vacation. He had graduated from Cape Bennet's Preparatory School three weeks ago, and unless he had a Color, he would never be forced to take classes again.

"Mom, I'm going out for a swim in the ocean," Kai announced after finishing his breakfast of eggs, rice, and fish.

"This early?" his grandmother interjected. "You are going to freeze. You should stay home, or go to a playground and train. The Festival is only four weeks away."

"Don't worry, I'll be training all afternoon," Kai promised. "Bye."

"Bye, love! Have a delightful swim," his mother said as he ran out the door.

Kai sprinted the entire way to the beach from his home in Brightside. It wasn't far, but he had worked up a good amount of heat by the time he got there, so it felt refreshing when he jumped into the lagoon. The water wasn't truly any colder in the morning, although it often felt like it was. It was a pleasant temperature on the surface and only got cold when Kai swam down into the ocean depths.

Kai swam across the lagoon with ease. In a few moments, he was out past the barrier reef and had cast himself into the waves of the open sea. He loved the feeling of getting sucked into a cresting wave, being lifted up-up-up, breaking over the top, and then falling back down on the other side.

Pretending he was a fish, he kicked his feet hard and dove down as deep as he could. He didn't get far before the cold and lack of air forced him to return. *Even if seabreath were a real thing, you'd certainly freeze to death before you could ever reach the ancient cities of the Old World.*

Kai lost track of time while he was diving down and being tossed about by the surf. When he returned to the shore, he felt refreshed. He sprawled himself out on the sandy beach and stared up into the bright blue sky to check the time. *It's only the middle of Red watch?* Kai was still bursting with emotional energy. *What am I going to do until Yellow?* He decided he might as well run a couple errands for his mother, so he got up and jogged over to Waterton.

As soon as he got to town, he spotted Talia crossing the street with her dad and older sister. Talia smiled when she saw him, but her older sister pretended not to notice him and hurried past to look through the window of a nearby clothing shop. "Hey, Tal," Kai sent a projection of his voice into his best friend's ear so she alone could hear him. "We're still on to visit Master Gnarles, right?"

"Yeah, it's going to be so much fun," Talia projected her voice back. "I've been working on something. I can't wait to show it to you. See you at the top of Yellow."

Kai was happier than he'd been in days. After he picked up a vial of Eucalyptus oil for his grandmother and checked when the new mop and cleaning supplies his mother had ordered would arrive, he spent the rest of the Red and Orange watches going to a few of his favorite places. He visited his father's shrine, then climbed up to the top of the communication tower, where he said hello to the timekeeper and held his hands out in the wind as he took in the view of the neighboring islands. He next walked along the Seastone Cliffs and then climbed up to the top of Kanaka Falls, where he drank his fill of the fresh river water. Finally, the Yellow watch was near, and Kai made his way to the spot where he was going to meet his friends.

Kai sat down on a large tree root, opened his hand, and examined the solitary finger of fire that burned in his palm. All this time, it had accompanied him. Neither the ocean waves nor the strong winds on the tower had managed to affect it in any way. The fresh river water left it unchanged. No matter what he did, the fire would not go out—it followed him everywhere he went. He longed to find a way to douse it out forever, but much to his dismay, he had no control over the flame that was cast from his unconscious mind.

Today, like most days, it was just a single tongue of fire, easily concealed by clenching his hand into a fist. While it caused him no physical pain, the stigma of it was a significant source of misery for him, and so—every once in a while—one of his friends would attempt to put it out for him. *I've got the best friends in all of the islands.* Kai stared deeply into the little flame that danced inside his hand. *I wonder if I'll ever be able to put it out.*

Fire had always fascinated him when he was a little kid, but he'd never expected something like this to happen to him. The flickering flame had been with him for so long, he felt like it was now a part of him; it was hard for him to believe that there was ever a time when he hadn't had it.

Where are they? It was now the top of the Yellow watch, but he was still all alone. Was he in the wrong spot? *No, Talia confirmed it.*

We were all going to meet at Master Gnarles. That was their name for the giant, ancient fig tree that grew far off the main trail in a remote part of the forest upon whose roots he now sat.

They can't all be late. He glanced up at the sun peeking through the canopy of leaves. *I bet they're already here, hiding.* Shortly after that thought, he felt something crawl across his foot.

Pretending not to notice, he gave a casual glance to the single ant that was now weaving its way up his leg. As soon as he saw it, he knew his wait was over. But, instead of getting up, he stayed right where he was: sitting in the dirt with his back against the trunk of Master Gnarles.

Two more ants crawled onto his other leg. Their little feet tickled his skin—*a little too much. This is definitely Snap*—but he resolved to pay the ants no mind and worked to keep his attention focused on the fire in his hand.

Then the rain came.

Big, wet drops the size of acorns fell and splattered on him—and on him alone. They fell from a miniature rain cloud that grew larger above him and spilled out water as if from a bottomless well.

Plop, plop, plop, plop, plop, plop, plop, plop.

As he had with the ants, Kai pretended not to notice.

Although the rain didn't bother him, it was a big problem for the three delicate ants zigzagging over his legs. They dodged the drops as best they could until a large plop of water fell on one of them, crushing it and washing it away. It was only a matter of time before other raindrops bombed the remaining two out of existence.

Snap's not going to like that, Kai mused as the rain's intensity and volume increased until it was as if a hose was showering down on him. It quickly destroyed the simple projected clothing that covered him, leaving him in nothing but his material shorts and shirt, commonly called threadbare.

This made Kai smile. *They really are the best friends anyone could have. But, it's not going to work.* He stood up and flung his flame hand out toward the rain cloud above him. He hoped the rain would be powerful enough to extinguish his fire, but nothing happened.

Then the rain became a waterfall.

Still nothing; despite its Power, the rain lacked the ability of even the gentlest breeze to alter the pattern of the flickering flame.

This isn't helping. Kai had had enough. He wobbled his hand back and forth to dissolve the rain cloud above him. But, instead of disappearing, the cloud poured an even wider flood of water down on him.

Huh. There's a lot of Power in this cloud. It can't be Talia . . . Weston must be here.

Kai wasn't going to let it get the best of him, so he squeezed his eyes shut and with all the determination he could muster he frantically shook his whole body about while blowing up at the cloud.

That didn't work either.

Oh great, Kai sighed. *I can't even blow it away from me. I bet they're loving this.*

But—where are they? Kai looked around the forest; his friends weren't anywhere in sight. *They must be projecting this at far range. I'm impressed. Snap's getting better.*

"Hey, where are you?" he called out.

No response.

Well, I might as well give them a good laugh.

He began to cower under the torrent of water, as if it were drowning him. He fell to the ground and flapped about like a fish. Then he sat up and began smacking his hand against his body, as if he were trying to smother the fire. He slapped his hand against his head, again and again. Finally, he put it up to his mouth and stuck out his tongue so that the flames appeared to be burning it. Play acting, he shouted and leapt about as if he were in excruciating pain.

And then he stopped, held his breath, and listened for the muffled laughter he sought. *Come on, that was funny.*

Nothing.

All right. I guess not.

Then the water stopped. In an instant, the cloud disappeared. Kai searched the forest for any signs of his friends.

Where are they?

Then a sparkle caught his attention. Something was moving—there!—in front of him. Light. A glistening infinity tree seed spinning in the air. It was a seed pod propeller, twirling round and round as it floated with grace to the ground.

Kai watched with quiet reverence as a gust of wind caught the spinning seed and flung it upward into the sky. When it stopped ascending, it hung in the air, whirling right in front of his face, oblivious to the laws of gravity.

As he watched, everything else in the islands disappeared for Kai. He forgot who he was, about the fire in his hand, about his friends watching, and even about their secret meeting place in the forest. The only thing that existed in that moment was this solitary whirligig. It was as if Tav himself had come down from the heavens and halted everything in the universe in order to focus all of Kai's attention on this one single object spinning in space.

He wanted the infinity tree seed to stay aloft forever. He would be content to live the rest of his life standing in this one spot, watching what could only be a miracle.

But then, all of a sudden, the wind changed. The whirligig gyrated, pivoted away, and took its leave. It spiraled over to the ground a few feet away, just close enough for Kai to reach it with his outstretched hand.

You could catch it. You could prevent it from falling. While most of him wanted to, he chose to listen and obey a different, deeper part of him that told him to leave the seed alone.

And so he stood still and allowed it to float by him.

In a moment, he understood that he'd made the right choice. *Seeds were not meant for the air. The soil is their home, and to be buried is their highest calling.* He watched it land in a sunny, open spot on the forest floor. *A good place for a new tree to grow.*

It was then that he realized he was no longer alone; his friends—Talia, Snap, Weston, and Luge—had snuck up and now stood with him.

Snap, as usual, was the one who brought him back to reality. She thrust out her arms and tried to push him over with a solid shove projection.

The sensation of a forceful push against his skin startled Kai. He stumbled, tripped over a root, and fell onto his back in the foliage.

"Oh, hey guys," he said.

"You're such a bloomer," Snap said, and they all laughed.

"Yeah," Luge agreed, "you totally dissolved into the Glory of Talia's projection."

Talia's projection? The whirligig wasn't real? Kai felt the daze wear off. "That was you?"

Talia nodded.

"Really? I felt sure it was real," Kai said.

"Unlike those raindrops," Snap interjected before Talia could respond.

"Hey, I was just trying to put out Kai's hand fire," Weston said.

"And waterbomb my poor, innocent ants in the process!"

"What can I say? They were unfortunate casualties of war."

"Weston, nice to see you. But are you sure it's worth the risk?" Kai asked with genuine concern.

"Hey, bud, Talia's been hanging out with you for years and look how talented she's become. I think I'll be fine."

"You know that's not what I meant," Kai said.

"Don't worry," Weston insisted. "No one saw me head out here. I'll be fine."

"Think again, ant-killer!" Snap twisted her upper body to the left, sprung it back in one quick motion, and sent out a projection of green goo that splattered him in the chest, followed by:

Orange—splat.

Blue—splat.

Yellow—splat.

"Didn't your mommy ever teach you to respect other people's projections?" She continued pelting him with more bright-colored goo bombs. Violet, red, indigo, and cyan. Splat, splat, splat, and splat. "Oooh, can you feel the love?"

Weston looked down at his color-stained shirt and a mischievous expression flashed across his face. "I guess your daddy never warned you about what happens when someone projects goo onto another person without their permission?"

Kai watched with delight as Weston ran the fingers of his left hand through his messy black hair while stroking his chin with his right. Immediately, a little slimy green frog appeared inside of Snap's ear.

"Aaagh," Snap squealed as she clawed at her ear to try to get the projected frog out.

"Oooh, yeah, now I'm feeling the love," Weston grinned as the frog croaked repeatedly.

Kai and Talia couldn't stop laughing as Snap—who hated little slimy frogs of every color—tried her best to dissolve it. But

Weston's projection was strong, and she lacked the necessary Power to remove it quickly.

Weston, now on a roll, began pulling on his right earlobe. Suddenly, all the copper-colored curly hair on Luge's head disappeared. A bottle appeared in his mouth, and his pleated trouser shorts were transformed into a kind of diaper. Weston blinked his eyes in quick succession, and projected tears flowed down Luge's cheeks.

"Ah!" Luge exclaimed, "What are you doing? Stop it!"

"Aw, Snap, you made the baby cry," Weston said.

"Oh, just wait! I may not be a mage, but I can pull Color out of me," Snap said as she sent a crimson-colored goo bomb at Weston.

"Buds, wait. Hold on," Luge said. "My mom just bought me that outfit."

"That was pretty obvious; it kind of made you look like a girl," Talia said. "The baby outfit is a big improvement."

Kai smiled in agreement; everyone knew that Luge's mom always bought him outfits from Ethon is-a Rose, a vivacious tailor who had a tendency to project clothes that were too tight and glittery.

"Don't worry, Budski," Weston said. "If you really want, I bet Kai can reproject your girly clothes for you later."

"No way. They're always worse than the ones I had before."

"So?"

"My mom notices and figures out I've been playing with Kai."

"Aw, it's not like she's putting any pressure on you to have a Color and become a magician," Weston said.

"And because of my help, no one will confuse you with Talia's sister," Kai teased. He turned his attention to Weston. "But you know, only degenerates make alterations to another person's clothing projections without their permission."

Before Weston could do anything, Kai jumped up and down two times and mumbled a few words under his breath; Weston's color-stained clothes instantly transformed into a pink tutu sparkling with iridescent jewels.

"Hey!" Weston exclaimed when he saw what Kai had done. The tutu only lasted a few heartbeats. Weston quickly waved his hand and it vanished, leaving him standing in nothing but his threadbare shorts and shirt. "Degenerates will be punished," Weston growled as he turned and started to chase Kai, who weaved around trees and jumped over logs to keep away.

Although they were the same age, Weston was bigger, taller, and stronger, so Kai knew it was in his best interest to avoid being tackled.

Snap delighted in this turn of events. "Wow, Weston," she called as she flung her arm at him. "Your threadbare is so fashionable!" Instead of another colorful goo bomb, a sequined sparkle quote appeared on his shirt, which read: 'Just a Bloomer Changing O'Ceea One Rhinestone at a Time.'

Kai kept himself a few feet ahead of Weston and dodged him while hooting and hollering at the top of his lungs. This was the life he loved. He could imagine no better way to spend his day. *I hope these moments never end.*

As he scrambled up onto the trunk of a giant fallen tree, Kai noticed Talia sneak away and duck behind a large bush. He could tell by the way she was moving that she was crafting some kind of projection. *This one's taking her a long time,* Kai thought as he and the others played.

"Hey, what masterpiece you workin' on?" Kai yelled at her.

"Be patient," she called back. "It's something new I've been practicing."

Yes! This one is going to be great. He could feel it.

Although she didn't have the same Power abilities that Weston had, Talia had a reputation for making projections with outstanding Glory. People said her projections were the best expressions of Glory the Island of the Four Kings had seen in a hundred years. That wasn't true, but her projections always moved Kai, who delighted in whatever came from her loving hands.

He had to find out what she was up to, but first, he needed to ditch Weston. "Hey, bud, looks like Snap tagged your outfit." Kai pointed to the glittery words that sparkled on Weston's body.

"What?" Weston stopped chasing him and looked at his threadbare for the first time. "Ah, Snap!" Weston said before he wiped the sparkly quote away with a wave of his hand. But, as soon as he did, Snap flung her arm out as if she were throwing a ball and plastered him with another quote: 'You can't buy Contentment, but you can buy Bling, which is the same thing.'

"Stop that!" Weston exclaimed as he wiped that quote away too, only to find that Snap had projected another on him. And another.

'I was ready to take on Evil when I saw something Sparkle.'

'Another Day, Another Opportunity to Glitter.'

Weston—who was now wiping away the projected quotes as fast as Snap was throwing them—turned his eyes on her and said with a huge smile, "I'm starting to feel really happy about coming here today."

"Oh, are you!" Snap exclaimed as she plastered his entire body with dozens of colorful sequined quotes. Weston gave up erasing them and turned to chase her instead.

"Yeah, if I stayed home I'm sure I would have croaked of boredom," he said as he projected a dark green rain cloud over her. Snap looked up just in time to see the cloud open and an army of frogs pour down onto her.

Snap let out a squeal and started to run, but, wherever she went, the cloud followed, showering her with frogs. They splatted against her head and shoulders and slid down her back, leaving a trail of gooey green slime behind.

"Oh, you'll pay for this!" she shouted as Weston burst out laughing.

Now that Weston's and Snap's attention was diverted—and Luge was following after them in his diaper—Kai darted over to the bush where Talia was hiding.

"Hey, no peeking," she said as soon as she saw him.

Kai ignored her and kept approaching until he stood right behind her.

"Come on, I mean it." Talia turned around and shooed him away.

But it was too late; Kai got the glance he coveted. She'd created a projection of a small man who marched along the forest floor, wearing a golden crown on his head. *Talia, you sly, clever girl. This is going to be fun.*

The Rebirth of King King

~Kai~

There once was a King named Bilmore,
Who wanted to be big so to build more.
His size began to change
And things got very strange
His transformation caused quite an uproar.

> —Master Leory is-a Wee, from the song *The King who was King King*

"Hey Kai," Luge said, "this baby outfit's gotten old, don't ya think?"

"Absolutely." Kai turned to face his diaper-clad friend. "Whatdaya want to be now?"

"I don't know. How about Devos Rektor?"

Ah, the Lord of Chaos. Good choice.

Devos Rektor was a popular villain from the famous Grand Projections known as *The Epics of the Cursed*. As the self-proclaimed Lord of Chaos, he both terrified and delighted audiences.

Projecting this outfit was not easily done. Devos wore an iconic suit of armor that was incredibly difficult to replicate. Kai was pretty sure he would botch the job and only manage to project some clunky Devos-like armor on Luge. Besides, after seeing what Talia was working on, he had something much more fun in mind.

"Perfect. Do you want to look like Devos when he was old or young?"

"Old, when he's decrepitly evil."

"You got it!" Kai threw out his hands toward Luge and grunted twice like a wild beast. The baby outfit faded and was replaced by a projection that made him look like a golden banana.

"Bud. Seriously? I asked to be the Lord of Chaos, not some stupid fruit." Luge paused when the scent of banana tickled his nose. "Aw, did you have to project such a strong smell on it?"

"You've always loved to be the center of attention, Luge."

"Actually, I don't think I do."

"No, honestly. Bananas like you love to be the center of attention. You'll thank me soon enough."

"Thanks," Luge said. "Is that soon enough?"

"Buds alive! That banana's high spun!" Weston said. "Where'd you learn how to do that?"

"Forecastle's friend Magpie taught me. We spent the whole afternoon yesterday turning Forecastle's family into fruits. It was hilarious."

Just then, Talia leapt out of hiding and said, "Ok, my King's ready."

Behind her was a creature that looked part man, part gorilla, and it was growing larger and more gorilla-like with every heartbeat. Talia swung her arms around and around in big circles until it towered thirty feet above them.

"Is that supposed to be a gorilla?" Luge asked.

Agitated, the creature turned back and forth on all fours. It wanted to run free, but it could not move from the spot where Talia had created it, as if it were locked inside some invisible cage.

"Gorillas like bananas," Snap said. "Gorillas really like Luge-like bananas."

"Oh dear," Luge said. "I'm glad you locked it up."

Come on buds, that's not just any gorilla. That's King King!

Unlike *The Epics of the Cursed*, the story of King King was considered one of the worst Grand Projections ever to come out of the Workshop. It aspired to be a horrifying story about a king from the Old World who lost his soul to vain ambition and was transformed into an enormous, terrorizing gorilla. Unfortunately, no one found King King—the king or the gorilla—scary at all. The story had been first conducted a year ago, and it quickly became the subject of many jokes.

But what Talia had just created was different; although it looked like a clunky, amateur re-creation of King King, there was something about it that commanded authority. Even though it was immaterial, it radiated the dreadful feeling that it could do real harm.

"Whoa, that's got mega levels of Glory, Tal," Snap said.

"Yeah, impressive. You're really hitting it today," Weston agreed.

Impressive? Are you kidding me? That's way more than impressive; it's unbelievable! She just made King King all by herself! And it's going to destroy us all! With a crazy look in his eyes, Kai started to run around in circles while bellowing, "Aaaaaaaagh!"

No one else did anything.

Kai stopped and looked at his friends in a way that communicated: *Come on buds, play along with me!* He then screamed, "It's King King, the kiiiiiller goriiiiiiiilla!" while jumping around. He then sent a projected command to the gorilla that caused it to stand upright and let out a terrible roar. It sent a shock wave through them all.

At this, the others finally understood and jumped into the fun.

Kai, satisfied with his contribution to the projection, smiled and returned to running around and wailing like it was the end of the islands.

"King King can't be stopped, O'Ceea is doomed!" Talia shouted a line from the Grand Projection as she flung herself around like a decapitated chicken.

"Run for the hills! The Old World king has invaded our island. Stand firm and fight!" Snap cried out another line.

Weston laughed at the absurdity of the line and shouted, "Run away! Stand firm!"

"Hurry everyone! Run firm and stand away!" Talia hollered. "The monster has been unleashed!" At the moment she said 'unleashed,' she clapped her hands and dissolved the invisible cage that had imprisoned the gorilla.

The massive monster burst out.

"Noooo, it broke its chains!" Luge shrieked another line. He tried to be serious, but he couldn't hold back his laughter.

Then King King spotted him. It took two leaps and landed right next to Luge.

Whoa!

Talia's King King was terrifying, and having it so close caused Luge to shriek—for real. Kai also felt the wave of fear that rippled out from the gorilla; although it was a projection, and couldn't physically harm anything, it sure felt like it could.

She added a terror sensation. Way to go, Tal!

Luge hurtled his banana-clad self behind a tree, placing it between himself and King King.

"Doomed. We're all doomed," Snap said. "If you're a banana, that is."

"Luge!" Weston yelled as loud as he could.

"What?" Luge trembled.

"You're a banana," Kai said.

"And a killer gorilla is gunna peel ya," Weston said.

"So—RUN!" they all yelled.

Luge did. He ran through the forest with King King never

more than a few paces behind him. Surging with adrenaline—and filled with glee—Kai and the others chased after them.

Snap threw one projected projectile after another: boulders, stumps, tree trunks, and branches. When these projections hit the beast, King King swatted them away, just like in the Grand Projection. Snap cried, "Noooooo, can nothing stop it?"

Weston, in the best adult voice he could muster, said, "Hello, my Queen, do you know why your husband isn't in court today?"

"Well, I have to admit"—Weston now raised his voice to sound female—"and this is a bit embarrassing, but I think he might have eaten a poisoned fruit and gone a bit . . . how shall I put it? Moldy. Do you perchance know where he is?"

Switching back to his own voice, he answered, "Why yes, I believe I do. Because he's flippin' trying to eat my best friend!"

"Maybe King King's just been misunderstood," Snap suggested. "Maybe, she just needs to see herself as beautiful."

"She?" Talia asked.

"Of course. Why do big scary monsters always have to be men?" Snap said.

"Uh," Weston stammered, "because King Bilmore was a man."

"Well, ours could be a woman. Maybe it was Queen Bilma who turned herself into a monster," Snap suggested, and she began to project objects onto the gorilla. With a flick of her wrist, a pair of pearl earrings appeared.

Flick, flick, flick. King King had a new stylish haircut, wore lipstick, and donned a sunny summer sundress.

"Maybe if she thought she was beautiful, she wouldn't be so angry," Snap said.

Nope. Nothing changed. The gorilla kept charging after the banana.

"Humm . . ." Snap reconsidered. ". . . or maybe she's just a fire-breathing demon straight from the whirlpools of chaos."

Fire-breathing, huh? Kai got an idea. He made eye contact with Talia and said, "Fire?"

She didn't have to speak her answer; her smile said it all. But then the expression on her face changed. "Wait," she said, "you know how you are with fire."

"I can handle it," he answered. In one explosive motion, Kai thrust both arms out wide, tilted his head, and arched his back.

Whoosh! The gorilla lit up. King King was now engulfed in a coat of blazing fur.

"Buds alive!" Weston shouted with a huge grin on his face as the beast still continued to pursue the oh-so-desirable banana-clad Luge.

"Uh, buds," Luge said, "when is it okay for me to start actually freaking out?"

"It's just a projection, Buddy," Weston laughed.

"Then why am I so terrified?"

"Because Talia made it, you moldbrain," Snap answered.

"I wanted to be the Lord of Chaos," Luge reminded them, "not be chased by him."

So that's it, Kai realized. *Talia put the essence of Devos Rektor into the gorilla. No wonder it's so terrifying! Good work, Tal. You're going to fill your globe with gold chips in four weeks.*

"Wimp," Snap teased.

"I'll accept that," Luge responded, "and now that we've established I'm a wimp, I'd like to make the wimpy request for someone else to take my place."

"Don't worry," Kai said as he sprinted ahead of the others. "I'm on it!"

In order to make his way forward to Luge, Kai needed to pass through the fire gorilla. Normally, something like this wouldn't be a big deal. Kai was real and King King was a projection; it couldn't block him, and he could move through it like stepping through a ray of sunlight. But, as soon as Kai entered Talia's projection, he felt a wave of terror wash over him.

It made him feel vulnerable, exposed, and frail, as if he were standing at the foot of a force so big and powerful that it could easily crush him without a second thought. "Woo hoo!" he shouted at the top of his lungs. *This is amazing!* Kai turned around and started to run backward as he shouted, "Unbelievable job, Tal! You totally captured the horror of Devos Rektor."

Smiling in the face of danger, he turned back and began running even harder than before. He emerged from the projection and in a flash was up alongside Luge. "I'll take the heat from here, buddy boy," he said. Kai made a few motions with his hands, grunted twice, and the banana outfit transferred from Luge onto him.

"You're so Orange," Luge said as he stopped to catch his breath.

Kai made a hard right turn. The blazing gorilla followed after him and away from Luge. The intense feeling of terror that struck him when he passed through the projection had faded some, but it was still present. It radiated out of King King, and the closer the beast got to Kai, the stronger he felt it.

People spend bags of gryns going to Grand Projections hoping they'll experience stuff like this. And here we are doing it ourselves— here, on our own home island. I don't want these days to ever end.

The boy weaved in and out of the trees in an attempt to confuse the beast. King King acted like the trees were real obstacles and tried to move around them.

The Island of the Four Kings still had several stands of ancient forest. Giant canopies of leaves covered the friends' actions like bandages on a wound. Ferns blanketed the forest floor, broken up by an occasional cluster of golden dewdrop or honeysuckle. Young trees fought for a sliver of sunlight. It was the perfect place to be chased by a terrible monster. Using a dodge-and-evade tactic, Kai managed to stay ahead—but just barely.

And then the fireballs came.

When the small rocky hill to his right was engulfed in flames, Kai's first thought was, *Excellent!*

King King threw another ball of fire at him. Kai managed to dodge it, and it landed at the base of a tree and sent projected flames lapping up the trunk. The next missed him also. He had to duck so low he almost fell to the ground, but the fireball went over him and engulfed a strand of immature kakui trees.

But the next one hit him right on target.

Kai looked back at his buds and saw Weston jumping up and down shouting, "Gotcha!"

Kai had been engulfed in projected flames many times before and he was used to it. *This is fine, there's nothing to panic about.* Projected fire was never hot or painful, but the fear it produced in him felt real enough.

The ability to project a sensation of heat was extremely rare—and thus extremely valuable. The fear was created by all the other senses: the sight of the fire, the crackling and popping sounds, and the smell and taste of smoke.

"You done?" Snap asked.

"No way! I can do this forever," Kai answered and set off again. He ran down the bank of Clearbrish Creek, leapt through the water to get to the other side, and turned downstream toward the beach. As King King continued to follow him, throwing fireballs all the way, Kai remembered something.

"The trick with fire," his grandfather had once said, "is to imitate the sensation of burning. In real life, one purpose of heat is to act as a warning. It's Tav's way to keep people from getting too close to fire, so they don't get burned. The problem with projected fire is that it has no heat, and so it can carry no warning. People who grow accustomed to projected fire forget the danger of the real thing. Thus, the most valuable skill when projecting fire is to make it feel like it's burning."

Since projecting heat was so difficult, his grandfather had to find another way to communicate the warning. When he found it, he coined what became one of his most famous maxims: "Forget the heat; focus on the hell."

Because of the unquenchable fire in his hand, Kai felt conflicted about this. He didn't want his hand to feel like it was burning, but another part of him was eager to master this skill. Anyone who could create pain-like sensations with projected fire had an invaluable talent.

So Kai had spent a great deal of effort learning to project the burning sensation of real fire. It wasn't something he was able to do often, but he figured he would give it a try right now. He threw back his hands and attempted to add a burning sensation to King King's fireballs. To his surprise, it worked. Kai was pleased when the next fireball hit the back of his neck and he felt the tingling sensation on his skin. When another hit his calves, he thought, *This is incredible. I did it! I can feel it burn!*

The projected monster chasing him, combined with his success, made him want to run faster to keep away, to keep alive. It seemed to place a feeling inside him that said, *Don't give up. Don't give in. Keep going. Never stop.*

But at the same time, there was another, deeper feeling inside him—one that did not come from any projection. It told him that all his efforts to keep going were an illusion. It told Kai that there would never be an end to the path this burning King King set him on. After he had created such a monster, it would always be there, following him. It would chase him forever, hitting him with one burning fireball after another.

No, that's crazy. I can stop at any time, turn around, and dissolve it.

But while that was true for this projection, it wasn't true of all others. The fire in his hand was proof of that; Kai was unable to put it out. Many times he felt the fire would go out only when he did. But, was this the only way? Was death the only way to stop the most terrifying projections? *Is that what Dad believed? Is that why he cut himself off from the magic and left us?*

Until this moment, Kai had delighted in running away from King King and her fireballs. Although it felt terrifying, Kai knew it wasn't dangerous. But at the memory of his father, his enthusiasm drained away. He felt the pain of running so hard, and the adrenaline surging inside him told him to be very afraid. Moments before, it was as if a bright yellow sun had filled his entire sky; but now it felt like the sun was nowhere to be seen, lost in an empty blue expanse. His situation felt hopeless. Yet, instead of giving up, he kept running. Everything inside screamed that the monster chasing him was real, and he needed to get away from it at all costs.

Hold on. This is a game. It's not supposed to be like this, Kai realized. So he decided to end it.

He looked over to his right. He was close to the ocean. With one final sprint, he turned, burst out of the forest, and ran onto the beach. As he arrived on the flecked sand, he turned to face the blazing beast.

The terror radiating from this giant grew as it drew near. Everything in Kai urged him to run, but he had made his choice. The game was over; it was time for him to play out the end of the story. He would allow their King King to get what she wanted, and so he stood before her and allowed himself to be eaten, just like Lillyanna had in the Grand Projection.

King King bent down, put her face right up to Kai's, and took two deep whiffs. She then stood up on her hind feet, thumped her chest, and roared. After giving Kai a fair warning, the beast swept her hand through his body,

grabbed the now flame-roasted banana

and

smushed it into her mouth.

But, as projections can only pick up other projections, Kai's physical body remained untouched, unlike what happened to Lillyanna in the Workshop's story. The gorilla's hand passed right through him, stripped away the banana, and left him standing in his threadbare.

After devouring the banana, King King no longer radiated terror. She had what she had desired, and she was now at peace. She stretched out her arms, yawned, and then lay down on the sandy shore and fell asleep.

Kai still couldn't move. The intense feelings of the experience were still ricocheting through his soul. Deep down he knew that something in him had changed.

As his friends came running up to him, hooting with joy, he felt his happiness return. He looked down at his hand and opened it, expecting to see the fire inside. But—it was gone! Somehow, his fire had been snuffed out.

The Rising Conflict

~Kai~

Malroy is-a Shield used to be a close friend of mine, but that was back before the unfortunate incident with his son, Flint. I never believed that boy had what it took to be a magician, so I wasn't the least bit surprised by what happened. It's quite tragic. Our island's never been the same.

—Tower Mage Rieta is-a Leaf, "Eye Opening Interviews and Outlooks," *The Weekly Word*

Whhooooaaa! Kai was in awe. He held up his hand to Talia. "Is it gone? Is it really gone?"

"What? I don't understand?"

"The fire, do you see any fire in my hand?"

"Uh, no."

Kai couldn't restrain himself. He looked up and joyfully shouted, "Woooooo hooooo!" He picked Talia up in his arms and spun her around in a circle. "You did it. You did it!" he shouted—and then he noticed that Talia wasn't shouting with him. Instead, she had stiffened with tension.

"Hey, bud, I know you're flooded with adrenaline, but . . ." Snap warned.

"No touchy-touchy," Weston reminded.

Right, touch. I always forget about that. Kai released Talia and said, "Oh yeah. Sorry."

"Touchy-touchy?" Snap said to Weston. "Who says touchy-touchy?"

"I do, right before I punch you in the jaw," Weston answered; he swung his fist through the air in front of her. Even though his knuckles did not physically touch her, Snap's face flinched from the sensation of the projected punch that smacked against her mouth.

"Ooooh, ouch bud," Snap laughed. "You're lucky I'm a lady, otherwise I'd show you what a real projected punch feels like."

Kai knew that Talia wasn't uncomfortable when he, on the rare occasion, touched her. But she had made it clear it would bother her if it happened in public. Most people went out of their way to avoid physical contact with others. Kai's mother did not believe in such nonsense, so he was prone to forget this social taboo when he was overflowing with emotion.

"I'm sorry, Talia. That was too much."

Talia looked back and forth at the others before she said, "Okay, just don't do it again."

"Bud, you only make things worse when you do things like that," Snap warned. "As if the fire in your hand isn't enough to make our parents nervous about you."

"But, look!" Kai showed them his hand. "It's gone!"

The others stared at his fireless palm in amazement.

"No way! Do you think it's gone for good?" Weston asked.

Oh, please Tav. I hope so. "I doubt it. It's gone away a few times before, but it always comes back." Kai turned his attention to Talia. "But, if there ever was evidence that someone was touched by Tav, this is it."

"I'm not so sure about that," Talia said.

"Well, there's no doubt your globe is gonna be filled with gold chips," Weston said.

"Yeah Talia, you totally kissed the rainbow with that," Snap exclaimed. "Let's wake King King up and do it again."

"No thanks," Luge said. "I've had enough bubbling skin for the day."

"Bubbling skin? Really? Aw, I bet eating cake is pure torture on your poor little teeth."

"I have sensitive skin. Touch projections really affect me, more than the average person. That's why my mom never let me go see *The Dancing Panda*."

"Oh, Luge," Kai said, and everyone laughed.

"Come on guys, I'm serious."

"I am too," Snap said. "Let's go do that again. Come on! I'll be the banana this time."

"You all can keep going, but I'm done," Weston said and then turned to Kai. "Can you fix my clothing, which you so wantonly destroyed earlier with that tutu?"

Kai shrugged his shoulders and said, "Sorry bud, there's nothing I can do to help. I think you're stuck with pink." Kai raised his hands, and Weston was once again dressed in a pink tutu.

Weston looked down at it and let out an annoyed moan. "Aw bud! Not again!"

Kai laughed. "The tutu just seemed to go so well with your eyes and—" Before he could finish, Weston jumped on Kai's back and wrestled him to the ground.

"Hey! What happened to no touchy-touchy?" Kai asked.

"Tackling isn't touching," Weston replied.

Kai broke free and ran down the beach away from Weston, who stumbled after him playacting like a hobgoblin. The others joined, and their tension broke into laughter as they ran in and out of the water, splashing each other with delight. *This is turning out to be one of the best days of my life.*

When they were done playing, Talia, Kai, and Snap did their best to restore Weston's and Luge's clothing to the ones they had arrived with. More or less satisfied, the five friends collapsed, exhausted, onto the sand next to the sleeping, but still burning, gorilla.

There was nothing but stillness and peace for a long time.

True friendship rests together with no need for words. Kai remembered a line from *Life of Rice*, one of his favorite Grand Projections.

Talia broke the silence with a whisper to Kai. "I told you, you're going to get into trouble one day unless you find a way to put out your fire."

He started to laugh and couldn't stop. "I knew you'd say something like that after I lit up King King."

"I'm serious. I'm glad your hand fire went away, I really am. But you know it's going to come back, right?"

"It always does."

"You've got to figure out what's going on inside of you that's causing it. Or, at least find a way to dissolve it for good before it harms you—or someone else."

"I was thinking I ought to embrace it. Everyone could call me Kai, the Fire Guy."

"Lame," Snap called over.

"But it rhymes."

"It's a wash idea; forget it," Snap said.

"Yeah, right. I'll drench my fire out. I'll throw it into the sea as soon as it comes back."

Talia sighed in the way she did when she knew that Kai wasn't taking her seriously. "I just want you to be free of it."

"And you're helping me, Tal, honestly you are. Look, your whirligig weakened the fire."

"It did?" It was clear she didn't believe him.

"Honest—you really moved me with that—I could feel the fire weaken. And now," Kai held up his hand, "it's gone."

"Hmm, maybe it did help . . ."

"Trust me. It did."

"Do you know what happened to the fire?" Weston asked.

"No clue. It must have gone away when I stopped and stood down this big guy."

"Stood down this big girl, you mean," Snap corrected. "Our version of King King is a beautiful lady, if you couldn't tell by her lovely sundress."

"That doesn't make any sense," said Luge. "If she's a girl, why are we still calling her King King?"

"Uh, because Queen Queen sounds dumb," Snap said.

"King King sounds dumb too," Weston said, and they all laughed. "Anyway, look at what our King King did—it took Kai's unconscious projection away. That's beyond mega!"

It is beyond mega. It had been a long time since something caused his hand fire to disappear. It had happened with some frequency when he was little. *I think it was easier to dissolve back then.* He thought back to the first time something had removed the fire.

He and Talia were eight. They knew each other—everyone knew each other on the Island of the Four Kings—but they weren't friends yet. This was one of Kai's best and most vivid memories. What Talia did for him on that day made her his lifelong friend.

"You did it again, Talia," Kai said. "Just like you did with your first butterfly."

"What are you talking about?"

Kai opened up his empty, flame-free hand to her. "Tav worked through you to help me—again!"

"Kai, quit it."

"Aw, he's trying to make her cry," Snap said with a laugh.

Kai ignored Snap and continued, "No, honestly, Tal. I don't know what would have come of me if you hadn't projected that butterfly for me back then. You were Tav's miracle to me when I was eight—and you still are today."

"Now I'm crying," Snap wailed, dripping with melodrama.

"Come on, Kai. Stop. I hate it when you talk about me as if I'm Tav's miracle and act like I believe in him like you do."

"I'm just trying to communicate how thankful I am for you."

"And I'm just trying to communicate how you're being rude. Look, you can't keep depending on me to put out your fire. I may not be there to save you the next time you dangle yourself like a banana in front of Chaos."

All right. Time to back off.

"C'mon buds. We're going to be together—in the Workshop," Weston said, "and soon! After what we just made, I bet we'll be signing the Magician's Covenant in a year's time."

"Yeah bud. Easy. No problem. All sixteen-year-olds have Colors, right?" Snap said sarcastically to Weston. She shot a blob of violet goo at him.

"I'm sorry Snap, I didn't mean any harm," Weston responded.

Snap was seventeen, a year older than the rest of them. Her opportunity to become a mage had come and gone last year when no Color was found in her. A person needed to have a Color to get into the Workshop; if Kai, Talia, and Weston went there, Snap would not be going with them.

"Hey, I'm over it," Snap said. "Becoming a mage makes people arrogant; I hope none of you have Colors."

Talia laughed in a way that Kai knew well; she was feeling conflicted. One part of her wanted to keep the swelling pride in her talents a secret. Kai, and everyone else, knew she was good—very good—and if she had a Color, she would grow up to be a highly honored citizen of their island. But no one in her branch of the Leaf clan had ever had a Color pulled from them—not a single D. Leaf, from the time of the Flood, had ever been a mage.

"Snap, please don't say that," Talia said.

"Yeah, yeah, don't mind me, I'm just the old, bitter friend. All three of you have far more talent than me, anyway."

"Three?" Luge said with a sideways smile. "Talia, Kai, and me? What about Weston?"

"Luge—you haven't made a projection in what, like sixteen years?" Snap said.

"I may have made one, by accident, when I was three."

"I bet it was a hammer," Weston said, and they all laughed.

Luge shrugged. "Yeah, that's probably true. But, Snap's right. All three of you are showing signs of Color, especially Talia."

"Of course," Weston said, "Talia is soaring ahead of me. She's going to take a mega slice of this island. Everyone knows that."

Kai stayed quiet, even though he also knew this was true. *Talia's talented enough to be a magician.* But that would never happen without a Color. If, four weeks from today, the puller found her void, all her talent would go to waste. She'd spend the rest of her life stuck in the Hall of Finance, managing properties like her parents did, dealing with the tenants and their never-ending complaints.

As much as Kai hated the idea of that life for her, he was also uncertain what would happen if she did, in fact, have a Color. Color changed people, and after what had happened with his own father in the Workshop, he couldn't bear it if she was changed, too.

"What do you think, Kai?" Talia asked.

Did she really just ask me that? "You know what I think," was all Kai said.

"That's it?"

Just stay quiet, Kai thought as he looked from Talia to Weston to Luge. *Four more weeks. When all of us are found void we'll be free to hang out all the time. Someone else can be become a magician and save the island.*

"Come on, don't you want to say anything about Talia getting into the Workshop?" Weston asked.

"Forget the Workshop," Kai said. "Let's just focus on filling our globes with chips and we'll live happily ever after, like kings."

"Yeah, chips are mega—like really mega—but the only way to live like a king is to become a magician," Weston said. "After we show all the testers at the Festival how talented we are, I bet the Master Magician will personally come here and stand before the elders to invite us to become the newest members of the two hundred eighty-eight."

Snap laughed. "Like that's ever happened."

"Look," Kai said, pointing at his neck, "I'd need a Color for that, and—"

"—and I hope the puller doesn't find one," Snap, mimicking Kai, interrupted. Then she, in her own voice, said, "Bud, wake up. This island needs a magician. Every year that we don't produce one, things get worse. You have to see that."

"Of course I see it. I just know I'm not going to be the one who fixes the problem."

"Why not? You have the talent, and it's the only way to prove to everyone in the islands that what they believe about your father and grandfather isn't true."

"Be quiet Snap," Talia said, but Kai knew she was right.

"No, I won't," Snap said. "The Festival is only four weeks away. We need to talk about this."

"He already knows what we think," Luge said.

Snap groaned. "You guys don't have the guts to speak about it, openly—with words."

"It wasn't Kai's fault. The shame didn't come from him," Talia said.

"Of course not," Snap said. She turned to face her friend. "Kai, I don't believe in any of the garbage that everyone else on this island has shoved down your throat. The problem is, you swallowed it. Bud, I can't come close to understanding what it's been like to have everyone look at you the way they do. None of us can.

"But, look, you can't hide who you are with that fire in your hand—and yeah, it's going to come back—so stop trying. Listen, you three are gifted. It would be incredible if all of you had Colors."

Ugh. Now you sound like my grandmother. A shiver shot down Kai's spine. "Well, that's not going to happen to me. I'm a third generation," Kai reminded them, and they all were quiet. *Please, Tav, don't let that happen.*

Talia broke the silence. "You all keep forgetting I'm a D. Leaf. What chance is there a Color will be found in me? You need to stop saying things that get my hopes up. No D. Leaf has ever had a Color. None."

"But look how talented you are. You just made a better King King than all the magicians in the Workshop!" Snap exclaimed.

"That wasn't just me. It was because of Kai," Talia said. "He makes my projections better. He makes everyone's better."

"That's not true. Everything you do comes from you," Kai said.

"Kai, please stop," Talia said. "I don't want to talk about this anymore. Everyone knows you and Luge don't want a Color. Weston's really the only one of us who has any hope of it. So let's just talk about him getting into the Workshop. Forget about me."

"But just imagine," Weston said, "if we all had Colors, we could all make projections like this together."

"We're doing that now," Kai said.

"In secret," Luge said, then added under his breath, "illegally."

"Yeah, and all that can end, Kai," Snap said as Kai bubbled with irritation. "I bet you could single-handedly redeem your family name by becoming a third-generation mage!"

"Weston, Snap." Kai looked at his friends. "Enough! No one understands Color. They say less than a quarter of people have one. But, even if we somehow beat the odds and all became mages, we'd still have to train for years to even have a shot at becoming magicians. It's not likely, and it's not the life I want."

"Then just speak for yourself," Snap said, "and stop wishing that all your friends will be void pulls. Everything would change if this island produced a magician."

"Including us," Talia said, half to herself.

It'll all be over soon; all this conflict will go away after the Festival.

They were all quiet.

No one made a projection or even shifted their weight. Everyone knew their group was about to change; nothing stayed the same for anyone after the Color Ceremony.

For a long time they lay there, disturbed and lost in thought.

Kai looked out at the ocean. Near the shore, the blue of the water matched the color of the sky. It was clear and calm, almost like a lake, but Kai found himself looking past it to the deep indigo of the open sea. A reef protected this beach from storms and kept the shallow water tranquil and blue. Out beyond the reef, the floor of the sea dropped off. It was out there that Kai could see the waves rolling in, cresting, and crashing with white foam.

Snap is right. This island needs a magician. If I'm void, all the pressure on me to fix things will finally go away, but the problem will remain. If Weston or Talia have Colors, though—and make it all the way to the Workshop—the islands will eventually forget about me and what my father did. It was a nice thought, but it meant their group of friends would separate. *Why are there so many things that divide people?*

A familiar voice returned them to reality.

"Hey, there you are! I've been looking everywhere!"

Kai glanced up and saw Snap's little brother, Thwack, running straight toward them.

Uh-oh.

"Hey!" Thwack exclaimed when he saw Kai. "What are you doing? You guys aren't allowed to play with him!"

"We aren't playing. We're relaxing," Snap replied.

"You're still with him. I'm telling!"

"No, you won't," Snap warned. "Not if you want to ever have a peaceful sleep again."

Thwack swallowed hard. Then, pointing to the sleeping gorilla, he said, "You've been making projections. Big ones."

"Thwack," Talia said, "I'd be really thankful if you didn't tell anyone about this."

"Yeah," Weston agreed. "I'll get in big trouble if my mom finds out."

"Then you shouldn't have broken the rules."

"It's okay buds, I'll take care of it. I have special talents that help me get my way—don't I, Little Brother?" Snap said.

Thwack swallowed even harder than before. Then he said, "Dad sent me to find you. Someone found a Glimmering."

"A new Glimmering? This early?" Snap asked.

"Yeah! Out on one of the Seal Rocks. Hurry, Dad's waiting!"

Snap said, "Sorry buds, it was great, but I'm outta here."

"Dad said you could bring anyone you want."

"Really!?" Weston and Luge exclaimed in unison.

"If that's what he said. Sure, come on." Snap grinned and they started to leave.

"Come on Tal," Weston called back when he saw that Talia hadn't moved. "You have to come too."

"I don't think so."

"Aw, come on," Snap insisted. "You know how my dad gets with stuff like this. It'll be a ton of fun."

Talia looked at Kai.

Go on Talia, don't stay behind for me.

She read the expression on his face and then said, "Okay, sure."

"Yay!" they exclaimed as they all ran down the beach.

All of them except Kai.

Snap stopped, looked back, and sent a voice projection over to Kai that said, "Sorry bud, you know my dad loves you, but, well, you know."

Kai smiled and sent a projection back that said, "I understand, go on, have fun. I'll check out the Glimmering later with my mom."

Weston also sent a voice projection to Kai. "It was fun. I'm glad I came. Luge wants me to tell you he had fun too—even though you made him a banana."

"See you soon? How about in two weeks?" Kai responded.

"I don't think I can risk it. Let's just wait until after the Color Ceremony."

Great, another four weeks in solitary confinement.

Talia was the last to send a message to Kai. She hung back a little and turned to face Kai as the others resumed following Thwack. "Sorry I got angry at you."

"Angry?" Kai projected back. "I don't understand."

"About Tav. I know you believe in him and all that kind of stuff is really important to you."

Kai sighed. *'All that kind of stuff.' Is that how she sees it? As if all the other things keeping us apart weren't enough.* "That's okay. Are you upset with how I hugged you?"

There was a long pause. *All right. This can't be good.* Kai ended the silence with another message: "I'm just happy we're friends. You've helped me a lot. I hope none of you get into trouble for spending time with me."

"I doubt it," Talia projected back. "But—oh yeah! Just make sure you dissolve King King."

"Of course."

"Can you handle that? I didn't put much Power into it; it should be easy to dissolve."

"No problem. Have fun at the Glimmering."

Once his friends were gone, Kai rolled onto his side and stared out at the crashing waves for the remainder of the Green watch. *As if living on a planet full of islands wasn't bad enough, I had to be born on an island where people want to isolate me even more.*

As heartbreaking as it was to have to keep his distance from them in public, he didn't blame his friends. Kai understood why their parents and the elders of the island wanted them to keep away from him. For as long as he could remember, everyone on the Island of the Four Kings had been desperate to restore their reputation. To most, this meant the island needed to produce a new magician—a good one. It seemed to Kai that this was the only thing that anyone ever talked about.

There were countless plans to turn out a magician, but all of them involved keeping Kai at a distance. Everyone saw him as tainted. They feared he would ruin the other children's chances at getting a Color, and they did their best to keep him away from their own children. *How is that even possible? People either have a Color or they don't. How could I affect that?* It didn't make sense, but no one wanted to take any chances.

And Kai was sick of it.

After the Color Ceremony, Talia, Weston, Luge, and I won't be children any longer, will we? None of us will have a Color, there will be no more fear of me corrupting them, and I'll be set free.

He felt good. Everything was going to work out.

As he thought this, he looked down at his hand. The fire had returned.

He closed his eyes and took a long, disappointed breath. *Why does it always have to come back?* He decided to stand up and not let it bother him. "All right, King King," Kai said as he turned to dissolve the giant projection, "time to say bye-bye." But when he looked to where she had been sleeping, his heart skipped a beat. *She's gone!*

And then he heard a faint and distant scream.

"Oh, no . . ." Kai didn't hesitate. He took off running.

The Accident

~Talia~

Devos Rektor—Deeeevooos the wrecky wrecky wreck-or.
He's just flippin' scary!
(Echo: Just flippin' scary, oh oh oh so flippin' scary)
He flooded the world! Talk about evil!
And, yet, I have this urge. I have this dee-sigh-er.
I kinda-kinda-kinda wan-ta be him.
I wan-ta, I really really wan-ta.
My ooooon-ly wonder: what does this say a-boooout meeeeeeeee?

—Mage Dondalon is-a Silk, as performed in the musical *Oops! I
Probably Shouldn't Have Said That, But Did*

With one final glance back at Kai, Talia set off running down the beach toward Waterton, the main harbor town on the Island of the Four Kings. While she enjoyed Glimmerings as much as anyone and never passed up an opportunity to see one, she knew her excitement was nothing compared to that of Snap's father, Limmick.

"Your dad must have flipped monkeys when he heard about this," Talia said to Snap with a laugh.

"Oh yeah!" Thwack said. "It's been a long time since I've seen so many come out of him. There's more monkeys than fish in the boat right now!"

"Great. Hasn't Mom dissolved them yet?" Snap asked.

"Nah. Dad begged her to let them stay for a couple watches."

He's so Orange. Talia couldn't help but laugh again. "I love how your family works: your dad is always super enthusiastic, and your mom keeps everything balanced. I can't imagine your family surviving without her."

"I guess that's one way to see it," Snap said.

She has a good family, but it's definitely not calm. It made perfect sense to Talia that Snap was always throwing projections at others.

When they arrived at Waterton's marina, Talia was surprised to see how many of the boat slips were empty. Glimmerings were a rare treat, so they always attracted a crowd; this was the first to appear in their region this year, and it seemed like the entire island had gone off to see it.

Talia looked out across the ocean and saw dozens of boats and ships sailing toward the Seal Rocks. One of the few vessels that remained at the marina—a rusty orange fishing schooner with bright blue sails—belonged to Snap's dad, Limmick is-a Wave. And, just as Thwack said, it was full of bouncing monkeys.

"Talia is-a Leaf," shouted Limmick from the deck of his ship, "Luge is-a Stone, Weston is-a Wave, hurry, quick!"

"We're coming!" Snap called back.

Limmick wore projected bronze armor, a helmet with dozens of short, sharp spikes, and warpaint all over his face. *That's impressive. I wonder how much an outfit like that cost him?* As soon as they got close to the boat, he thrust his hand into the air and shouted, "To triumph!"

Limmick's eyes were like great whirlpools of water, sucking in everything. And no matter what they saw, a smile was never far from his face. Of all the fathers on their island—aside from her own—Talia enjoyed being with Limmick the most.

Snap and Thwack rushed on board and joined their other siblings on deck: Smack, Whack, Slap, Flap, and the new baby girl, Crackle, who was held close by their mother, Meridian.

Projected monkeys crawled over every surface of the ship; they climbed up the rigging, walked along the railing, and jumped about on the deck. Talia smiled when she saw Meridian cause one of the monkeys to disappear with a subtle flick of her finger. *Good thing they aren't material, or there wouldn't be any room for us.*

As soon as everyone was aboard, Limmick called out, "Are you ready for the best experience ever?"

The monkeys onboard locked arms with one another and started to dance around. Weston joined in.

"I'm ready, Master Limmick," Talia said. Although she was ready to leave, she was still preoccupied with thoughts of the conversation with Kai on whether their futures contained Colors. *I can't get my hopes up. No one in my family has ever had a Color. Why would it be any different for me?* Still, everything in her desired to become a magician.

"Come on, then! Let's go! I've demonstrated more restraint than I ever imagined possible—don't you agree?" Limmick said with a wink to his wife.

"Tremendous achievement, dear," Meridian answered.

Limmick wasted no time launching the ship. As soon as they set sail, he grabbed an oar and started rowing with his sons to make up for lost time. It didn't take long until they were far from shore and on their way toward the Seal Rocks.

Feeling the fresh ocean air on her face always made Talia breathe easier. Even though this wasn't her family, she felt at peace with them. They were good, honest people and she was beginning to relax.

"Can you believe it's Glimmering season already?" Limmick asked the group. "The Grand Projection is still sixteen weeks away."

"I think they're coming out early because the Workshop needs this year's to be a success," Talia said.

"Everyone knows that," Snap replied. "The question is whether it's a good or bad sign. If they have a really good Grand Projection in the works, why are they planting a Glimmering so early?"

"That's a good point," Weston said. "I bet they're probably just trying to move on to the next one as soon as possible."

Yeah, moving on. That feels right. Here, out on the beautiful sea and away from the pressures back on land, Talia felt wonderful. She loved the Island of the Four Kings, and it would always be home. Still, with the Color Ceremony only a few weeks away, it was nice to get some space, even if just for a few watches.

Talia sighed with contentment. "There's nothing like hanging out on a ship full of monkeys to remind you of the important things in life."

"And what would those be?" Snap asked.

"Oh, lots of things: friends, the sea air, silliness, family, projections, just basic things like that," Talia replied with a smile. But then, just as she was about to let go and sink into the peace of the moment, everything changed.

"RAWWWWWWWRRR!"

They all heard it, but Talia was the first to identify what it was. And when she did, the feeling of peace dissolved into terror.

Oh no!

She turned around and looked back at Waterton. There, standing on the dock and watching them leave, was none other than their flaming projection of King King.

The giant gorilla looked out at them with clenched fists, then let out a second terrible, lonely roar. It was so loud that Talia imagined everyone in the Penta-Islands could hear it.

"RAWWWWWWWRRR!"

"Aaaah!" Weston exclaimed.

"No. No. No. No," Snap muttered under her breath.

"Uh, buds?" Luge said with a frown. "Didn't Kai say he was

going to take care of that?"

"Oh, this is bad. This is very, very bad," Talia said as she felt the terror she placed into the projection waft over her from across the water. *If I can feel the dread this far away, anyone left in town must feel it, too.*

"Ha ha! That's what you get for playing with Kai!" Thwack teased.

Then Meridian turned and saw King King standing on the dock. "Where did that come from?"

"They made it with Kai!" Thwack answered. "I saw."

"Did you make it in a playground?"

Snap lowered her head in shame. "No."

If I don't stop this now, we're going to be in so much trouble. Talia thrust out her hands, closed her eyes, and tried with all her might to dissolve her giant gorilla of a mistake. It didn't work. *Am I too far away?*

"Where did what come from?" Limmick asked. He was so focused on where they were headed, he hadn't looked back yet. But when he did, a wild smile came across his face. "Whoa! That's the most flippin' awesome thing I've ever seen!"

"It is?" Snap and Thwack asked at the same time.

"Stars above! Look at how huge and terrible it is. You kids made that? Fab-u-lous! What is it?"

"King King," Weston said.

"It is?" Limmick stared at it. "The Kingdom's pretty grainy, but yeah." He squinted. "Yeah, I can see it. It's unbelievable!"

"And unbelievably illegal, dear," Meridian said.

"Of course it is and all of you are totally going to get dipped for making it," Limmick said. "But you should be really proud of it, really proud."

This is not the way I wanted the island to experience my first public projection. Talia scanned the beach for any sign of Kai, but he was nowhere to be seen. *Run, Kai. Please, get to it before too many people see it.*

"Hey, I sense something. There's some Glory that's part of it that feels familiar." Limmick thought for a moment, then exclaimed with a look of joy, "That's it! It's Devos Rektor, right? It's the way we feel in *The Epics* when Devos is about to face off against Migo the Marauder. Am I right? I have to be right."

Talia nodded and said, "Yes, Master Limmick."

"That. Is. Amazing! You totally hit it!"

Yeah, great, and now we're going to all get hit with a prohibition unless we can stop it—fast. No matter how much she waved her arms to try to dissolve it, she couldn't.

"Look, there's Kai," Weston said.

Sure enough, Kai was finally there, sprinting across the dock straight toward the giant beast while making big sweeping movements with his hands as he tried to dissolve it. His efforts clearly weren't working either. *What's going on? Kai has always had more than enough Power to erase anything I've projected.*

When Kai met King King at the end of the dock, the beast let out another roar, jumped right over the boy, and lumbered away—straight for Market Street.

Kai turned and chased after it and soon disappeared from their view behind some houses. The gorilla was far taller than the buildings and they could still see it—but they were blind to what Kai was doing and to how the few people left in Waterton were reacting to this rogue creation.

"Forgive me, Meridian, but projections are erupting inside of me, and now that we're safely out at sea, I have to flip a few monkeys or I'll explode." Limmick held out his hands, projected a little monkey into them, and flung it up in the air. When the monkey landed on the deck of the ship, it bounced up and down like the others a few times before it jumped overboard.

Talia hardly noticed, though. She drilled her eyes into King King. *Why won't you dissolve!?*

Snap winced and turned her head away from shore, as if watching caused her pain. Luge just stared out over the water in a daze. Weston seemed to be taking it the worst. He had crouched low and was mumbling about not wanting drops in his eyes.

Limmick was the only one who didn't seem upset by what was happening. He kept tossing new monkeys into the sea, shouting, "Go! Rescue our fair island from your Supreme Monkey Overlord."

It seemed to Talia that he would have just kept projecting monkeys all day, but his wife interrupted him. "Dear, don't you think we ought to be doing something about this?"

"I'm sending monkeys to help—isn't that enough?"

"Well, the gorilla seems to be terrorizing our town. Shouldn't we do something real to stop that?"

"I count seven monkeys swimming back to shore. Wet monkeys are an extra-potent weapon against flaming gorillas."

"I was thinking of something . . . substantial. Something other than adding more illegal projections to the problem."

"How about passing blame! That's substantial." Limmick turned to Snap and said, "What part of that giant, naughty monkey did you project, little girl?"

"I only added the sundress and bling."

"Excellent. Good work. Adds a sassy touch that was missing in the Grand Projection. What about you Weston? Do you want some? There's always plenty of blame to dish up when things like this happen."

Before Weston could respond, the gorilla started throwing fireballs.

Oh no. Fireballs? They're definitely going to place a prohibition on us now.

"It can do that, too!? That's incredible!" Limmick shouted. "That's what the real King King needed—less romance, more fireballs.

See what the future magicians from the Island of the Four Kings can do! We're coming back. This year! I know it. Right, Talia?"

Someone should have stopped it by now. Kai has more Power than I do. Did he help me while I was making it? Is that why it's so strong?

She had never had such a colossal failure before. She didn't know what to do other than cry out, "I'm sorry everyone. I really messed up with this." *Please! Someone, take it down!*

"Oh, dear, there's no need for that," said Meridian. "Don't be so distraught."

"Yeah! You've made something amazing," Limmick said.

Talia frowned. "And illegal."

"That's true," Limmick agreed. "And the fireballs will certainly cause your prohibition to be a whole lot worse."

Weston groaned louder.

"Talia," Meridian asked calmly, "what happened?"

"It was me. It's my fault," Talia admitted. "We were off in the forest alone when we made it. But I didn't put much Power into it at all. It should be easy to stop."

"Uh . . . yeah . . . you should know that, um . . . I should probably tell you . . ." Weston faltered, then shifted his weight to his back foot as if preparing to run away. "When you were making it, I put as much Power into it as I could."

Snap's eyes exploded open. "You bloomer! Why would you do that?!"

"I thought it would be more fun if it was a challenge for us to defeat," Weston said. "With all the excitement about the Glimmering, I guess . . . I guess . . . I forgot."

Oh, great. We've left Kai alone to deal with something he didn't create—and can't stop.

"Okay. So, come on—stand up—you need to extinguish it," Luge said.

"It's no use, I've already tried everything—I started trying as soon as I heard it roar."

"See?" Thwack said. "Stuff like this is exactly the reason you're not supposed to play with Kai."

Snap rolled her eyes. "Right, because 'stuff like this' is so common."

"It is when Kai's involved!" Thwack said.

Talia turned away. She tried to ignore everyone and focused all her attention on dissolving King King. She had to hurry; the gorilla was almost at Market Street. If it wasn't dissolved soon, it could cause some real damage to the projections that were for sale there.

"You kids are going to become magicians, I have no doubt about it now," Limmick said. "Who else other than a magician can make something like that?"

"Kids," Meridian asked, "do you have the power to dissolve it?"

"I'm trying, but it hasn't worked yet," Talia said.

"We're too far away," Weston groaned.

"Honey, turn the ship around, we need to get closer."

"No, that will take too long, and I have a better idea," Limmick said. "Let's focus all our Power on it. We'll destroy it together—like they do at the end of *The Epics*!"

"In case you haven't noticed, this isn't a Grand Projection."

Limmick ignored her and shouted a battle cry, "Magicians, mages, and commoners unite together against this great evil!"

"We're all commoners, Dad," Snap said.

"Even better. Let's do it. Shout if you're in."

Everyone shouted and gathered together at the edge of the boat, and all—even Luge—labored to send every bit of Power they had across the water in an attempt to dissolve the rogue projection.

Despite their combined effort, the monster remained unaffected.

"It's not working," Luge said.

Another fireball went out from the gorilla. This one struck a small shack at the marina, and the detailed and expensive-looking projected decorations on the shack were quickly obliterated.

Nothing that Talia and the others did seemed to affect it. They were losing hope, and one by one they gave up. Only Talia kept at it, driven by pure determination and strength of will.

"It's no use," Snap said. "Dad, we need to head back."

Two more fireballs shot into Market Street.

Limmick's face showed his disappointment as he turned the wheel of the ship and said in a whisper Talia could barely hear, "Why can't real life be as great as Grand Projections?"

Come on! Please, dissolve!

And then, all at once, the gorilla flickered and started to fade.

"It's fading! It's fading!" Snap's younger siblings cried out.

King King was dissolving, slowly, bit by bit, until—with one last, ferocious roar—it was completely gone. A surge of relief mixed with the weight of despair hit Talia, and she nearly collapsed against the railing of the ship.

"Woo hoo!" Luge and Weston cheered.

"Wow, Talia, good work!" Snap said.

"It wasn't me," she said. Deep down, she knew she'd failed to overpower it. "Kai must have had help from someone there."

"I bet it was the IP," Weston said.

"Probably," Talia sighed. *I hope he did it on his own and the IP didn't see it.* "I'm just grateful it's gone." *Okay, now, please run Kai—get far away until we get back and I can explain that it was my projection and not yours.*

Although King King was gone, Talia feared it would continue to chase them for a long time.

The Shame

~Talia~

There are three domains commonly attributed to every projection. The domain of Power. The domain of Kingdom. And the domain of Glory. All competent trainers expect their young mages to exercise complete control and mastery in all three domains. There is no greater shame than to lose control of one's projection.

—Magician Qyennta is-a Smooch, *Power, Kingdom, and Glory: The Gift of Projections*

When Limmick's ship finally arrived at the Seal Rocks, they found the entire belt around the cluster of small, rocky islands crammed with boats. It was a chaotic mess of vessels from small dinghies to the largest schooners. Every sailor was vying for a spot near the Glimmering.

"Whoa," Luge gasped, "it looks like everyone from the Penta-Islands is here!"

That's good. It means there weren't many people who experienced our King King disaster.

All but one of the Seal Rocks were too rocky to sustain any life beyond prickly brush and the odd stunted tree. The exception was an island, slightly larger than the others, where there was enough soil to support a healthy grove of trees. On it were a small shack and a ramshackle dock, built and occupied by a peculiar, secretive man named Horatio is-a House, who was rumored to be a bootlegger. Although this was his private island, he was nowhere in sight, and the whole area was jammed with people.

"We're never going to find a spot," Snap said.

"Have faith, children! Do you think I would risk us not getting to see the first Glimmering in our region?" Limmick pointed toward the east side of the island, to a ship that looked like his, except it was greenish-yellow and had red sails.

"Uncle Trimmick!" Snap's siblings cried out when they saw Limmick's brother standing on the deck. He was shooing away several other boats that circled him like sharks, trying to get him to leave.

"A little late to the show, aren't ya?" Trimmick laughed. "I wasn't sure how much longer I could hold this spot!"

"Ha! Well, we had a few delays . . ."

"You're telling me." Trimmick yawned. "But, this year's Glimmering is quite unique, completely interactive and—"

"STOP! Stop," Limmick exclaimed. "If you spoil it for me I'll have your ship incinerated with fireballs from the new, improved King King that's risen up from *The Depths of Helldoro*."

"What are you talking about?" Trimmick asked. "King King wasn't in that Grand Projection."

"Oh, you'll understand soon enough."

Yup, we're going to be paying for this forever. Kai, go, run away, and wherever you go make room for me.

After Trimmick sailed his ship out, Limmick sailed his ship in. As soon as he set anchor, Limmick dove into the water and swam like a frantic fanatic toward the shore.

"We own a rowboat dear," Meridian called after him. "Remember, we bought it instead of replacing our old chipped dishes?"

Despite the fact that they'd come here to see the Glimmering, Talia was reluctant to join the others in the rowboat. Drained and discouraged by all that had just happened, she wanted to stay behind. But more than that, the mere thought of interacting with another projection made her stomach clench tight.

Her friends wouldn't listen to her protests, however, so she reluctantly joined them in the rowboat.

Once they were on the shore of the little island, they followed a path through the brush. It led them to a crowd gathered in the grove of trees.

And what they found there surprised them all.

Every Glimmering gave some hint or revelation to the nature of the upcoming Grand Projection, but some—like this one—were more mysterious than others.

"It's . . . a boy?" Snap asked when she saw it.

Everyone's attention was fixed on a masterfully crafted sixteen-year-old boy. When Talia first caught sight of him, he was in mid-air, leaping across a small ravine. After he landed, he sprinted over to a coral tree and scrambled up into its branches.

Limmick was entranced, just as Talia had expected, and followed every move the boy made—even going as far as to climb up into the tree to be with him.

"Come on up here," she heard Limmick call to them. "This kid is a kick."

The others pressed forward through the crowd to interact with the projected boy and follow him around the little island. Everyone was curious about the mysteries he might reveal.

Talia, however, stayed back and remained disconnected from all that was happening. Though she was present in body, her mind and heart were switched off.

And so she sat.

Silent.

Still.

It was impossible to tell how much time had passed. She barely even noticed when her friends came back and sat down next to her.

"This is mega mold," were the first words she registered. "This is the most boring Glimmering ever. I bet Dad's going to keep us here until sunset."

"Sure, but I'd rather spend the rest of my life here than go back and start what's waiting for us," Weston said.

"Don't remind me of that," Snap muttered. Everyone was quiet.

Luge broke the silence. "Hey, I bet that boy is hiding something that no one's found yet! It's like a mind puzzle or something."

"He'd better be," Snap said. "Otherwise, I'd say it's a pretty drench Glimmering. The kid doesn't have any special abilities or anything."

"I don't know," Luge shrugged. "I kind of like him."

Snap laughed. "You would. 'Color, no Color.' Who talks like that?"

"It's a good message. More people should think that way."

"If it were true, then they would," Snap said. "But the islands don't work like that. It does matter if you don't have a Color. I know, firsthand."

"I guess you're right," Luge said with a sigh. "But, I still think O'Ceea would be better off if more people thought that way."

They sat still for a long time, which was fine with Talia.

Snap said under her breath, "I wish we could ask him our questions about the Glimmering."

Talia glanced up. A few feet away from them stood a Green magician, the one responsible for making the Glimmering.

"Isn't it strange?" Luge asked after a pause. "Right there, right in front of us, is a real, living person with all the answers we could ever want to know. And yet, we're only allowed to talk to the projection he made to try and figure out all its mysteries."

"Yeah, pretty strange," Weston said casually. He then sent Talia a private voice projection. "Tal, won't it be great once we're in the Workshop? Then we'll be the ones who make Glimmerings and know all the secrets."

Up until now, Talia had been only listening to this conversation with tepid interest. However, when she saw the magician, her heart leapt and her mind switched back on. She turned away as soon as she saw him, but after a moment, she turned back and couldn't take her eyes off him. *Could I really have what it takes to become someone like him?* She studied his every detail like a student preparing for the most important test of her life.

Elden is-a Bone was a magician in his early twenties from the Island of the Golden Vale. She recognized him right away. He was the one who had created the boy, and he controlled the boy's every action and every word. Magicians like Elden were masters at their craft; they could keep their projections under complete control.

A projection is not supposed to act independently of its creator. That's one of the fundamental rules. So what was I thinking? I shouldn't have even considered making something as ambitious as King King. Look at the mess it caused.

Some people felt stifled under the myriad of rules put in place by the IP and the IIRP to ensure the safe use of projections, but not Talia. She believed the ancient elders had been wise when they decided to make regulations. She agreed that only certain people, in certain circumstances, should project.

Those with the proper authority were easily identifiable by the collar they wore around their neck. These collars bore specific marks that indicated the wearer's projection-making credentials. Everyone except children and a few outliers wore a collar. As Talia hadn't yet come of age, she didn't have one, which meant that she—like all children—was permitted to project only as long as she kept within certain parameters. Talia knew these boundaries, and yet she had allowed her actions in the forest to fall outside of them.

Limitations are important for the majority of kids. But how am I supposed to get better if I can't train? How can they expect Kai, Weston, and me to get high scores if they limit us to playgrounds? Talia's heart was set on getting a Color collar. With one, she would be free to project all the things she felt stirring inside her, the things that longed to get out.

She looked at the Green magician's collar. Even if there were people on this little rock of an island who didn't know his name, everyone knew what kind of man he was just by looking at the strip of cloth around his neck. Moving about in the otherwise lifeless black fabric was a Green light, vibrant and dynamic. But the thing that really caught her eye was the single thread of platinum metal, bright and sparkling, woven along its top edge. This marked him as a magician of the First Magnitude.

This Glimmering was Elden's performance. If the projection was a puppet, this Green magician was the puppeteer. Talia had tremendous respect for all magicians, but she had extra admiration for Elden. He was responsible for creating Narlo, one of her all-time-favorite characters in the otherwise forgettable Grand Projection from two years ago.

Without a second thought, Talia was on her feet. She took two steps toward the magician, but stopped when she heard Snap's voice projected in her ear. "Tal, stop! What are you doing?"

At first Talia didn't grasp what Snap was getting at, but when Snap pointed her head in the direction of Elden, she understood; no one was to interact with a magician during a Glimmering. The audience acted as if the magician was not there.

"You thought I was going over to him?" Talia projected back to Snap.

"You were staring at him like you couldn't wait to have his babies."

"What! Don't be ridiculous!" At moments like this, Talia was glad no one else could hear them. "He just caught me by surprise. You know how much I liked Narlo."

"Yeah, yeah. Tell yourself whatever you like. Just don't do anything foolish."

"Don't worry. I'm not going anywhere near him. We've broken enough rules for one day," Talia replied as she turned away from them and headed straight toward the projection of the boy Elden had created.

It's time to get a really good look at this Glimmering.

The Glimmering

~Talia~

Some people feel the practice of using numbers to represent the regions is rather bureaucratic and dystopian, but honestly, the problem is far worse. Everything in O'Ceea is tangled and confusing: 9 Colors, 5 regions, 1,000 gryns per lyke and 1 million gryns per whisper, 288 magicians, 3 privilege levels, 7 days in a week and 42 weeks in a year, 9 watches but 7 nightmarks. Ugh! Why our ancestors didn't base everything on one round number like 10 is beyond me. I find it hard enough to remember everything as it is.

—Historian Alfie is-a Hive, *Confessions of the Aged and Ornery*

The crowd had thinned by more than half since they first arrived. As Talia drew close to the boy, she heard Meridian say to Limmick, "I think it's time we go."

"Aw, do we have to? It's so amazing. I can't stand that I have to wait so long for this Grand Projection—sixteen weeks is like forever," Limmick whined.

Smack, Snap's brother, smacked his hand to his forehead and said, "That's the point of a Glimmering, Dad."

"Yes, and that's why they're so brilliant! Mass manipulation, totally works on me. I should become a Glimmering Hunter, I'm made for it. Honey, can I abandon you and all my lovely little urchins to go roam the islands looking for Glimmerings?"

"Absolutely dear, after you take us home."

Oh no, we can't leave yet. "No, wait. I haven't looked at it yet."

"You haven't? Where have you been all this time?" Smack asked. Talia didn't answer.

"I guess we have to stay," Limmick said to Meridian. "You can head back to the boat if you want. I'll stay here with Talia and suffer through until she's finished. That's what good parental role models do, right?"

"I'll try to be quick," Talia said, and she slipped through the thinning crowd to get close to the projection.

The boy was marching around the base of a tree, humming some song and speaking to a Red mage in the crowd about the upcoming Festival. "I've been so excited I haven't been able to fall asleep. See! Look at me now, I can't stop moving. I don't know how I'll be able to wait."

"You're that excited? But aren't you worried you won't have a Color?" the Red mage asked.

At this, the boy stopped his march, shrugged his shoulders, and said, "Color, no Color, nothing will stop me from laughing and playing!" He sprinted away across a bare patch of ground, laughing as he went. Talia ran after him. The others in the crowd had grown tired of following after this energetic boy, but she kept up with him.

"Hey, you're fast," he said to her when they arrived at a different tree.

This is so mega! It's talking directly to me. "I've had a lot of practice running through forests."

"I like forests," he said as he grabbed onto a branch of the tree and started dangling from it. Even though the branch did not move—projections were not able to move material things, after all—it looked just as if an actual boy had slung himself over it.

Wow, that's impressive. Elden must have a lot of Kingdom to be able to make it look so real. "What else can you do?"

"Lots of stuff."

"Like what?" As soon as Talia asked this she knew she'd made a mistake. The boy dropped down and started marching around the tree, humming a song. *Yeah, Elden isn't going to give up information that easily,* she thought, and so she tried again. "If you like forests, what's one of your favorite kind of trees?"

"Any that I can climb," the projected boy answered.

"But, can't all trees be climbed?" The question came out of Talia's mouth before she'd had a chance to think. *I bet it'll run off to another tree after that.* Instead, the projection froze and blinked in and out of existence for a moment.

Limmick, who stood nearby, burst with delight. "Way to go, Talia! You clattered it."

When the projection started moving again, the kid leapt up into the tree and wriggled himself into a sitting position on a branch. He looked out over the crowd and said, "I like climbing this kind."

Talia asked the boy more questions, but got only the same plain, uninteresting answers it had given to everyone else earlier. She soon came to understand why Snap and the others thought this Glimmering was so drench. The projection appeared to be just an ordinary kid, like them. Other than his being unusually energetic and playful, there didn't appear to be anything unique or special about him.

From a technical point of view, the boy projection was a marvel. It was clear by the way he climbed up into the tree and sat on a branch that the Workshop was making great strides in crafting projections that looked and acted more real. *But what's so important about this boy to make it the center of a Glimmering? I bet Luge was right about this being some kind of a puzzle.* As Talia pondered this mystery, she heard an all-too-familiar voice say, "This way, gentlemen."

Walking in her direction with two identical-looking men at her side was none other than Kai's grandmother. Talia's heart skipped a beat when she saw her. *If she's here, maybe that means Kai is here, too.* She looked around but saw no sign of her friend.

If the older woman noticed her, she gave no indication. Kai's grandmother was in business mode, escorting what Talia suspected were two tourists—apparently twins—to see the Glimmering. Talia couldn't put her finger on it, but she felt some unusual sensation coming from these two men. After observing their pale skin, strange orange hair, and light violet eyes, she decided they must be from some other region and dismissed the feeling.

Why are they keeping their distance from everyone? It seemed like they were taking extra precautions to make sure no one would touch them, even by accident. *I bet they're wearing really expensive, delicate projections and don't want anyone to damage them. That would explain it.*

Kai's grandmother had not been there for more than a moment or two when she became displeased with the boy. "Get down from that tree, now!" she called up to him. "There are important guests here who have come a long way to meet you."

Talia stifled a laugh. It was just like Kai's grandmother to demand her way with everyone. *Apparently even projections.*

As commanded, the boy started to climb down, humming the same tune that he had been humming earlier.

"What is your name?" she asked.

"What name do you want me to have?" replied the boy. "Colors are names, and so are no Colors. I wonder what name I'll get in three days?" It was the same answer it had given Talia earlier. *Clearly, the Workshop doesn't want us to know his name yet.* The boy bounced about excitedly.

"No one is that excited about being tested for a Color," Kai's grandmother informed him. "Are you not worried about what will happen if no Color is found in you?"

"Color, no Color, I expect life will be the same," he answered.

"But your family will be disappointed."

"Color, no Color, nothing will stop me from laughing and playing!"

"But what about your family?" she asked again, but the boy ignored her and gave a joyful laugh as he skipped away.

"Come back. I want to know what will happen to your family."

The boy ignored her and kept on skipping.

Kai's grandmother didn't give up. "Surely your family would be devastated if you never made it to the Island of the Magician's Workshop?"

The boy stopped, turned back, and gave a confused look. "The Island of the Magician's Workshop? What's that?"

He's excited for the Color Ceremony, but he's never heard of the Workshop.

"Fascinating!" Limmick's eyes lit up as he spoke.

Kai's grandmother stared back at the boy and said, "Everyone knows it is the island where only magicians and their families can live."

At this, the boy laughed. "Why would magicians want to live on an island and be separated from everyone?"

"Because everyone lives on an island," Talia said, "and the Island of the Magician's Workshop is the best one."

"What do you mean? Everyone doesn't live on islands."

"Ah ha! He from old age!" one of the twins exclaimed.

"Before Flood! This be very good story," the other agreed.

The boy ran off, climbed up another tree, plucked a projected apple, and started to eat it. He didn't say another word, no matter how much he was pestered.

"Jade, you brilliant old donkey," Limmick cried out. "You cracked it. We have an Old World Grand Projection to look forward to. Woo hoo!"

This new revelation also excited Talia. Most of her favorite Grand Projections were set back then, where roads connected different peoples together, before the waters rose and transformed 'the world' into 'the islands.' If the Master Magician was going to tell them another story from the Old World, there wasn't a doubt in her mind that it was going to be a success.

Suddenly, the hidden identity of the boy became much more intriguing. *Who could he be?*

*   *   *

Even though the projection was still active, eating one piece of fruit after another, the Glimmering was essentially over and everyone began to leave. Limmick, of course, wanted to stay longer, saying, "Why battle a log jam of boats when you can gape at an Old World character stuck in a tree? He kinda looks like a monkey up there, doesn't he?"

"Hmm, I worried he would look like that," a voice answered from behind them. When Talia turned, she was shocked to see the Green magician. "Hi, I'm Elden is-a Bone. I was hoping you would linger after I finished; I wanted the opportunity to greet you."

He came over to speak to us? What's going on? On the outside, Talia tried to look like nothing special was happening, but inside, she was exploding with an arsenal of emotions she didn't understand. Apparently, the same thing was happening in Limmick, because all of a sudden, a startled monkey projection popped out of him, stumbled around for a moment, and then fainted.

Elden seemed unphased by their looks of surprise. He addressed her directly. "You're Talia is-a Leaf, is that right?"

He knows my name? How does he know my name? Talia nodded and stared back at him, unable to speak.

"I always appreciate the opportunity to meet with someone who is able to clatter one of my projections."

Oh, no. I knew I shouldn't have asked the boy what kind of trees he liked climbing. "I'm so, so sorry," she blurted out. "I didn't mean to."

"There's no need to apologize, Talia is-a Leaf; it is true, all trees can be climbed. I hadn't seen that before. Thank you, it will make this boy's performance in the Grand Projection stronger. I must leave, but I wish you well going into your Color Ceremony," he said, and then he turned away.

Limmick, who was bouncing from foot to foot, finally managed to speak. He called out to the magician, "Wait! How do you know who we are?"

Elden stopped and glanced over his shoulder at them. "When I heard you call her Talia, I knew who she was."

"But why would you know anything about me?" Talia asked.

"The Workshop makes a point of knowing the names of those who show promise among the next generation. I suppose it's natural for magicians to want to know about anyone who might one day displace them."

Displace? That's a terrible thought. "No, no, you've got the wrong idea. I don't want to displace you."

"Of course you don't," the Green magician chuckled. "It is, however, the way it works; for the good of all the islands, the Workshop needs to have the best. So take my words as encouragement, Talia is-a Leaf, and know your talents have not gone unnoticed. Maybe someday I'll meet you on the Island of the Magician's Workshop."

He started to leave, but before he got too far he stopped again, as if considering something. "I must apologize. While it's true your talents have not gone unnoticed, I cannot predict whether Color is in you. Thus, I ought to take a lesson from my own projection: whatever happens with you before the puller, Color or no Color, I do hope you'll still laugh and play."

✳   ✳   ✳

The Green magician's words weren't an encouragement to Talia. Instead, they unsettled her. Something about what he said caused all the events of the day to weigh down on her. In most circumstances she would have waited to speak about it with her father, but the pressure was too great. She felt like a wave of emotion was about to crash over her. *No. I can't let this happen here.*

Tears began to well up in her eyes. She tried to hide them from Limmick, but he saw her distress and said, "Oh, no. Here, let me get you to Meridian."

"No, please don't, I'm fine." *I'm not fine at all. I need to talk about this with someone. I need to get it out.*

"You sure?"

"Yeah, I'll be fine." *But will I? No D. Leaf has ever had a Color. It's no use. I'm never going to meet anyone on the Island of the Magician's Workshop.*

Limmick looked as if he weren't sure quite what to do. "You . . . don't look fine."

"It's just that it's been a long day." *I only need to wait this out. Eventually I'll get back to normal.* She tried to stop her tears from falling, but one came out of her left eye and streamed down her cheek.

"What's wrong?"

"Uh . . . I . . . ." Talia stammered.

"Just let it out."

"I . . . I mean . . . Everyone seems to think I'll . . . that . . . I'll become a magician. Everyone on our island believes it's going to happen. Even . . . even Magician Elden thinks so."

"I know, wasn't that flippin' amazing? He actually knew who we were!" Limmick exclaimed, but when Talia gave him a look that said 'not now' his expression changed. "Oh, right. I'm listening."

"It's no use. It's not going to happen. None of my oh-so-great ability is going to matter unless I have a Color. I'm going to stand up there—in front of everyone—and nothing is going to come out of me."

"You don't know that! Look, while it's true no D. Leaf has ever had a Color, it's also true no D. Leaf has ever had anything close to your talent. Your ability has to come from somewhere."

"You can't understand—there's Color in your family. Your brother's a mage." Talia regretted these words as soon as she had said them. *I need to learn to keep my mouth shut.*

Limmick pointed to the black collar around his neck and said, "Do you see any Color there? Don't you think I was disappointed when I was found void at my Color Ceremony? No, I wasn't. I was destroyed."

"But there's—" Talia stopped when they heard a distant, grating roar. Even though it was loud, she was too upset to care. "But there's Color in your family," she continued.

"Think of Snap," Limmick said with a sigh. "You know how much she wanted a Color. She was found void as well. She had much higher aspirations for her life than what's available for her now as a commoner. I'm sure you don't know this, but I had big aspirations when I was your age. I didn't plan on becoming a fisherman. Everyone knows how much I love projections, and here I am rowing all day, working with fish. Trust me, Talia, I understand."

"But you're so happy. You don't show any of that—at all."

"I'm not happy all the time. I expect Snap has told you some negative things about me."

"No, not really."

"Well, that's nice to know. I'm just trying to do the best with the life I've been given."

"It seems to me you found a way to still laugh and play, just like the boy said. I just don't know if I'll be able to if I'm void and can't compete to get into the Workshop."

"Hold out your hands," Limmick said, and Talia obeyed. "Now I want you to project a monkey like one of mine, right here onto your hand."

"Um, but . . . I don't think I should be making any more illegal projections."

"It's okay. I'll say it's one of mine. I'll take the blame if we get caught. I don't mind prohibitions so much. So, go on."

"Mmm. I don't know. I've never tried to project a little monkey like yours before—it will probably take me awhile."

"It doesn't need to be any good—just throw it out."

"Uh, I don't usually do that."

"Come on, I'm not going to score it. I just want to show you something. You can dissolve it right away."

Projecting like this made Talia feel uncomfortable; she didn't like anyone observing her do poor work. But she agreed—in part. Instead of doing it in an instant, she spent about a moment crafting a monkey. It was misshapen and didn't move much, just scratched its head and blinked its eyes, but it did look like a monkey.

When she was finished, Limmick pressed his lips together and grunted. "Hmm. It took me twelve interminable weeks to figure out how to project a monkey as good as that, and there you did it in a few heartbeats."

"That doesn't matter . . . talent doesn't guarantee a Color, everyone knows that."

Limmick took a deep breath and collected himself before he said, "That's not my point. Look at your monkey. It's different from mine, right?"

"Yeah. Mine's pretty drench."

"No, no. I'm not talking about how it good it is. Even if it looked just as good as mine, it wouldn't be mine—not in the least, right?"

"I guess not."

"Look at it. The Glory of it is totally different."

Talia saw it. Her monkey wasn't as lively and spirited as Limmick's. His monkeys always made her feel better. Something about them gave her hope. Hers didn't.

"Now, I want you to project something that's a reflection of you. It can be anything—the first thing that comes to you. No, wait, don't do that. Try to find something inside you that's begging to come out. Don't try to figure out what it is, just find it and let it come out."

Talia didn't have to think hard. She knew right away. She lifted up her hand and a dozen bright, colorful butterflies fluttered out into the air around them.

"That's it. Look, those little guys are a reflection of you. Aren't they wonderful?"

She looked up and saw how they filled the darkening blue sky with luminous color. They were pretty, but they didn't delight her like Limmick's monkeys did.

"Making projections is such a common thing for us," he said. "But think about it. You just made something that looks and acts like something alive. Isn't that amazing? And then, there's the boy we just saw. How is that possible? No one really knows how we're able to do it—we just can. It's so easy to lose sight of what a miraculous thing projections are. When I'm happy—when I'm really happy, and not just trying to avoid stuff—I think that comes out in the wonderful and magical things I project, even though they're just silly little monkeys."

Talia had never thought of it like that before. She looked up at her butterflies. They fluttered to and fro and seemed oblivious to what anyone felt about them. In each she saw something, or rather, she felt something. Every butterfly radiated a tiny emotion, one she recognized as originating from inside of her. *They really are magnificent!*

"Can you imagine not having the ability to project, Talia? Wouldn't it be horrible?"

It would be. "But that's what will happen to me if I'm void. Commoners aren't allowed to make projections."

"You've got more talent than anyone I've come across in years. Even without a Color, you're sure to earn enough chips to get yourself to the third privilege level. Then you'll be able to project anything, anywhere—just like a mage can."

But I'd never become a magician.

Limmick continued. "I have no idea what the Workshop is trying to say with that boy repeating 'Color, no Color' over and over again. But, to be honest, as a commoner, the first time I heard it, it felt like a slap in the face. Mages and commoners aren't the same. But everyone who's alive is able to make projections. I don't think anyone should take our ability to make them for granted. So, Talia, I hope you don't stop making projections, or enjoying them, if it turns out you don't have a Color."

Talia still didn't know if that would be possible, but at least now she had a spark of hope that her universe wouldn't end if she was found void.

"Thanks, Master Limmick. I always knew there was more to you than the childish Orange fisherman everyone sees."

"Is that how people see me? Wow, that's great; I've fooled them all." Limmick grinned.

Talia walked back to the boat with a light heart.

✳   ✳   ✳

Limmick and Talia had been away from the others for quite some time, and it was now the middle of the Indigo watch. When they stepped out from the brush and onto the beach, they saw that there was only one boat left in the water: Snap sat there in the rowboat, waiting for them.

"You won't believe what just happened," Snap said to them.

"A handsome young magician came up, started talking with you like you were best friends, and gave you VIP tickets to the next Grand Projection?" Limmick asked.

Even though he was her dad, and she should have grown used to his ridiculous statements long ago, Snap looked confused. "Uh, no. But, Kai was here, and he got into a mess by projecting another King King."

"Wow!" Limmick laughed. "That kid sure has spunk, I'll say that for him."

Talia sighed. *Oh, Kai. Why would you go and do that?*

8

The Tourists
~Jade~

A friend took me to the former Region 6 once—shortly after they were taken in by Region 5—and goodness me, what an experience that was. Not much to see, and even less to do. Maintaining our health was quite the challenge. I believe we spent more gryns on flasks of water than we did on food and travel. But, oh my, the people! I've never met anyone as kind, funny, or welcoming anywhere.

—Magician Agatha was-a Cloud, *Meet the Magicians*

It was never easy for Jade to stand in front of her former home and see how badly it had fallen into ruin after only eight years. She'd much rather ignore it, but here she was, staring straight at it, along with two foreign tourists. This wreck of a home was, after all, a key part of the show.

If there was one thing Jade had learned in her sixty-seven years living in the islands, it was that people—no matter what region they were from—loved to witness the misfortune of others.

"Oh! Very good house," Kiranik said.

"Yes! Ruined, but very good," Daganok agreed.

Jade forced a smile. *Yes, delight in our misfortune. This is what happens when someone falls from grace. Just wait until everyone sees us when our family rises once again.* "Yes. My husband and son loved this home. We all did. It was a fitting residence for a magician. When we had it built, everyone considered it to be the grandest building on the island."

The two men, twins from the Whoosh clan, nodded in agreement. The eight-bedroom mansion still commanded attention, even in all its decay.

"Yes. Very nice."

"Very good . . . uh . . . why no one live now in?"

Ah ha, good, this part of the story always gets people from Region 6. "You come from Region 5, right?" she asked them.

"No, no. Region 6. Is very good place."

"Yes, much good. You come visit us. Ours very nice islands."

"I have heard such wonderful things about the far west. Thank you for your most generous offer. Anyway, we have not lived in our real home since Flint cut himself off from the magic—inside it."

"Inside? Here!?" Kiranik was visibly shaken.

Daganok blinked and asked, "In this house?"

"Yes, did you not know?" Jade answered.

"No."

"No know."

Kiranik looked intently at his brother for a short, silent moment before saying, "Now we understand. No one can live in house."

"No more living. It same in Region 6."

Yes, I know, Jade thought, but she said, "Oh, really! I did not know that."

The twins paused for a long moment and looked into each other's eyes as if they were projecting a conversation.

This is working out quite well. Jade had grown rather adept at finding ways to benefit from cultural differences. *Thank goodness no one holds to such foolish taboos here. No more living? Who wouldn't want to live in such an exquisite place—no matter what happened in it. After all, it's still one of the most valuable pieces of real estate on the island.*

Then Kiranik asked, "You own?"

"We want to know if you own big mansion."

They had to ask that. "It certainly is our house, there is no question about that. I did all the work. I hired the Stones to build it, and I was here every day to make sure they did everything right. I designed it specifically for my family—it really would not work for anyone else. But, technically, the Workshop owns it now."

"Whoosh! The Workshop owns?"

"Whoosh! The Workshop very rich."

"Of course they are, which is why the seven-year clause in the Magician's Covenant is so ridiculous. My son earned his place in the Workshop—honestly—and they really ought to have given us the deed to our home after all the nonsense we have endured. But look at it now. Our beloved abode is empty while we sleep in a shack in Brightside, surviving on the charity of others. Now we only go in to spray Eucalyptus oil on the mold and refresh our family icons."

"Shield icons in this house?"

"Ancestors live here?"

"Of course! They deserve a far better sanctuary than our little shack. This is our true dwelling place after all"—*and when Kai becomes a magician we'll move right back in and everything will be just like it was*—"even though the memories here will always fill us with great sorrow. Declarious can't even walk past without crying."

"Very sad! We go inside, look at your mighty family projections?"

"Yes! Very sad. I cry. I want go see family icons. They mighty strong?"

"Of course they are still strong; we have always spent the little we have to keep them alive. I would rather die of hunger than to see our ancestors fade away. They are very precious to us, so I must be careful who approaches them." Jade paused for dramatic effect, knowing that this would keep them eager to find out if she would allow them in or not. "Oh, all right. Go ahead."

Kiranik and Daganok ran up to the house like children eager for mischief. They pressed their faces against the window, peered into the house, and spoke to each other in hushed voices. Kiranik opened the door and they dove inside.

After Jade had lost her son eight years ago, visitors from all over the islands came here to get a glimpse into their lives. She had yelled at the first tourists and chased them away. But later, when Jade realized there were many people willing to pay her to give them a tour of her family's tragedy, she welcomed them.

Jade wasn't sure what she thought of these two. It was rare to see anyone from the former Region 6, which was quite a different culture. But she believed she knew enough about it to solicit the most money from these twins. *Anyone who comes to visit from that far away is after something very important.*

However, Kiranik and Daganok were unusual. They were sophisticated in a way that indicated they had traveled the islands. Based on the yacht they arrived on and the way they insisted that everyone give them space at all times, Jade knew that they had to be incredibly wealthy. Yet, the way that they spoke, the level of childlike excitement they displayed over every little thing, and their ridiculous choice of clothing caused her to think they weren't all that intelligent.

They could be the jackpot we've been waiting for. They are certainly wealthy enough to pay for Kai to get a Tier One trainer.

She couldn't figure out how anyone could tell the difference between the brothers. They seemed to be identical twins: pale, short, and thin, with the exact same orange, cropped hair. There was nothing to differentiate them physically. But from the moment they introduced themselves, Jade made a conscious effort to keep track of who was who so as not to offend them by using the wrong name. This was no easy feat, especially because they also wore the same projected clothes: a green tunic suit with a red shirt. It was a ridiculous outfit, made famous from the Grand Projection *Neckies and Nobodies*. That was one of her husband's favorites and made him laugh harder than any other Grand Projection, but Jade couldn't stand it; Green and Red were Conflicting Colors, and, like Yellow and Blue, they simply didn't belong together.

Jade was still brooding about how much damage that one Grand Projection had done to the islands when the twins came out of the house. Before *Neckies and Nobodies,* people knew their place. After it, a whole generation grew up believing a life of fun and adventure was possible for idiots dressed in Red and Green. *At least these idiots are rich.*

Just then, her grandson ran past on the path from Waterton.

Excellent timing. "Well, look who it is. Where are you off to in such a hurry?"

"Sorry, can't talk now. I need to see Mom!"

Jade smiled and called out to him again. "Your mother can wait. We have visitors, and I am sure they would love to meet you."

"Oh hi, it sure is nice to meet you. I hope you have a lovely visit on our island. But, please excuse me, I have something to attend to that's really important!" her grandson called back as he raced off down the path toward home.

More important than his grandmother? Jade kept herself composed. *I'll catch him at home.* "Forgive my grandson," she said, "he trains so hard these days. Nothing would please him more than getting into the Workshop so he can support his poor mother and me."

The eyes of the Whoosh twins grew wide.

"Grandson?" Kiranik gasped.

"He be poor Kai?" Daganok asked.

Good. They care about him. Empathy doubles the donation. "Yes, that certainly is my sweet boy. Such a treasure. Talented, even more than his father," Jade replied. *He'd better be, or we're going to collapse like this mansion.* She stopped that train of thought. *No. Kai will become a magician. He has to. Everything depends on it.*

Kiranik and Daganok stared intently at one another for a long moment. *They must be projecting some private conversation,* Jade deduced. *I know what they're discussing: they want to experience what Kai can do for them.*

The two men turned and faced Jade.

"We must meet!"

"Yes! Very must!"

This is going to be easier than I expected. Jade couldn't help but smile. "Follow me, darlings." Jade stepped away from the remnants of her old life and led them onto the cobblestone path that led to her current home.

As much as she hated coming back to this house, she did miss Little Hills; all the best people on the island lived in this neighborhood. Despite being close to Waterton, every home here possessed a sizable plot of land. The Little Hills community controlled the nicest beach on the island, and the parties they hosted were fantastic.

If Malroy had played things differently, we'd still be here. But no, he chose to abandon me to go off and worship Tav, while I had to stay and be reduced to a tour guide showing everyone the mess our son created. If only I'd been the one to marry Nyles, not Waddlebee. Then I'd be the one living in that mansion on the Island of the Summer Breeze.

"Very nice icons in house," one of the twins said as they walked.

"Yes, family have very good history house. We like."

"Thank you. Our ancestors should not be separated from their family like this; maybe someday, we can go back to them."

"Kai special. He help make happen. Much of honor in Shield family."

"Yes, family be very special when Kai become third mage in row."

Jade asked, "Do you really think he will?"

"No chance no."

"Yes, no possible he become no mage."

Ha ha. Even they know it. Waddlebee, you old hag, you think you've won. But your son doesn't have half the talent of my Kai.

As they left Little Hills and made their way deeper toward the center of the island, the nicely maintained path changed. Here, the cobblestones were no longer orderly and level. The well-manicured yards with projections of flowers and ornate foliage gave way to ordinary vegetation. The path went into the forest and became increasingly neglected and broken down, until they were walking on what was essentially trash and rubble.

"Home is—uh—very far?"

"Very long, far?"

"Yes," Jade answered. "We can no longer afford to live close to town."

"Ah, very sad. True life tragedy," Kiranik said.

"Tragedy. Life so sad," Daganok agreed.

All at once, a jubilant expression crossed Kiranik's face, and he said, "Tragedy! Just like *Life of Rice!*" Then, with a wave of his hand, he changed his outfit so he now looked like one of the rice farmers from that Grand Projection.

"Yes! *Life of Rice!*" Daganok immediately copied his brother.

Oh dear. These two are practically poozers. Jade took a close look at their black collars and saw the star pattern that marked commoners who had achieved the third privilege level. *At least they're doing it legally.*

The rest of the way, the two brothers did nothing but quote lines from *Life of Rice*. They didn't stop until they stepped out of the forest and into Brightside, the poorest neighborhood on the Island of the Four Kings.

This part of the island was dreary. Instead of beautiful mansions, manicured bushes, and fresh flowers, Brightside was filled with long rows of simple, hastily constructed shacks, all crowded together and punctuated by the occasional communal outhouse.

There were few projections to decorate or cover over the drabness. Those who lived here were too poor to afford decorators, and because most lacked the proper projection credentials, they were not allowed to make their own decorations. Instead, local business owners offered to pay to have projections placed on the shacks—that is, if the residents allowed their homes to be used as advertisements. Many people chose to do this because it gave them a few extra gryns. Everyone knew that advertisement projections were better than no projections at all.

Jade led Kiranik and Daganok down row after row of houses until they came to the one that had sheltered her family for the last eight years.

Unlike many of the other shacks in Brightside, theirs didn't have the projected blue and green paint of Ronnie's Rowers or the pleasant songbirds of New Leaf Estates. Even both of the neighbor's homes were covered with the bouquets and aromas of Daeya, the Flower Girl. Jade resented this. Daeya was a J. Shield, and not an S. Shield like them, but she was a Shield nonetheless. *How hard would it have been to project a few flowers and pleasant scents onto our home?* But no—the only advertiser who was willing to do anything to their home was a high-end vacation spa on Island of the Crystal Lake, all the way over in Region 3.

The advertisement was a projection of a gorgeous, tanned woman in a summer dress who lounged playfully on the roof of their home next to her muscular, shirtless partner, a man with bouncy cyan hair. Every time someone approached the entrance to the house the couple would say in unsettling unison, "Greetings, did you know the mistakes of the past can be washed away at the Cyan Spa?" Then when someone left, they would exclaim, "We look forward to seeing you at the Cyan Spa, where the mistakes of the past can be washed away!"

Aside from this horrid projection, Jade's home was quite plain. The standard whitewash paint was faded and peeling, the wood siding was rotting, and the roof sagged so badly that it leaked whenever it rained. The only good thing about it was the view. Out the back window they could see the forest instead of another shack. Jade hated it here, but—like everything in her life—it served a purpose.

After they arrived and had triggered the Cyan Spa advertisement, they found Kai and his mother, Declarious, standing just inside the door. They were engaged in what looked like a serious conversation. Although Jade couldn't hear what they were saying, it was clear something was wrong.

"Masters Kiranik and Daganok," Jade said as she approached, "I would like to introduce you to my son's widow, Declarious is-a Shield.

"Ah, very generous we greet you," Kiranik said.

"We celebrate your generosity with greetings," Daganok said.

Declarious smiled in response but did not say a word, and Kai quickly ducked into the shack.

"Kai," Jade called after him, "our guests would very much like to visit with you."

He turned back and stood inside the doorway.

"Masters Kiranik and Daganok, this is my grandson."

"Kai Master," the twins said at the same time. "Very pleased for meeting you!"

Although they were clearly excited to meet Kai, they kept their distance.

Declarious leaned over and said to Jade in a hushed voice, "Now isn't the best time."

Oh dear, I need to talk to her again about how to compose herself. This look of concern is most unbecoming. Jade ignored her daughter-in-law and faced Kai. "This is Masters Kiranik and Daganok. They are from the Whoosh clan, a very prestigious family from Region 5."

"Region 6," Kiranik and Daganok corrected.

"Of course, my apologies. This old brain of mine is nothing like it used to be." In fact, her old brain was still quite sharp, but Jade was prone to fake forgetfulness when she thought it would work to her advantage. Earlier, the twins had informed Jade that the Whoosh clan refused to acknowledge the assimilation of Region 6 by Region 5, even though it had happened over thirty years ago. "Yes, Region 6 really deserves to recover all that it lost. It is such a tragedy when good, honest people like you lose something so precious. Do you not think so?"

"Yes, yes. Region 6 very good place."

"Yes, yes. Our home very precious."

"It certainly must be. Now, let me show you our home," she said, and she showed them the inside of the shack.

"This your house? Is so small!" Kiranik said.

"Very small. Like for mouse," Daganok agreed.

"Ha ha! Small house. Small mouse. It true. Ha ha! So funny," Kiranik laughed and laughed. Then his face suddenly turned serious and he looked at Jade. "I apologize for little brother. He joker in family. Can no longer take to meetings. No one ever get work done anymore. Everyone laughing. He very funny brother. We very sorry."

Daganok shrugged his shoulders, lifted up his hands, and made an expression with his face as if to say, 'I just can't help myself.'

"Oh! Ha ha ha. There he go again. Brother so funny."

They have to be idiots—actual idiots. Jade stumbled over her next words. "Uh—yes. Very funny. He should help the Workshop. They need good comedians; it would be nice if one of their comedies was actually funny."

"Oh no. Little brother have no Color. But Kai. Yes, he have Color."

"Yes! No Color in me. But Kai big Color. Three in a row. Make history."

The two Whoosh twins nodded together.

"That would certainly be wonderful," Jade said.

"Where—uh—is Malroy Mage?" Kiranik asked.

"Yes, where famous trainer?" Daganok echoed.

"My husband has been away a long time." Jade did her best to sound sorrowful. "It has been hard for him to find work after what happened with my son. Many considered him responsible, as he trained Flint."

"Malroy Mage best trainer in Region 2."

"The best, Malroy Mage."

"Oh, thank you. Everyone used to believe that."

"Used to? No anymore?"

"No today?"

Jade crinkled her nose and motioned to their home in such a way that said, 'Would we be so poor if people still trusted him?' *And everyone would still trust him—if he hadn't run away from everything we built.*

"We think he great man. Many fans in Region 6. He earn much fortune there."

"Yes. He work great for Region 6 and he earn whispers."

Whispers? Jade was surprised by the mention of the ancient—and extremely valuable—platinum coins. A single whisper was equal to a million gryns. *They can't be serious.* No trainer has ever made that kind of money. Jade had heard rumors that her husband's skills were still in high demand in some far corners of the islands—places where her son's infamy would be an asset. Apparently, Region 6 was one of them. Malroy had received a few offers for work after his fall from grace, but he had rejected them all.

If only wealth motivated Malroy. He had to go and throw everything away. And for what? So he could live a backward life on the Island of the Cloudy Peaks while we remain in squalor? What a waste. It pained her to think of what she could have had. She was once again reminded that her childhood best friend, Waddlebee is-a Stone, had made the better choice. *Look at Waddlebee's life: the mansion she lives in, the parties she's hosted, the yacht, all the servants, and all the other splendors reserved for the family of a magician.* Jade looked around at her house, at Kai standing next to his mother, and at the tourists. *And look what my choice got me.*

Declarious finally spoke. "That is very kind of you. Malroy is a loving, kind man—he has always treated us far better than we deserve. It's good to know there are still a few people on O'Ceea who remember him."

Declarious dear, you really ought to let me do all the talking. "But, nobody remembers him anymore. He is not able to earn much, but we get by," Jade said, returning to her script.

"Yes, yes, very sad," Kiranik said.

"Very sad your story. I grieve," Daganok added.

"But please," Jade raised her voice, "there is no need to pity us. Everything will be made right when Kai has his Color pulled and gets the training he needs to enter the Workshop."

Kai shifted uncomfortably and said the words his grandmother had directed him to say in situations like this. "Yes, Grandmother, I will make everything right. I only wish we had enough lykes to hire a decent trainer."

Oh, come on Kai, you need to put more emotion into it than that. Your reluctance is so obvious. Jade said to the tourists, "Now that we have found Kai, I suggest we go see the new Glimmering. There is little else to interest us here."

"New Glimmering? Here in Region 2?" Kiranik looked shocked.

"Glimmering? How you know—we no know?" Daganok said.

I know far more than you can imagine. "It was just discovered, so all of us should go now, before it dissolves and we lose the opportunity to get a taste of what the Master Magician intends to serve up for us this year."

"All of us—together?" Kai asked.

"Yes Kai, these men have come a long way for you."

"Yes, we have very big boat. Room for everyone."

"Yes, big room. We all go."

"Kai," Jade said, "I expect you are eager to see it."

"Uh, Grandmother, I . . . um . . . something happened earlier . . ."

Jade raised an eyebrow at Kai when she saw the resistance in his eyes. "Excellent. I am sure it is something absolutely wonderful," Jade interrupted. "Kai is always doing wonderful things."

"Yes! Kai big third-generation mage."

"Kai special big ingredient!"

"Come along, Kai. We must not disappoint our guests. They have come a very long way to meet you. A Glimmering is a perfect occasion to show them your talents." *Don't be reluctant, Kai, this is what we have to do in order to survive.*

Kai turned to his mother. It was clear that Declarious didn't want him to go either, but thankfully she understood this was essential for the family, and so she played her part to the best of her ability.

"I'll see what I can do about . . . what you told me," Declarious said.

Kai sighed. "All right, let's go."

"Hurrah!" Kiranik and Daganok cheered.

"We shall be back soon, darling," Jade said to Declarious.

✳   ✳   ✳

After Jade offered them a ride to the Glimmering in her rickety rowboat, Kiranik and Daganok—as expected—insisted they all come aboard their yacht instead.

The Whoosh twins' boat was far more decadent than Jade had envisioned. It was a fairly standard, medium-sized yacht currently rigged with four sails. Although it could hold about ten people comfortably on the deck, the yacht felt cramped because dozens of projected characters were crammed onto it.

I bet they paid more lykes for the projections than they paid for the actual boat. Jade recognized that these were masterfully crafted, likely placed there by a magician. Everything on board was from a Grand Projection, and while some might see this collection as a nice homage to the Workshop, Jade found it tacky.

"What a delightful assortment of projections," Jade said.

"Thank you, Jade Mistress. We love Grand Projections."

"Grand Projections make happy our love."

While the twins peered around at them with adoration, Jade turned her attention to the captain of the yacht, a stout little man who shouted down at the rowers in the hull, "Get into formation! Time to launch!"

When the oars went out, Jade counted each one. *There are*

fourteen rowers down there! That's far more than they need. A yacht this size might have—at most—six rowers to supplement the power of the wind, or to keep the boat moving when there was none. *But fourteen! These two must be far more wealthy than I first imagined.*

"You have done such a nice job with your boat," Jade observed. "Have they not done a nice job, Kai?"

"Yeah. It looks great." It was clear that Kai was trying to sound interested, but—even though he was surrounded by the projections of great heroes, villains, and monsters—he kept glancing back toward Waterton, as if he was searching for something.

What could he be looking for? Owing to the announcement of the Glimmering, the town was almost entirely deserted. Only Markus is-a Shield, the captain of the Island Patrol, could be seen moving quite quickly through the streets. *I bet Kai's looking for that D. Leaf girl. I'm sure he's been boosting her. I wonder when he'll find out she's just using him. No D. Leaf has ever had the talent she's showing.*

Suddenly, the boat lurched away from the dock.

"Whoa!" Jade exclaimed as she tried to keep her balance. Daganok was the nearest person to her and could have easily reached out his hand to stabilize her, but instead, he moved away as she struggled to stay on her feet.

"Hang on, Grandmother," Kai said as he took a step toward her, but Jade waved him away, asserting she was fine.

"Many rower make boat go fast! Woo woo Whoosh!" Kiranik cheered from his position next to the wheelhouse.

"So fast, we Whoosh like wind!" Daganok echoed gleefully.

Jade looked at the younger twin with a mixture of annoyance and admiration as he followed his brother below deck and into their private cabin. She was relieved he hadn't actually reached out to try to help her when she almost fell. *That would have been entirely inappropriate.* The idea of a stranger touching her sent a shiver through her. *But he should have at least taken a step toward me, out of common courtesy—like Kai did.* She shrugged it off as a cultural difference.

The boat was soon cutting through the crystal blue waters at a speed few boats ever attained, and to her surprise, she found she quite liked it. *Hmm, yes. This is much faster than I expected. Imagine how jealous Waddlebee would be if I shot past her on a yacht with fourteen rowers!*

✳   ✳   ✳

It wasn't hard to find the cluster of small islands where the Glimmering had been spotted. Even if they hadn't known the way, it was impossible to miss: nearly all the vessels in the surrounding area were there.

It also wasn't hard for the Whoosh twins to secure a spot alongside the crowded ramshackle dock. Jade watched closely as the captain of their boat opened his coin pouch and paid another boat to give up its spot on the west side of the island.

Yes, I knew they weren't afraid to spend money.

The spot they'd secured was right next to a small but elegant boat that was advertising the most successful smell projection restaurant chain in all the islands: Nosy's.

"Nobody knows you like Nosy's!" a short man standing on deck crooned. "Nosy's knows you better than you knows yourself!"

Jade tried her best to avoid looking at him. Like every advertiser for this restaurant, the man had dozens of small noses projected all over his face; it was impossible to see his eyes or mouth. *Oh, how I used to love going there,* Jade thought as the captain and crew secured the lines.

After the boat was docked and the lines coiled, the captain and all the rowers left and went onto the island. *That's strange.* It was a few more moments before Kiranik and Daganok came out of their private cabin.

"Kai, time to go," Jade called.

"Projections never smelled so good!" the advertiser continued to call out to them. "At Nosy's, we knows what youse needs!"

"Oh! Nosy's very good! We needs," Kiranik exclaimed.

"Yes. We needs! We needs!" Daganok shouted.

"Region 6 very best, even though no Nosy's."

"No Nosy's to knows what we needs." Daganok sounded sad.

What? Are they saying there are no Nosy's in Region 6? Jade found that hard to believe. She was sure the chain of restaurants had spread over all of O'Ceea. *Must be because of all the poverty there.*

"Come on, Kai," Jade said from the dock, when she realized he hadn't moved.

"I'd rather stay here."

This caught the attention of the tourists. "You no want see Glimmering?" Kiranik asked.

"What? You no want?" Daganok gasped.

Jade stared at Kai. "You have been looking forward to Glimmering season since last year's ended."

"It's not long before the Festival; I really ought to be working on my projections."

Jade's face became serious. "Kai, what is really going on?"

"Nothing. I just don't want to go—and there's nothing you can do to make me."

Honestly? You're really going to do this to me now? But Jade knew by the look in his eyes that trying to force him would not be effective. *Fine. I can make this work.* She turned back to the twins and put on her best smile. "Kai wants to stay on board so he can make you a present. He would like to add to your collection of projections." She motioned to the ones that covered the boat.

Kiranik and Daganok exchanged a look of delight.

"Projection on our boat from Kai is-a Shield!? We say yes!"

"We say mega yes, and Kai make projection!"

"Wonderful! So, what is your favorite character from a Grand Projection? Perhaps one that you do not have yet." *If that's even possible.*

"King King!" they answered at once.

"Really?" Jade was caught off guard by the request; if this was another joke, she did not understand it.

"Yes, King King. Please!"

"Please, yes, make King King."

No one in their right mind would want a monument to that atrocity on their boat.

Kai peered out at them. "King King? Are you being serious?"

"Yes. King King is newest and best."

"Best popular in Region 6!"

"You make for us!"

"You add for our boat!"

Kai looked away. "I'm . . . I'm not so great at that one, and I'm still a child. I'm pretty sure I'm not supposed to do that."

"Region 6 different rules. No so strict."

"Strict rules, we no have."

"You be big magician one someday. I know you do King King good. He Whoosh favorite."

"He favorite Whoosh. You make one good King King, great as Master Magician!"

Their genuine excitement over this amused Jade. *Are they completely unaware? Or*—the thought made her uneasy—*what if King King really is something people in Region 6 relate to? The current Master Magician was born and raised there, after all.* "All right Kai, do you want to stay and make a King King, or do you want to go with us?" Jade asked.

Kai scratched the back of his head and looked nervously at all the boats nearby. "I guess I'll stay here and see what I can do."

"Woo woo Whoosh!" Kiranik and Daganok cheered.

"But, I'm not promising anything. It probably won't look much like King King."

"Delightful!" Jade tried to sound positive. *We're going to have to have a long talk about his behavior later.* Something was going on with Kai—something unpleasant and dangerous—and she determined she was going to root it out.

The Attack

~Jade~

There's nothing quite like the gift we've been given in projections. However, serious problems have been known to occur due to underage misuse.

—Island Patrol Captain Markus is-a Shield, "Eye Opening Interviews and Outlooks," *The Weekly Word*

Jade could hardly believe her eyes when she saw the projected boy running freely around the forest. *So the Master Magician is going to make another attempt to glorify idiocy. Hasn't he learned?*

She became disgusted with the Glimmering as soon as the boy said, "Color, no Color, nothing will stop me from laughing and playing."

Everyone knows having a Color changes everything for the better. Jade didn't stop herself from calling out to the boy trying to flee from her, "Surely your family would be devastated if you never made it to the Island of the Magician's Workshop?"

It pleased her that the boy stopped and answered her. "The Island of the Magician's Workshop? What's that?"

How ridiculous. He's never heard of it? Why would the Workshop make a projection about a character who didn't know about the Workshop? The Master Magician is an even greater fool than I thought. He's going to have another clinker on his hands with this one.

"Fascinating!" she heard the nutty fisherman Limmick say.

I can't believe this is the sort of thing people get so excited about. "Everyone knows it is the island where only magicians and their families can live."

"Why would magicians want to live on an island and be separated from everyone?"

Oh dear, it's going to be another Old World Grand Projection that says, 'everyone's the same.' Well, they're not. Magicians are better, and they have a right to live separate from all the chaff taking over the islands. Caught up in her thoughts, Jade no longer paid attention to the conversation taking place around her.

"Ah ha! He from old age!" Kiranik spouted.

"Before Flood! This be very good story," his halfwit twin agreed.

The boy scampered away to a tree, where it looked and acted like some deranged monkey. *Good riddance.*

"Jade, you brilliant old donkey," Limmick shouted so loud the entire crowd could hear.

His comment cut her. *How dare you call me names! I'm a lady, and a very attractive one at that. I've had many suitors in my day. Very few women have managed to keep their looks as well as I have. Waddlebee, for example—you should look at her before calling me names.*

She was done, but her guests—*of course*—were fascinated and spent an unfathomable amount of time staring at the annoying boy up in the branches of the coral tree. It was one of Jade's least favorite kinds of trees. *It's a tragedy they weren't all cut down during the purges.* Jade was certain the Workshop had chosen this island on purpose because it was full of these trees. *It suits their abominable message, to have that boy sitting up in a tree that burns with Conflicting Colors whenever it blooms.*

I'm glad my Kai isn't as rebellious as that little monkey-boy, she thought, right before she caught sight of the D. Leaf girl her grandson liked so much. Then she reconsidered. *Kai is susceptible to love. I wouldn't be surprised if it's something about her that's influencing his mood today.*

After everyone but Limmick and the D. Leaf girl had left—and because nothing else had happened with the projection that was interesting in the least—Jade suggested it was time to leave. To her relief, the twins agreed.

"Ohhh . . . such mystery! Who be this boy?" one of them asked when they started to return to their boat.

"I like boy. He big mystery."

Jade didn't care to differentiate between them anymore, and she stopped paying attention to which one of them was speaking.

"'Color, no Color'—be same. All laugh play. Good message. New Grand Projection be very successful. Master Magician very good. He have many projections more he tell." Kiranik and Daganok spoke in their back and forth manner.

Oh dear, what are the islands coming to?

As soon as they stepped out of the trees, Jade sensed trouble. There was a strange smell in the air that did not seem right, and she thought she heard shouting.

All the boats on the west end of the island were gone. When they stepped around the bend and the Whoosh yacht came into view, Jade saw it had been splattered with brightly colored goo bombs. Standing on the deck of the boat, with his back to them, was Kai, completely covered with the Nine Colors of the rainbow.

"Look! Kai make King King, and King King make enemies! Oh! This be good adventure!" Kiranik and Daganok said.

What's going on? The only other vessel in the area was a rowboat occupied by four young people between the ages of seventeen and twenty. By the way they were yelling insults at Kai, it was clear they were the source of the damage. *Why are they so angry?*

"Didn't you learn your lesson?" one of the young men in the rowboat jeered.

"Learn? Shields are too dumb to learn," said a young woman.

That's Gromer and Glender is-a Wave! You two will get the prohibition of your life for this. I'll make sure of that. Jade was about to storm onto the dock when the twins called her back.

"Stop, Jade Mistress. We watch, hide here," they said. Not wanting to insult her guests, she resigned herself to step back, out of the line of sight, and crouched next to them behind some brambles. *The things I put up with for donations.*

"A shield is meant to protect, but all your family's done is destroy," taunted Gropher is-a Wave, a young Violet mage.

The fourth person in the rowboat, Tiepan is-a Leaf, a Blue mage, said, "You should run away and ask to join the Sword clan." He then flung out his hands, sending twin swords to stab into the side of the boat.

"After all the destruction your fireballs did on Market Street, maybe the Fire clan would adopt you. Kai is-a Fire is perfect for you; it even matches your hand!" Gromer teased, and suddenly the hull of the boat became engulfed in a blaze of fire.

You terrible, awful children. I knew Kai should have come with me. He needs me to protect him. Jade stood up to go, but one of the twins stopped her.

"No, Jade Mistress! You stay here," he commanded her with a force and authority that Jade hadn't imagined they possessed.

Who are you to command me? For the first time since meeting them, Jade wondered if there was something more to these two rich, entitled idiots.

"You stay, we see what Kai King King do," the other twin said.

King King? What is he talking about? Jade wondered until she saw a pitiful projection of a gorilla beside Kai. It was a quarter the size of her grandson and was waving its arms in the air and roaring—although it sounded more like chirping.

Kai wasn't paying any attention to the gorilla, however. He was attempting to dissolve the goo bombs that covered the yacht, but it appeared he didn't have enough Power to do anything about them.

"Look, he can't even dissolve a simple color stain. I didn't put even half of my Power into them, either," Gropher mocked.

"Come on, Gropher," Kai said. "This is a really expensive yacht. You shouldn't be doing this."

"Then you shouldn't have stolen it."

Kai looked confused. "What? I didn't steal it."

"Then why are you the only one on it?"

"The owners are here, on the island," Kai explained. "They're really rich, important, and powerful people—when they come back, you'll be in big trouble."

Kiranik and Daganok exchanged a confused look.

"We be rich?"

"Kai say so, must be true."

I'm crouching behind a thornbush with two throttlewogs.

"No," said Gropher. "We won't get into any trouble at all—if anyone comes back, they'll find you, alone, on a boat that's been wrecked. You'll be the one in big trouble then."

At this, Kai's miniscule gorilla began hollering at the top of its lungs.

"Kai very smart. He stay quiet and let King King yell for him," one of the twins said, causing the other to look back with a puzzled expression.

Gropher kept on taunting. "Look at his pathetic gorilla! Ha ha! Here Kai, let us help you with that." He whispered something to the others and all of them began making big sweeping motions as if they were projecting something monumental.

Jade saw no indication that any new projections were being created, but then she noticed that something was happening to Kai's gorilla. It started to grow in size and in ferocity. *They've taken over Kai's projection. I need to put an end to this.*

"You wait," one brother said, followed by, "You see." Both of them pointed back into the forest, where Jade saw—for the first time—that all of the rowers of the boat were crouched behind them. *Oh my. I guess I won't have to do anything at all—they will put an end to this.*

The loss of control over his projection startled Kai, and he leapt back from it. Then, recovering, he thrust his arms out and put all of his effort into dissolving it. But it was no use; the projection had far more Power than he possessed.

Jade shivered as she watched the now raging gorilla climb up the rigging and grab the first projection it came across: a small wallaroo. King King slammed it against the mast several times until it went limp in the monster's hands. King King then dropped it and continued to another projection and did the same, then on to another.

Kai tried to stop it any way he could. He tried again to overpower it. He tried to strengthen the projections that were being torn apart. He even tried to project a banana suit onto Gromer to distract the gorilla, but Gropher quickly dissolved it.

No matter what Kai tried, nothing worked. He was helpless.

"Enjoy your new girlfriend, Kai," Tiepan taunted as the others, now bored, took up their oars, preparing to row away. But before they left, the Blue mage made one last modification to the gorilla, and in an instant, it was wearing a bright yellow sundress. "There we go. Look at her! I think she's a much more attractive girlfriend for you than Talia. Goodbye, Kai! I hope you enjoy your prohibition."

You won't get away with this. I can't wait to see how much you all enjoy your prohibitions. Jade looked to the twins. *Come on, now's the time to get them, before they row too far away.* But the men from Region 6 remained still and watched with strange delight as the deformed gorilla pounded their expensive projections and trashed their yacht like an undisciplined two-year-old throwing a tantrum.

The rowboat was soon out of sight, and the gorilla roared so loud that anyone in the immediate area was sure to hear it. *These fools don't appear concerned at all. How is that possible?*

"It okay. Boat insured," one of them said, as if he knew what she was thinking.

"Insurance always make life better."

Kai looked miserable and crawled over to a corner of the boat, where he slumped down and hid from sight.

"Ah ha! Very sad adventure story. Kai no cry out for help."

"No cry, so no one come and save his day."

Of course not. Kai knows if he cries for help, whoever comes will only blame him for all this.

One by one, the projections on the boat were disabled by the twisted beast, and it became clear to Jade that their owners would continue to do nothing. *Do they not care about any of it?*

Just before everything had been laid to waste, three children burst out of the forest, sprinted across the beach, passed by them, and leapt onto the dock.

"You will stop, NOW!" Weston shouted as he held out his hand. The gorilla froze.

"That dress wasn't meant for you," Snap said, and with a flick of her wrist, it was gone.

"Stop hurting Kai," Luge joined in. He had what looked to be an actual rock in his hand that he was about to throw, but before he did so, he stopped short.

Weston crouched down with a look of fierce determination on his face. Within a few heartbeats, King King was gone.

Kiranik and Daganok leapt up and started making whooshing noises. "Whooooooosh-ay, Whooooooosh-ay!" They were shouting at the top of their lungs.

"Big surprise!"

"I no see big twist coming!"

"Story have very good ending!"

"Everyone very love happy good ending!"

I need to go to Kai and make sure he is okay. Leaving the whooshing behind, Jade hurried over to the yacht and hovered over her grandson. When Kai saw her, he got up and said, "I'm all right Grandmother. Really, I'm all right."

It appeared that Kai's spirits were lifted by the sight of his friends, and Jade was also pleased. When she expressed her gratitude to Weston, Snap, and Luge, they responded that they were just doing the kind of thing Kai would do for them.

"Plus," Luge said, "we left Kai once already today, and we couldn't let that happen to him again."

"Sorry we didn't get here sooner," Snap said. "We were waiting on the other side of the island and didn't notice anything was wrong over here until we heard the roar."

Kai turned to Weston, who was hard at work dissolving the color stains from the boat. "Thanks," he said. "I knew you'd have enough Power to stop it."

"Well, I kinda owed you," Weston responded. "I probably still owe you, and will owe you until the end of time." Weston finished erasing the projected fire from the yacht. Kai looked confused, so Weston explained, "I put all the Power I had into King King—the other one. That's why you couldn't dissolve it after we left you. I'm really sorry." Weston turned his attention to cleaning all the color stains that were covering Kai.

What are they talking about? Jade knew there was something she was missing. *All this interest in King King is making me sick.*

"So that's why I couldn't do anything to stop it." Kai paused, thinking. "That makes me feel better. Sure, I forgive you."

"Really? For real?" Weston asked as he dissolved the last of the stains from Kai.

"Of course. We're buds, right? But, I'm glad you apologized, otherwise I'd have to hold a grudge against you until we were old men," Kai joked. "Thanks for cleaning this all up for me."

"Yeah, it's the least I could do." Weston looked around at the carnage on the yacht. "I wish I could help with the rest of this, but I don't have anywhere near the Kingdom to repair any of it."

Kai looked up at all the devastated projections strewn across the yacht and said, "And I thought what happened earlier today was aw—" Kai stopped speaking when he heard a commotion. The unspeaking pack of rowers was marching down the dock toward them. "Grandmother! What are your guests going to do to me?"

I have no idea. But someone has to pay for this. They might force you to serve them until you work off the debt. "They have no right to do anything; you did not do anything wrong. It is those rapscallions who should be punished. Plus, they witnessed the entire thing and did nothing to stop it."

"What?" Kai said, but before Jade could explain, the rowers were aboard the boat. To Jade's surprise and delight the crew took no notice of them and went straight below deck. Right behind them came the captain, who immediately instructed Weston, Snap, and Luge to leave.

"Wish me luck," Kai said to his friends as they stepped off the boat.

The captain didn't speak to Kai, or even look at him; he set to work preparing the boat for departure. Only after the yacht was ready did Kiranik and Daganok finally come aboard.

"Masters Kiranik and Daganok," Kai said as soon as he saw them, "I humbly apologize for all that happened and—"

"Kai, you make us big happy with new entertainment."

"We very long no see big good entertainment. We happy."

Kai looked as stunned as Jade felt. "But—your projections—look at them. They were very valuable."

"It okay. We be rich."

"Kai say so, must be true."

Are they really not upset? Impossible. No one can lose anything this expensive and not care. The more time Jade spent with these men, the less she understood them. This made her uneasy. *No matter how rich they are, I'm ready to be free of them.* "It is time for us to leave," Jade ordered the tourists. The two looked at one another, shrugged, and gave their own order to the captain to cast off.

✳   ✳   ✳

No one spoke for most of the journey back. Instead of disappearing below deck to their cabin as they had on the way to the Glimmering, Kiranik and Daganok stayed up on deck, where they were silent but looked intently at each other. *They're projecting some secret conversation, no doubt.* By the way they kept glancing at Kai, Jade was certain the twins had something they wanted to communicate with him.

The eerie silence was finally broken when they said, "So good, Kai! You real talent! Master Magician one day. We know!"

"Thanks," Kai replied in a way that conveyed it wasn't something he wanted, "but I'd need a Color for that."

"Color, no Color. No difference," one of them said. Kai—who hadn't seen the Glimmering—looked confused.

There it is. See how the Master's stories influence people. The Workshop is directly responsible for why no one knows right from wrong anymore.

"Ha ha, Little Brother. Good funny, but now time for important meeting."

"Okay, I be good and make no funny," Daganok promised.

"Kai," Kiranik said, "it true. Color, no Color, you still real talent. We have big stadium in Region 6. You come in future and make Grand Projection for all us, Color, no Color. You and friends very welcome."

Kai nodded politely but said nothing.

Go on Kai, this is the time. You know what to say.

"One question," Kiranik said. "We hear you have special talent with projection. You make projection better for other people. This special gift."

"My projection be better with you. Very rare special gift."

"We travel to all islands to make happy meeting with this talent. We hear rumor you special, so we come and see you."

"We come to see."

Ah ha, there it is. Jade smiled. *Time to show them what's really going to mark our family's place in history.*

While very few people knew about Kai's secret ability, word was leaking out. It had become increasingly common for people to come and directly ask to have it used on them. In the beginning, it was very infrequent. It only happened once a year, at most. Now, it was more like once every four weeks. But Jade liked this, for whenever someone came to them for Kai's gift, she knew it meant a large donation.

"You have seen our home. We are a very poor family," she said. *That's your cue, Kai.*

He lowered his eyes and continued to say nothing.

Come on Kai, this is the big one. Jade said, "Kai always helps others—when they are in need."

"Oh, yes. We same. We own insurance company."

"Insurance always make life better."

"Kai," Jade said as she turned to him, "are you able to help our guests make their projections better?"

"Yes, Grandmother." He faced the twins. "But, I

ask—please!—don't tell anyone else about it; too many people know already."

"No, no! We never tell."

"No. I know. Even though I big joker, I keep very good secret for you."

"All right," Kai said. "Hold on." He closed his eyes for about ten heartbeats. He didn't move. Nothing about his nature changed. When he opened his eyes, it seemed like he hadn't done anything at all.

"When you begin?" Kiranik asked.

"I am still same?" Daganok asked.

"I'm finished," Kai informed them.

"Finished?"

"That all you do?"

Kai, come on! You know how important it is to make it look impossibly hard. Whenever someone sees how easy this is for you, they always pay so much less.

"Yeah, I don't need to wave my hands or anything."

"I no feel different." Kiranik looked at his hands. "You feel different, Little Brother?"

"No." Daganok looked completely let down, as if the one thing he was looking for most in his life proved to be nothing more than an illusion.

"Go on, project something," Jade encouraged. "Make it something you've projected many times before."

The twins looked at each other. Kiranik instructed the captain to bring him a piece of fluff cake. Once it arrived, Kiranik took the airy, white, and otherwise tasteless pillow of flour, raised it up, and wriggled his fingers wildly in the air. His eyes were fixated on his brother, who stood very still with a big smile, as if bracing himself for great things to come.

When Daganok smelled it, his face nearly exploded with joy.

"Oh! Oh! Oh! It smell so so good!" He leaned over and took another big whiff of the cake. "Me smell more more better than ever!"

The two began to dance around on the deck as if they had obtained some life-changing gift. "You very special," they shouted. "You Kai. You very sure next Master Magician. We thank you more."

Yes, laugh and play, you Colorless fools, but don't forget— nothing in life is free. Then, as if reading her mind, Kiranik turned to face her.

"Jade Mistress, we have most nice present for Kai."

"We give you later, when Kai return to home island."

Jade smiled and, trying her best to sound genuine, said, "Oh my, how unexpected."

✳   ✳   ✳

As soon as they came into the marina of the Island of the Four Kings, Jade caught sight of the Island Patrol gathered on the dock, watching them approach.

"IP here," Kiranik observed.

"I allowed?" Daganok asked.

How convenient; I won't have to run around the island trying to track them down to report those rapscallions. "Hello, Markus," Jade called to the captain of the Island Patrol, who stood with two officers at the dock. "I must inform you of some unpleasant business we have experienced."

"Indeed. An unfortunate turn of events."

"Oh? You know about it then?"

"Of course," Captain Markus said. "Unfortunately, the prohibition is going to be quite severe, but rules are rules."

"Absolutely. I understand completely." Jade was delighted as she stepped onto the dock. "Severe punishments are necessary to ensure our young citizens know their place."

"I'm glad you're in agreement," Captain Markus said.

He quickly boarded the boat, reached out, and grabbed Kai.

"Excuse me?" Jade's eyes grew wide. "You have the wrong person. The crime was done by Tiepan is-a Leaf and the three Waves he keeps company with."

Captain Markus ignored her and directed his words at Kai. "Kai is-a Shield, you are charged with projecting a giant, fireball-throwing King King, which terrorized the citizens of this island with the ethereal presence of Devos Rektor. How do you plead?"

"Markus, what is going on? I do not . . . Kai don't say anyth—"

"Guilty," Kai replied.

What is he talking about? That little King King didn't terrorize anyone but Kai, and it certainly didn't throw fireballs! "Masters Kiranik and Daganok, please explain who attacked your yacht," she said, but when she turned back to see why they were being so quiet, she realized that they had disappeared into their private cabin.

Captain Markus continued, "May it be publicly proclaimed that Kai is-a Shield, a minor, pleads guilty to the creation of a public projection. The aforementioned projection became free of its creator's control and overpowered and extinguished commercial projections in the central market and docks. As this is your first offense—and you have admitted your guilt—I sentence you to three weeks of prohibition: all ten fingers, both hands up to the wrist, and both eyes."

"This is outrageous!" Jade exclaimed. "I forbid you!"

"Jade is-a Shield, you are not an elder of this island. You do not have the authority to govern me, nor will I allow you to obstruct justice," Captain Markus commanded as he pulled out a small vial of liquid. "Are you ready Kai? This will be a lot less painful if you don't fight it."

"I won't fight you," Kai said. He held out both of his arms for the two officers to grab hold of.

"Good, I'll do your eyes now," Captain Markus said as he

pushed against Kai's forehead, tilting his head back until his eyes were positioned straight up.

"Three weeks! You must not do this," Jade exclaimed. "The Color Ceremony is only four weeks away."

Kai made fists with both his hands and prepared himself to receive the drops. Captain Markus raised his hand and pulled out a dropper from the vial. Quickly and efficiently, the officer of the law squirted two drops into each of Kai's eyes.

Jade watched helplessly as her grandson twisted his body and tried to break free. He let out a startled gasp—"Wash it out!"—and blinked his eyes wildly. "Wash it away!" He shook his head. Finally, he dropped to his knees. Tears began to roll down his cheeks.

It took everything in Jade to restrain herself from reaching out to pull Kai away from them. *This isn't right! The IP have too much power. When did they become so eager to judge others?*

"Your grandson will not be able to see reality clearly," the captain told Jade, "so make sure you keep a close eye on him. Someone will come by every morning to re-administer the drops until his prohibition is over. And, please, ensure this doesn't happen again. Kai is a valuable asset. It would be a shame for him to miss the Ceremony because of any further disobedience.

"Come Kai, I'll lead you to the courthouse where we will administer the treatment to your fingers and hands. Mistress Jade, I will personally deliver him back to your home tonight."

"I'm sorry, Grandmother," Kai sniffled. "We were playing with projections earlier today, and—"

"I would advise you to be silent right now, Kai. I don't want you to say anything that would force me to lengthen your prohibition."

And so, without another word, the captain and the officers led Kai away, leaving Jade alone. *Kai didn't do anything wrong. What's going on? We're being targeted. Someone is trying to get us banished from the island.*

As soon as they were out of sight, the tourists reemerged.

"Very strong men!" one of them said.

"Island Patrol very strict in Region 2," the other agreed.

"It appears Kai is being punished for what those other children did to your yacht. Are you going to do something about that?"

"Yes, yes," they agreed. They sent their captain off to speak with the Island Patrol and give a full report of the actual events.

Satisfied justice would be done, Jade said, "I thank you for a lovely day, gentlemen, but, due to these unfortunate events, I need to say goodbye. Before I go, I believe you mentioned something about a present for Kai?"

"Yes, yes. Proper way be show you after meal."

"We take Jade Mistress to Nosy's."

Nosy's? Jade looked at all the famous creatures and characters dangling limp around the brothers. A little weasel with broken legs dragged itself to the edge of the boat and looked up at her with helpless eyes. *They can't possibly think I'd want to eat at a time like this.* "I apologize, but I really must go."

"Oh, very serious."

"No one say no for Nosy's."

"Yes, I am afraid it is very serious," Jade said. "Now, the present."

"Very sorry. We present present for you now."

"We offer you special treasure for Kai."

Although she had been eager to receive payment from these men all day, coins no longer seemed important to Jade. Wealth, for this short moment, had lost its pull on her. As she leaned in to see the gift, she had only one concern: Kai. *I must get home as soon as possible and get everything ready for him. He will need a comfortable place to rest and recover from this atrocious mistake.*

But when she saw the gift, Jade's blood began to boil. The payment for all she had done wasn't like anything she had expected.

The Orphan

~Kaso~

The Epics of the Cursed *are—without a doubt—going to become timeless masterpieces. Never before in the history of O'Ceea has there been a villain so deliciously evil as Devos Rektor. We loathe and simultaneously love this Lord of Chaos. Greydyn is-a Ring has breathed real life into this new-made myth. I wouldn't be surprised if he rises to the level of Master Magician someday.*

—Opinionator Kasal was-a Quill, after the original release of *The Epics of the Cursed*

"It'll start soon, right?" Coby couldn't mask the eager anticipation in his voice. "It's gotta be soon!"

"Yeah," Kaso said for what felt like the hundredth time. It was still the bottom of the Crimson watch, but judging from the lightness of the sky, it wouldn't be long before the sun rose and beams of Red light spread across the islands, heralding the beginning of a new day.

"It's going to be better this year. I know it." Coby squirmed with delight. "It's going to be the best one ever."

Although Kaso was only sixteen—six years older than Coby—he'd lost most of the excitement of anticipating new Grand Projections. They just didn't move him like they once had.

Must be because I'm getting older. Deep down he knew this wasn't true, but he wasn't ready to face the real cause. He looked around. In the early light he was beginning to make out the faces of the people who had surrounded them all night. Hundreds of boats from every island in Region 3 had gathered on the sea, filled with people, young and old.

"Kaso, can you make me another juggling bear projection?" Coby asked.

"No, you'll enjoy the Glimmering more if you have to wait. Plus, I don't want to have to focus on dissolving it once everything starts."

Glimmering season had begun early this year. After the first few Glimmerings appeared a few weeks ago, they had started popping up all over the islands. Most were hidden and needed to be discovered, but others—like the one they were about to experience—were pre-announced and thus drew big crowds.

"Hey Kaso, can you at least refresh your blanket projection? I'm feeling a bit cold," asked Bront, who was sitting behind him. Despite being eighteen, Bront was still happily dependent on others.

"No problem," Kaso said. He stretched out his arms, closed his eyes, focused on warmth, and began to make a humming sound through his nose. The projected blanket that covered the two dozen boys crammed into their small boat grew thicker and felt softer on their skin. The projection also made them perceive the sensation of warmth, even though their actual bodies remained the same temperature.

"Thanks! It really is a shame you can't test this year," Bront said.

"Yeah, if any orphan has a Color inside them, it'd be you, Kaso," said Klofen, the only fourteen–year-old Kaso had ever heard of who could grow a full natural beard. "You're going to be a mega successful mage. I'm sure of it."

"No way." Macea, a fifteen-year-old girl who was in the boat next to them, joined the conversation. "Kaso's going to be a magician of the Second Magnitude!"

"Why not one of the Third Magnitude?" Bront asked.

Macea laughed and said, "He probably will, but I don't want to be the person who said it—it might cause Kaso to become arrogant."

"That'll never happen," Klofen said, "right, Coby? Can you imagine your brother growing up to become like Migo the Marauder?"

"Nope, he's nothing like that guy."

Kaso responded, "I'm a lot more arrogant than you think."

"Which proves you're not arrogant at all," Macea said with a laugh.

"It's so stupid that we're not allowed to get our collar until we're nineteen," Bront said.

"That rule was made to protect us," Macea replied. "Orphans have more than enough struggles as it is. The last thing we need is to have our hopes and dreams dashed at the feet of a puller."

"But, Kaso's different. I agree with Macea: you're going to be a magician," Klofen said.

"You will be. Even Auntie knows it," Macea projected to Kaso.

She does? Kaso squinted his left eye.

"I overheard her talking about you with one of the island elders," her projected voice continued. "They agreed that if any orphan had a chance to become a magician, it would be you."

Kaso had never heard Auntie say anything like this before. She usually discouraged speculation about Color because she didn't want the children under her care to get their hopes up. Color was notoriously difficult to find in orphans, and—even on the rare occasion it was found—orphans had a severe disadvantage in becoming magicians. Because they weren't allowed stand before a puller until they turned nineteen, they entered training three years behind others their age. *But if Auntie does, in fact, believe I have a chance—that would change everything.*

"Hey, Auntie," Macea yelled to the woman a few boats away from them. "We all think Kaso has enough talent to earn a place in the Workshop. You agree, right?"

"You know how I feel about giving false hope, Macea," Auntie replied. "A person needs to be a mage to get into the Workshop, and it's impossible to predict who will become one."

"Yeah, but Kaso is different. Everyone knows that."

Kaso was different; he stood out in many ways, the most obvious being his size. Naturally strong and tall, he rose a head above most adults. While he had no collar and was still legally a boy, he had the appearance of a man, and a formidable one at that. And it wasn't just his size. He had the countenance of someone who had taken on adult responsibilities at too young an age.

Auntie continued, "We've all experienced his Täv-given gift of being able to warm others, and he'll surely find a lifetime of ways to love people with that gift, just like he has right now by making these blankets for us."

"But, don't you think he'd be a great magician?"

"He'll certainly earn his chips when he goes for testing, but that won't be until he turns nineteen and checks out. Unless someone decides to adopt him, he won't be able to know if he has a Color for three more years. So, right now is not the time for any of you to speculate about Kaso's future; we're already sitting on a sea full of speculation—enough to create another flood," she added with a laugh.

"And Kaso, you can stop wondering also," she said to him. "Täv is going to take care of you. He's active and real in the islands. I don't presume to know what plans he has for you, but they are far better than anything that you can conjure in your most wild imagination. So please, wait. There is no urgency; you have nothing to worry about. All I want right now is for you to enjoy all the wonders we're experiencing here, in this present moment."

"Does that mean it's about to start?" Coby whispered to Kaso, but Kaso didn't respond. All his focus was on what Auntie had just said. From the moment he arrived at the orphanage and was introduced to her, the two of them had a connection. They somehow understood and accepted each other. *Macea's right. Auntie could only mean one thing. She believes I could get into the Workshop.*

"Hey." Coby poked Kaso in the ribs. "Do you think it's about to start?"

"Auntie doesn't lie."

"Wooo hoooo!" Coby shouted, and then a frown came on his face. "I wish we were closer."

"You have it in your power to choose to be happy in all circumstances. We're fortunate we're here at all," Kaso said.

"Yeah, yeah. You don't have to quote Auntie to me. I'm choosing to be happy. I just want to be able to see better. I'm not as tall as you."

"No one's as tall as Kaso, or as strong," Bront laughed. When Kaso had hit a growth spurt about two years ago, he grew from an average-sized kid into an imposing man who could win a fight with any of the older boys at the orphanage.

"Don't forget, last year we couldn't come here at all," Kaso reminded Coby.

"Ha! I bet everyone who was here last year wants to forget what happened," Klofen said. "What were they thinking? If this year's Grand Projection is another clinker, I'd say the Workshop better choose to be happy by choosing a new Master Magician."

Bront smacked Klofen across the head with a projected punch and said, "You'd better choose to keep thoughts like that to yourself—if you want your body to choose to be happy. I hate it when people believe they can kick someone out of the house just because of a little bad luck."

Coby ignored the others and spoke to Kaso. "This year's going to be the best one ever—I just know it. The Master Magician must have fixed the problem."

I don't know. Kaso didn't want to express his doubts to anyone, especially his younger brother. There was something about last year's Grand Projection, *King King*, that still didn't sit right with him. The magicians of the Workshop—for some reason—had been unable to cause people to care about it. *But, why?* This question had gnawed at him for weeks, until he finally figured out what it was: the Grand Projection lacked warmth.

He would know.

He also knew Klofen wasn't alone in his opinion. The Master Magician couldn't afford another failure. *The Workshop has always been known for giving us stories and characters that really move people. That's why everyone calls their projections Grand.*

Kaso knew there was something wrong at the core of the Workshop—the last several Grand Projections seemed to have had the same problem. *And it seems to be getting worse every year. Grand Projections used to be fun and full of life. King King should have been terrifying, or maybe funny, but instead it was way too serious and humorless. What changed?* He had no idea, but now that he had started thinking about this, he couldn't slow his thoughts.

"I think it's starting!" One of the other kids gasped as a ray of sunlight cracked over the horizon behind them.

"Yes! There. Look!" Coby exclaimed as three bright, Red pillars of light shot straight up into the sky, indicating that the Red watch had begun.

Twin violins began to scratch out a haunting, staccato tune.

"Many years ago . . . we watched as the sea turned black . . ." a deep voice boomed across the water.

"Wait . . . I recognize that song . . ." Coby's eyes grew wide as many of the other kids started to murmur amongst themselves.

"It can't be. It can't be," Klofen whispered.

"It's a trick," Bront exclaimed.

"No way! That's the song!"

Kaso felt a bolt of excitement shoot through him as bright flashes of red and indigo exploded around them in the early morning sky.

"Far beneath us lies a lost, forbidden world . . . But we have not forgotten it . . ."

All around them, Kaso could hear the crowd cheering and clapping.

"You asked to know the story . . ."

His mouth dropped open. "No way!"

"He . . . is ready . . . to show you."

A dark crimson slash burned across the sky and a grinning version of the creepy white mask of Devos Rektor appeared.

"YES!" Coby leapt out of his seat, screaming his delight along with every other person on the water. The cheering and screaming was so loud Kaso couldn't hear the rest of the Glimmering.

What followed was a series of flashing images, smells, sounds, sensations, and tastes that overwhelmed Kaso with euphoria and nostalgia. His father had taken him to see *The Epics of the Cursed* when he was six years old. They were re-projections, of course, as the Workshop had projected the originals thirty years ago. Like most boys his age, Kaso was fascinated by Devos Rektor and his villainous ways. Everyone wanted to know the origin story, but Greydyn—the creator of Devos and the current Master Magician—had kept the secret well guarded all these years.

"I'm . . . I'm really surprised," Kaso said after it ended. *I can't believe the Workshop is finally going to tell the beginning of Devos Rektor's story.*

"I told you!" Coby exclaimed as he leapt up and down. "I knew it would be a good one!"

"We don't know anything yet. The Grand Projection is what, thirteen weeks away. It could still turn out to be another flop," Kaso said. Although he was as excited as everyone else about seeing Devos Rektor again, something about the Glimmering didn't feel right to him. *Something's still wrong.* He mused. *What is it?*

"How could it be a flop?" Bront asked. "Any new story about the Lord of Chaos is going to get every single person on O'Ceea to go experience it! Even really old ladies and dumb little kids who can't even talk yet! It's gonna be mega!"

"Oh, Bront." Macea laughed.

"Meh. There's a reason no one's adopted me." Bront laughed back.

"I bet they'll have to extend the run to three, maybe even four weeks," Klofen said. "It'll be the biggest hit the Workshop has ever had!"

"See, I told you," Coby said to Kaso. He paused, then asked, "Is it going to be about what I think it is?"

"What do you think it'll be about?" Kaso asked.

"How Devos Rektor became a villain."

"That's what it looks like."

"People have been asking for this story for decades!" Klofen said.

"So, you still want the Master Magician to be thrown out of the Workshop?" Bront asked.

"I never said that," Klofen responded.

Ignoring them, Kaso and Coby looked around at the growing number of golden visionariums that were appearing around them.

"Look! The Opinionators are already projecting!" Coby said as he pointed at the sparkling cubes.

It barely even played once. What can they have to say so soon?

The IP allowed those who had an opinion about their experience of select Glimmerings, like this one, to project their views into golden-hued cubes that floated in the air. If Kaso placed some part of his body inside one, he could experience the opinion it held. *But why would I want to?* These golden visionariums came in a variety of sizes. Most were small, just large enough to place a head inside of; others were as large as a whole person, and a few were large enough for two or three people to enter.

Anyone who had the right credentials could project a golden visionarium, but just because someone projected one did not mean many people would enter it. Where the orphans were, far out from shore, the Opinionators were largely unknowns. It was the famous Opinionators who got all the attention, and to experience the better golden visionariums, one had to travel closer to the shore.

"Can we go on the island this year?" Coby asked. "The island is where the best of the best are."

"You know we can't," Kaso answered. "But we'll probably be able to get a little closer than we are now."

"Aw, I promise I won't get lost."

"You can't promise that. Being there alone wouldn't be safe for someone your age."

"I don't want to go alone. I want to go with you. You'd protect me. You said you always would."

"And that's why I'm saying we need to obey Auntie and stay in the boat."

Many people would spend all day going from one golden visionarium to another, sometimes waiting a whole watch to experience the ones created by the most celebrated Opinionators. It would take the orphans a long time to row home, though, so Auntie wouldn't allow them to linger too long. But she was okay with them spending some time paddling around. So that's what they did, placing their heads into one golden visionarium after another.

Kaso didn't participate. He found the Opinionators not only a waste of time, but also a huge distraction from what Grand Projections were meant to be. To him, Opinionatoring about a projection was like dissecting a living thing. It cut the projection up into little bits and pieces until all that remained was an unrecognizable pile of nonsense. Opinionators were just trying to get famous on the back of the Workshop. And, just like Auntie said, there was enough speculation here to cause another flood.

"I can't wait to see it again. When are they going to replay it?" Coby asked.

Kaso looked back at the nearest communication tower and saw two Red beams of light in the air. "It's the middle of the Red watch now. They won't play it again until the top of the Orange."

"Why does it have to take so long?"

"So there's time to go to all the golden visionariums," Kaso said in a tone that came out angry.

"Why don't you like them?" Coby asked.

"I just don't."

"I know, but why?"

Kaso was silent, but a sense of wrath burned inside him. *All these people care more about a Glimmering than they do about things that really matter. Like finding us a family.*

Since Kaso didn't respond, Coby turned his eyes back to the island. "Can we row to shore and go to all the good ones on the beach?"

"I already said no. Auntie doesn't allow that. Why'd you even want to? They're worthless. Everyone's just guessing what it's about, same as usual. It doesn't matter, so just calm down." *Why am I so angry?*

"It matters to me!" Coby's eyes were wide as plates. "I want to know everything I can possibly know! We won't experience this Grand Projection for weeks and weeks! I want to go to shore."

"So does everyone in our boat. Get used to it. We're orphans." *Why can't you accept that? It's been four years. Father's not coming for us.* Kaso took a deep breath, trying to still the anger that was welling from somewhere deep inside him.

He sat and stewed for most of the watch while the orphans rowed the boat from one Opinionator to another. There was something stirring inside him. *What's troubling me?* He knew he shouldn't be so hard on his little brother. Coby was only six when he had been separated from their father. Kaso moved them into Auntie's orphanage, but every day since arriving there, the little boy waited for their father to walk through the door and take them home.

How long will he keep thinking that's going to happen? Kaso knew wishful thinking was dangerous for orphans. The best hope the two of them had was for Kaso to get enough chips, to earn enough credentials, so that he could get a good enough job.

The two of them were the only family they had. He would have loved it if Auntie could be their mother, but she had the honorable responsibility of being the mother to sixty-three kids right now. There was enough weight on her shoulders as it was. One day he would pay her back many times over for all she had given to them.

His plan had always been simple: prepare in the orphanage until he was nineteen and declared an independent adult. With his projection skills, he knew he would earn enough to support himself and Coby. Then, after he worked his way up in his job, he would send as many extra lykes as he could back to the orphanage so that the good work Auntie was doing would no longer be such a burden on her.

But, if Auntie really thinks I have a chance of one day working in the Workshop . . . Kaso felt a wave of uneasiness hit him as he considered that possibility. *I can't test here. But what if I went to*

Region 2? Orphans are allowed to test there at sixteen. Do I have the guts to sign us out? Traveling alone to a different region is risky. He wasn't worried about physical harm. *No one will touch us, and if they do they'll be sorry.* The problem was more practical. He didn't have a single gryn. There was no way he could pay for passage there and back. *And what about food? And what if one of us gets sick?* He thought through each risk, one at a time. *Could I really pull it off?*

Kaso wished he were under water. All the chaos and noise were making it hard for him to concentrate.

"Kaso, guess what," Coby exclaimed after pulling his head out of one of the golden visionariums. "This Opinionator is certain the Glimmering of the boy found in Region 2 is none other than the young Devos Rektor."

"Coby, they don't know anything for certain."

"They know some things!" Coby exclaimed. "It also says there's much more to hear on shore, and that we should go there to find out. Please, can we?"

"No. And I wish you would stop listening to them." *What's going on with me? Why don't I want them to influence Coby?* While looking up into the deep blue early morning sky, part of the answer came to him. *The white mask. There was something about it that wasn't right. But what?*

All these thoughts consumed his attention for many moments and he lost track of time. Suddenly, he felt a finger tap him on his temple. It startled him. He turned, but no physical finger was there. *Who's projecting on me?* As he looked around and tried to figure out who wanted his attention, he realized Coby was no longer sitting beside him. *Oh Coby, you didn't.* But Kaso knew he had.

Luckily, Bront, Klofen, Macea, and the others were so focused on finding new golden visionariums that they didn't notice when

Kaso climbed over the rail of the boat and slipped soundlessly into the water.

After the warmth of his projected blanket, the coolness of the water sent an uncomfortable chill through him, so he touched his fingers to his chest and cast a coating of heat onto his body. The ability to project warmth was not common, and being able to do it while in water was extremely difficult. But Kaso had spent a lot of time practicing this over the years and had become quite adept at the skill. After arriving at the orphanage, he started submerging himself in the depths of the ocean whenever he wanted to get away and forget.

"It's like you have seabreath," Macea had said to him many times. "I don't know how you manage to go down so deep and stay there for so long."

A strong, fast swimmer, he arrived at the shore without trouble. He immediately began looking for his brother. This was not an easy task as the little island was crowded with people. He saw many famous Opinionators and passed by long lines of people who were waiting to get into their golden visionariums. These Opinionators were more talented and projected larger cubes, providing more space for a full range of opinions that stimulated all five senses. Kaso passed by a variety of configurations, but the most common was a long rectangle projected close to the ground. To experience these visionariums, Kaso would have to lie down on the sand, as if he were going to sleep. *I don't know why people do that. It makes them so vulnerable.*

He weaved past one person after another lying on the ground and overheard people's reactions to the Opinionators. Apparently the Glimmering was getting fantastic evaluations, and there was great praise for the Master Magician. *Everyone wants this—no, needs this—to be a hit. They're so desperate to restore their faith in the Workshop.*

As he maneuvered through a tightly packed section of the shore, his head brushed the corner of a golden visionarium, and he heard a few words spoken inside: ". . . it has heart."

Kaso stopped. *That's what's wrong!* He didn't agree with that. *It didn't have heart. It lacked warmth.* He had sensed this throughout the entire projection.

Devos Rektor's creepy, lifeless white mask was an icon that people throughout the islands recognized. As the symbol of a great villain, it had a strange, attractive power over people. Even though it was inflexible and never changed shape, it somehow stirred up a wide range of emotions. In real life, the metal mask would be cold—it was a piece of armor after all. Devos Rektor challenged the gods, and when he wore that mask, it somehow projected the feeling that he was a god himself, and that nothing could stand in his way.

But the mask Kaso had just experienced in this Glimmering felt hollow, as if no one was behind it. *Everyone thinks it's the same, but it's not.* It felt more like the face of a ghost than that of a god. *If I'm right, then the Opinionators are spreading a lie. People trust them, but they're liars!*

But right now he had a more pressing problem. Where was Coby? He searched for the remainder of the Red watch and stopped only when he heard the gentle melody of a violin.

Looking up into the sky, he saw that the beams of light rising from the nearest tower were now Orange. A new watch had arrived, and the second performance of the Glimmering was about to begin.

"*Many years ago . . . we watched as the sea turned black . . .*"

Kaso had never stood so close to a Workshop projection before. *It's different. It's far better!* Before, the deep voice had traveled across the water to him, but now it wrapped around him like a snug cloak. The sensations that felt dim and distant from his spot in a boat full of orphans were now rich and intense. He'd never realized a projection could be this moving.

No wonder people spend so many gryns—no, probably lykes—to get up close to the magicians as they create their Grand Projections. When he was a child, Kaso had dreamed of the wonder he'd feel if he became a magician and had the honor of working inside the Workshop. Now, he realized his imagination had grasped only a fraction of that wonder.

But, it still isn't warm. He knew this now even more than before. *Something's wrong in the Workshop.* King King *made that clear. Now this! What happened? If they don't find someone to fix the problem— and soon—the entire Workshop is in danger of falling apart.*

As Kaso thought this, it became evident to him what he must do. *I need to check out of the orphanage.* He could stay and project warm blankets on a few people or go to the Workshop and project warmth across all the islands. But he hesitated. Something was holding him back. Was it fear? No. There was no reason not to go.

He needed to try.

He would try.

He would leave the orphanage and go to Region 2. The only question left was: how? He tried to think of a plan, but his thoughts suddenly became thick and heavy. He couldn't see or hear clearly; it was as if he were in a fog. He began to shiver.

"Far beneath us . . . lies a lost, forbidden world . . . But we have not forgotten it . . . "

The crowds started chanting, "We have not forgotten! We have not!"

Kaso started to feel dizzy. The projection was so intense. It was beginning to overpower him.

"You asked to know the story . . . He . . . is ready . . . to show you."

Kaso fell to his knees, and then, as Devos Rektor's mask appeared, a chill rippled over him, stripped off his warmth projection, and exposed him. He was cold and alone.

His will gone, he passed out on the sand.

The Poozer

~Kaso~

The only logical way to understand poozers is to view them like I do: kids who've never grown up. Who else but children would impersonate characters from Grand Projections and play act like they're really them? They claim it's just innocent fun, but I'm not so sure. You never know who's really hiding behind those masks.

—Mage Rouwand is-a Stump, *Insights from the Insightful*

Kaso woke to see Macea's concerned face. She knelt beside him and gently shook his shoulders.

"That did not just happen," he groaned as he sat up. "A projection did not make me pass out."

Macea's eyes danced with amusement as she said, "No way! It absolutely, certifiably did not."

"Ugh. Only little girls pass out like that."

"And old men . . . But hey, at least it was from the Lord of Chaos and not some rainbow rabbit."

Kaso glared at her, but his countenance changed when he remembered why he was here. "Where's Coby? Have you seen him?"

"No, I thought you two were together."

"Wasn't it you who tapped me to let me know he'd left?"

From Macea's face, he could see that she didn't understand what he was talking about. *Huh. I wonder who it was then. Auntie?*

After Macea explained to him that Auntie had sent her to shore to look for them, she agreed to help Kaso look for Coby, and the two of them set off to search the little island. As they made their way, Kaso tried to explain to her how unsettled he was by the lack of warmth in the Glimmering.

"What do you mean?" Macea asked.

"It didn't feel alive—like a real thing."

"Oh, I get it. Yeah, I see what you mean."

"Do you really?"

"I just told you I did."

"I know, it's just—" Kaso tried to find the right words. "I mean, it's really important that I'm seeing this right."

"I think you are. I sensed something too. To me, the Glimmering felt kind of desperate. It reminded me of an old person who was close to dying but didn't want to face it."

"Wow, that's kind of disturbing—and morbid. How could you possibly know what that feels like?"

Macea stared back at him and said, "You know why I live at the orphanage, right?"

Oh, of course. "Sorry, I forgot. Yeah, I guess you would know. I'm sorry."

"Forget about it." Macea shifted uncomfortably. "But, I do think you're right. All the Opinionators are just drenching their threadbare over this being a new Devos Rektor projection. People have waited forever for this."

"Yeah, and everyone is also desperate for the Master's touch to be back. They're just placing their own expectations onto it."

"Must be," Macea said after a brief pause. "Said with the perfect insight of a future Violet mage."

People said that kind of thing to him all the time, and Kaso was never sure how to take it. "We'll find out one day, I guess. Possibly even next week."

Macea stopped. "What do you mean? You know that's not possible."

"It's not possible in Region 3. But this isn't the only region on O'Ceea."

"What are you talking about?"

"Our Festival starts today, but Region 2's doesn't start for several days."

"You're thinking of leaving, now?"

"I don't have much time if I'm going to stand before a puller this year."

Macea looked straight into his eyes. "Are you serious?"

"Yes. I've decided. But just because I want to go doesn't mean I can. I need to find a way to get Coby and me to Region 2 for their Festival of Stars. That will cost money, and we don't have any gryns."

"You're going to take Coby?"

"Yes," Kaso said. *I would never leave him behind.*

"Do you really think Auntie will allow him to go with you?"

"I'll only go if Auntie agrees to both of us leaving. I'll explain all of the reasons to her, and I won't go unless she believes it's right and gives me her blessing."

"Auntie loves you, and trusts you—but I don't know if she'll agree," Macea said as she stared off in the distance.

I expected she'd be happy about this. "Everything okay?"

"It's just . . . I didn't expect you'd go now. I thought you'd wait until you were nineteen."

"Why?" Kaso asked. "You were the one who said I'd become a magician of the Second Magnitude. The Workshop has a big problem. It's missing warmth and that's my gift."

"But are you sure that's your problem to solve?"

"I don't know, but Tav has given me the ability to project heat. That's not common, and it's something they need right now.

In three years, it might be too late."

Macea was quiet for a moment as she considered all this. "You've thought this out?"

Kaso stared at her.

"Okay, of course. You think everything out. I mean . . . have you already decided this is what you're going to do?"

"I still don't know how I'm going to get to Region 2, but yes. It seems right."

"Well, Auntie will be there for you, no matter what, and you'll always have the option to come back to us—even if you pass out again and prove to everyone in Region 2 that you are, as you said, a little girl."

"Ha, ha, very funny," Kaso said. "But, I do appreciate your support. It's a big deal to leave."

"Huge."

"I just hope I'm doing the right thing," Kaso said.

"Are you ever wrong?"

*   *   *

It wasn't until the bottom of the Orange watch that they finally found Coby, over on the other side of the island. Kaso saw him first, but it was Macea who spoke what they were both thinking: "What's he doing with them?"

Coby was chatting with four men who appeared to be old, grizzled veterans of the sea. They were bearded and hairy, with deep, bloody scars across their bare, muscled chests. Even their faces were bruised, making it look as though they'd just come from a fight. Their clothes were ragged and torn, yet they wore circular gold earrings, gemstone-covered bracelets, and platinum rings.

Those men are just wearing body mods, Kaso told himself. *They have to be. No one can be that scary-looking in reality.*

"Who are they? Performers?" Macea asked.

Kaso wondered. There was something odd about them. "Could they be poozers?"

"Those costumes are better than any I've ever seen before," Macea observed. "Poozers aren't that good."

"One of them is a mage," Kaso told her as he noticed that one wore a Yellow collar.

"Then they're certainly not poozers. What do you think they're mashing?" Macea asked.

"Probably *The Pirate's Gamble* and *The Adventures of Wolly and Wog*. Something about this doesn't feel right. If they're performers, then why are they just standing around talking to Coby? He bonds with strangers too easily. Come on, let's get him as quickly as we can."

As they approached, the Yellow mage faced them and spread his arms open wide. "Well, 'alloo wee ones!" he greeted them.

"Kaso!" Coby said when he saw his brother. "I'm sorry I left, but the Opinionators kept calling me here to learn their secrets! But when I got here I found something way better—these are real life poozers!"

"Poozers?"

"The most popular poozers partaking in this most peculiar production," the Yellow mage said. "Quite a surprise, this announcement of Rektor's return, isn't it?"

Yup, poozers. It's time to leave.

"Aren't they grand?" Coby whispered to his brother.

No. Poozers were known to target orphans. "It's time to go," Kaso said.

"My, my, we've become affixed with a rude squiggler, ain't we Captain?" a second man said.

"Squiggled squalor, I'd call them," the Yellow mage corrected.

Kaso tried to pull Coby away, but he wouldn't budge. "Stop, they're really nice. They only look scary. I don't want to go yet."

"Of course not! Each and every Blank we make the acquaintance of wants to be sticking to us."

He knows Coby's an orphan? Kaso became grave. "Coby, what have you told this man about you?"

"Nothing," Coby answered.

"Lower your sword, Big Brother—you're Violet fabric, no query there—no one has given your dear sweet brother any requirements to speak secrets. I recognize all Blanks because I am a Blank myself."

"You were an orphan?" Macea looked at him with intense interest. "But you're so—"

"Old?" The man began to laugh. "Just costume play, my little dove. Bankfort here isn't much older than you, I reckon."

"No, I wasn't going to say old."

"Attractive?" the third suggested.

"Definitely not. Stupid's more like it," Macea said.

"Oooh. Kersplunking on a portentous poozer!" the Yellow mage said to Kaso. "I like her, Big Brother. No wonder you've clasped her selfishness to you. But, stupid wasn't what you were going to say, was it little urchin?"

"Time to go," Kaso insisted.

"No, he really was an orphan, and the others still are—just like us. They're really funny," Coby said.

"Oh, come now, my pretty precious. What was it you were going to say?" the Yellow mage pestered Macea. "I've caught the death quakes anticipating what your compassionate Blank heart feels about us poor poozers."

Enough. Kaso picked Coby up, slung him over his shoulder, and started to carry him away.

"I'll catch up," Macea said to Kaso. "There's something I need to know."

"Truth. She's speaking truth, Big Brother," the Yellow mage

said to Kaso. "There's always something we need to know. Now you have to stay."

"No, I don't," Kaso said.

"My, my. Now there's something I need to know. Can a big, strong, honorable big brother such as yourself leave a little defenseless lass behind with a bunch of terrifying old sailors?"

"Don't worry. I'll be fine," Macea said, but Kaso didn't move; he wasn't about to leave her now.

The Yellow mage nodded. "You see, boys, this here proves there still are decent men in the islands and thus hope for all womenfolk! And now, my curious carbuncle, what truth do you seek?"

"What's your name? Your real name, not the character you're pretending to be," Macea spoke it more as a demand than a question.

"Captain Quint the poozer, at your service, Mistress."

"Okay, Quink. How old are you, for real?"

"Oooh, 'Quink!' My-my. Big Brother, she's even more squiggly than my boon-swuckling imagination had imagined imagining."

"Yeah, wow. Imagine that," Macea groaned. "Now, your age—your real age!"

"My dearest, can't you tell?"

"No, and that's the only reason I'm still here."

"Ah, ha ha ha. We've swash-buckled 'em, boys," Quint said to his gang. He turned back to Macea. "To reward your devotion, my super squiggler, I'll give it up. First, since you're seeking truth, this here is Treau. He's sixteen. I already introduced you to Bankfort, who is seventeen. Last we have poor little Forcemore, who's only thirteen. And, as for me? I'm nineteen years from the womb."

"I asked for the truth, Captain Quink." Macea had lost her patience.

"It's true," Coby said. "I've seen them."

"Can we go now?" Kaso asked, still holding the kicking Coby. He was certain these men were lying to them. *Poozers can't be trusted.*

"What is truth, Mistress?" Quint became grave. "Is truth what one sees . . ."

As he spoke, a ball of fire appeared. Inside it they could identify a young family: a father, mother, and many children. They looked happy.

". . . or smells . . ."

The sweet smell of oranges emanated from the flame. It was a fresh, enlivening scent that enticed Kaso, Coby, and Macea to draw in deep breaths. But then the smell changed. In an instant, they were overwhelmed by the stench of a corpse.

". . . or feels?"

Abruptly, the fireball exploded and radiated a bone-chilling wave of cold through them.

The Yellow mage burst out laughing. "Perceptions—like projections and expressions—are deceiving."

Macea wrinkled her mouth in disgust and walked away. Kaso followed. But before they got far, Quint called out to them, "I've discovered the people you ought to trust most are the very ones you shouldn't trust at all."

Nonsense.

"Captain Quint," Coby yelled as he was being carried away, "show them what you really look like."

"Fine idea, wee one," Quint replied. "Let me present myself to you naked, as I really am: a desperate Blank, with nary a clan to call my own—abandoned in my most youthful years. Behold me now as Tav has fashioned me."

Quint opened his arms wide and bowed, and the projections that covered his true appearance dissolved. Standing in the place of the old threatening sailor was a skinny blond teenager with tangled, wavy hair. His threadbare were old, tattered, and stained; the condition of his physical clothing was nothing like what civilized people wore under their projected outfits.

It was a dramatic change, and Macea stopped walking away to look at him. "He really is nineteen!" she said with shock. Quint dissolved the costumes from the other three and revealed them all as they really were.

They're a bunch of scrawny kids. They could be orphans after all.

Once Kaso saw these poozers stripped of their projections, he knew there was no danger. He could easily deal with all of them if they tried to cause trouble, so he put Coby down and said, "Those projections were amazing! Who clothed you with them?"

Quint bowed deeper, and the triumphant blast of a trumpet sounded all around them. "At your service, Big Brother."

"No, really, where did you get them?"

Quint lifted his arms, then pointed his fingers at little Forcemore and began wiggling them in a frenetic manner. "I'm a meager soul who can only speak the truth," he said. At this, Forcemore's appearance was transformed. He was now an ancient hunter with skin as dark and tanned as Kaso's. He had long, thin, honed muscles; wore animal skin pants and a necklace of bones; and held a long spear in his hand.

The Yellow mage did the same to Bankfort, Treau, and himself.

That's impressive. Really, really impressive.

"I told you!" Coby said. "They were dressed like Old World soldiers when I first saw them. I bet you want to stay now!"

"You're right, we can stay a bit longer—but not very long." Kaso was curious, so he allowed Quint to create a variety of body mods and clothing for them. It was fun to see themselves looking vastly different. *How could an orphan learn all this?*

Moreover, everything Quint created had the highest levels of detail. *He must have a Kingdom level high enough to earn a spot in the O'Ceea Championship Games.* Kaso gave Quint a serious look. *So why is he a poozer?*

"You're really talented. What team do you compete with?"

"These honorable and praiseworthy lads are my teammates and true brothers." Quint paused. "Which delivers us to the topic of the day. Rumor has it you've been endowed with a particular flair for one of the more fascinating—and fantastical—facets of projection: heat. Coby has testified it's your fanciest forte."

"Coby! You said you didn't tell them anything about us."

"No, I didn't say that. You asked me, 'Coby, what have you told this man about you?'—I have a very good memory, even if you say I don't—and then I said, 'Nothing'—about me. But, I told him a lot about you. Quint says you have to go get your Color now, this week."

Coby, what did you say about me?

"I'm always looking for upstanding folk to join my crew," Quint said, "and I can guarantee I'll get you standing in front of a puller, free and proud as a poozer."

"I have no interest in becoming a poozer," Kaso told him. "And don't try to deceive me—I know the rules. Poozers aren't a recognized clan, and orphans can't test until they're nineteen."

"You indeed are a mighty sage, my pre-Violet mage. These are the rules in merry ole Region 3. But all we need to do is take a jolly jaunt over to Region 2—where they allow poozers to play and sixteen-year-old Blanks like yourself to stand before the Staff of Light. It really is a glorious assembly of islands—and quite a forward-thinking collection of clans, if you ask me."

Kaso considered the Yellow mage who stood before him. He didn't know all the rules that governed testing in Region 2, but he knew that going there was his best opportunity—probably his only one—if he was going to stand before a puller this year. *Why does he want me to join him?* Traveling with a bunch of poozers was far from ideal. *But it ought to get me there.* Kaso's mind raced as he weighed the benefits and dangers of joining Quint.

"How do you propose I get there? I don't have any gryns for the fare, or a bed."

"Gryns? Those squigglers are so sparkly; everyone goes crazy for them. I think you've been wise to avoid 'em."

"But they are necessary to pay for passage on a ship to Region 2," Macea stated.

"Not on my ship. All passages on *Castor's Choice* are free."

He owns a ship, too? Who is this young mage?

"*Castor's Choice?*" Macea scoffed. "That sounds like something you'd see on a bottle of medicine."

"Captain Quint has an amazing ship," Bankfort said. "A ninety-foot schooner, with masts so high that if you climb to the top, you can pick a cloud out of the sky and eat it!"

How does a nineteen-year-old have his own ship? Though, I suppose with his talent he could have earned enough to buy one.

"Do you really have a ship that big?" Coby said.

"Certainly, and it—by mere chance—has a firm and fixed schedule to travel to Region 2," Quint answered. "Young Treau here is fixin' to be tested there—owing to the same unique circumstances as yours. So, problem solved. You can just hitch a ride with us."

This is too easy. There has to be something else he wants from me.

"Will you train him?" Macea asked abruptly.

"What?" Both Quint and Kaso were shocked by her question.

"You're clearly an exceptional mage," Macea said. "Kaso's never had proper training. He needs all the help he can to get into the Workshop."

"Don't we all, Mistress Squiggler? Don't we all. But, that's why we live on the sea, free from rules and clans and elders and their boss-tentatious ways. No distractions at sea. All that happens is trainin' and feastin' and plunderin' stuff."

Macea glared at him.

"Er—plunderin' is more of an expression," Quint said with a nervous laugh. "But we do train, all day, every day. If Big Brother wants to pop his numbers, we'd be honored for him to join our republic."

"It's a good offer," Treau said. "Much better than slinking around an orphanage. Leaving mine was the best thing I ever did."

He seems sincere. Kaso knew few orphanages had an Auntie as loving as theirs.

Macea said, "Tell me, Captain Quink, where did you learn to make projections so well?"

"Ah, sweet damsel, you beckon me to sing my song. Alas, my family failed to perceive my poor heart," Quint stated.

His family?

"But as a poozer," Quint continued, "I've been free to train and traverse every region, soaking in every bit and bittle of knowledge." He pointed to the projections covering him. "I'm flesh and blood proof every poozer is priceless."

Kaso hesitated. *He's deceiving me about something. Why is he so desperate for me to come with him?*

"Kaso doesn't need to be a poozer. He needs to have his Color pulled," Macea said.

"And it will happen," Quint affirmed. "It's as clear as the Nine Colors of the Dyemoon that radiate through the storm clouds encircling the Island of the First Watch. His Color shines the watch after sunset."

"See, he thinks so too. Everybody does," Coby said.

Could I really have Violet in me?

Quint smiled at Macea and said, "Well, my pretty, it will be so enriching to travel with a lady such as you."

"Me?" Macea raised her eyebrows. "I'm not coming. I like slinking around my orphanage. They're the best family in the islands."

"Second-best to making your family with me," Quint said. "Ole *Castor's Choice* has been searching for a mistress."

"I'm pretty sure I'll find a better option. And, if you really are looking for a mistress, you should consider changing the name of your ship," Macea goaded.

"Ha ha. I like you. Don't count me out. Life, like all good stories, is full of unexpected surprises. So, Kaso, what do you say?"

Before Kaso could say anything, Coby jumped in. "Wait, are we actually going with them?" All the light in his eyes went out.

Oh no. Coby needs to be excited about this if it's going to work.

"Give us a moment alone, to talk," Kaso said, and the three of them stepped away from the poozers.

Coby looked deeply concerned as he spoke. "Are we really going?"

"You want me to try to become a magician, right?"

"Yeah, of course," Coby stammered, "but, do we really have to leave?"

Of course we do. But Kaso knew that look well. "This is about our father, right?"

"It's okay Coby. You can tell us what's wrong," Macea said.

They waited a long time for him to muster the courage to speak. "What if Dad finally finds out that we've been at Auntie's orphanage all this time, and when he comes to get us, we're gone? Then he'll have to try and find us all over again!"

Kaso was silent, then sighed. *He doesn't want to hear the only real answer to that.*

"But," Coby said after a moment, "you have to get your Color. We don't have a choice, right?"

"That's right."

"And if you get a Color and train real good with the poozers, maybe you'll actually become a magician. Then you'll earn lots of lykes and Dad won't have to work so hard and leave us all the time, trying to find jobs—right?"

Kaso let his little brother's words hang in the silence before he replied. "Lots of good things will happen to us if I become a magician."

"We'll have a home of our very own, with Dad!"

What do I say to that? Coby was so young when we left. Kaso had never told his little brother why they had gone to live with Auntie, and now wasn't the time to reveal what kind of man their father was and crush Coby's false hopes that they would be a family again.

But what if he did come back? Kaso didn't know what he would do if his father came and found them only because Kaso had become a magician. He'd probably punch him in the face.

"C'mon, boys," Quint yelled. "You're at risk of falling into the sea of Opinionators. Do you want to slug about at home and speculate about projections or set sail with us and make magnificent ones of your own? Join us, and you'll soon be weaving magic with masters."

He's still trying to convince me to go with him. Can't he see I'm going to say yes? He's really desperate.

Macea said, "Quink seems a little too eager, don't you think? I don't really trust him. I think you might be rushing this decision."

"I certainly don't trust him. But it was only the bottom of the Red watch when I decided to leave the orphanage to attend a Festival, and now I have someone offering to take me there. How else can we explain it? Things don't work out like that unless they are meant to be."

"Are you saying Täv is behind this?"

"How can I know that?" Kaso said. "But it sure seems like it. Things are working out so well, just like Auntie says they do when Tav is involved."

"Will we be safe?" Coby asked.

"I'll always be there to take care of you," Kaso said. "You know that! I just need to know if you're willing to leave."

He nodded.

When they rejoined Quint, Kaso spoke directly to him. "I accept your offer to take us to the Color Ceremony in Region 2, but I have no interest in joining you or your crew. I just want a ride. Is that acceptable?"

"Wonderful," Quint said with a big grin. "Even a single step in the right direction is better than standing still."

"Also—you can see how big I am."

"It is hard to miss," Quint said.

"If you do anything to harm us, you'll regret it." Kaso's face was serious as he said, "I don't lose fights."

"I'm certain you don't."

"I'm not going to allow you to take us as prisoners, or lock us up as slaves, or bind us into any kind of contract. This came up all too easily, so let me make something clear: there will be no tricks. Or you'll no longer need to project fake bruises on your face. Understood?"

"It's as clear as the waters of the Crystal Lake. You'll be my guest, and I promise we'll take good care of you. We've already warmed up to you. You'll warm up to us soon."

"All right," Kaso said after a brief pause. "We'll do it. Pick us up tomorrow at our orphanage, on the Island of the Sunny Rock."

Quint looked confused. "Tomorrow? No, no, no. We're leaving—together—now."

"Why?"

"That's how these things work."

"What do you mean?"

"That's how it always works in Grand Projections."

I think all the poozing is starting to affect his brain. "Well, this is real life—my life—and I need to get my auntie's blessing."

Quint sighed. "Then let's go speak to this woman of wisdom and be off with us."

"No. I'll talk to her when we get back to the orphanage. Coby and I will spend one more day and night with our family. Just family."

"We're family, aren't we, Big Brother?" Quint flashed a grin.

Kaso chose to ignore him. "I will share this news with my family. We're not going to slink away without having a proper goodbye."

"You promise you won't change your mind?"

"Kaso keeps his word," Macea said.

"Fine, fine," Quint relented. "Do what you must. We'll meet you tomorrow then—you and your squiggler's heart won't be regrettin' it!"

The Blue Wallaroo

~Kalaya~

Once, when I was young and foolish, I fell in love with a merman. He gave me the gift of seabreath, and I rode with him down under the sea on the back of a leviathan, all the way to the ancient cities. Yes, that's right—the Workshop stole the story of my life. Igar must have overheard me talking about it, and then they went and turned it into the Grand Projection Love Sinks. *But they got it all wrong. That merman turned out to be a real throttlewog. What they really should have called it was* Love Stinks.

—Mistress Mazannda is-a Moon, *Spooky Signs in Wicked Times*

The sun had nearly set over the ocean, but Kalaya is-a Cloud was far from being done with her wallaroo. It was supposed to be dancing, but as she watched her creation bounce back and forth on the sandy beach, Kalaya knew it lacked the smooth and realistic flow of true motion.

And it was bright, sky blue.

What am I doing wrong? Why can't I get this right?

"Relax, Kalaya. You're doing fine," her boyfriend, Jaremon is-a Twig, reassured her.

"Oh yeah? Then why does it keep coming out blue?"

"You're just nervous, that's all."

"But I've never been able to make it brown."

"Well . . ." Jaremon said as he sat down in the sand and

watched her every move. "It's a strange creature. I don't think it's easy for anyone."

"Color is easy. Even children can control that. Why can't I get it right?"

"That's a good question," he said. "I'm not really sure."

Kalaya glanced over her shoulder at him and raised her eyebrows. "Really? Can it be? Has the all-wise Jaremon finally admitted he doesn't know something?"

"Guess so." He grinned. "Wow. So this is what it feels like."

"Yup. Welcome to reality," she said with a laugh as she fiddled with her hair. *I wish I could make projections as easily as he can.*

Jaremon was two years older, and in the time since Green had been found in him, he had soared to the top of his team and outshined most of his clan. Even now, as he watched her practice, he masterfully projected beautiful dolphins in the ocean beside them. Every so often one would catch her eye, and she'd watch in awe as it effortlessly leapt through the air and slipped back into the water with a realistic yet harmonic splash. Each time one entered the ocean, it sent out a wave of glowing green phosphorescence that made it look as if the dolphins were swimming in a sea of stars.

He's infinitely better than I am. Will I ever get to that level? She was lost in these thoughts when she felt something squeeze her hand. "What are you doing?" she asked in shock when she looked down and saw that a faint pink shimmer had encased the fingers and palm of her right hand. "This isn't the time for romance. The Festival starts tomorrow! I need to focus if I'm going to be able to make this work."

"I just want to support you."

"I get that, but holding hands is not the kind of support I need right now."

She was thankful that he didn't push the issue and quickly

erased the touch projection so she could continue to concentrate on her wallaroo. She'd been laboring on it all through the Blue and Indigo watches and probably needed to work beyond Violet if she had any hope of getting it right.

"Kalaya, time to come home! Your father wants to talk with you before he goes to bed!" her mom called to her from the path by the trees.

"What? But first nightmark hasn't even started yet," Kalaya called back with a frown.

"He's got to go to work early tomorrow," her mother said, "so he won't get a chance to see you until after the Color Ceremony."

"But . . . I haven't quite figured out how to make my wallaroo dance!" *Or stop being blue.*

"Oh." Her mother hesitated. "Well, in that case, take as much time as you need. Your father will understand. I'll leave the door unlocked and your dinner on the table."

"Thanks!" Kalaya called as her mother disappeared down the trail and back into the forest.

"Your mom's quite thoughtful," Jaremon said. "My parents don't really understand the need to practice so much."

"Yeah, she's okay, I guess," Kalaya said. "She can get a little obsessive about all this though. She's probably said 'this is your big moment' ten times today."

"Well, it is. People only get one chance to stand before a puller."

Kalaya turned and furrowed her brow. *Come on, not you too!* The pressure on her was unbearable; she hadn't been able to sleep for at least a week.

"What? What did I say?" Jaremon asked.

"Nothing. It's just . . . I already know how big of a deal this is. I don't need people reminding me all the time."

"Sorry," Jaremon said.

"It's okay. I just . . . I just really want to become a mage—like you."

"Well, if we keep practicing, I'm sure you will."

Kalaya looked at him for a moment. *He's right.* She returned all her attention to the wallaroo. After a long period of twisting and squeezing her fingers, trying to get everything positioned exactly right, she took a step back and asked nervously, "Do you think it looks realistic enough?"

"Sure," Jaremon replied with a wry smile. "Aside from the fact that the ones in *The Roo and the Rower* were brownish-red."

I knew that bothered him. "Yeah, yeah. I meant besides the color."

"I know. I was just teasing." Jaremon stood and looked at it more closely. "You are very talented, and your skills are developing more and more each day. From a technical—Kingdom—standpoint, she looks quite authentic."

"Great—authentic in every way but the most visible." Kalaya let out a defeated sigh and dug her toes into the sand.

Jaremon turned away from the wallaroo and faced her. "Look, don't let the blueness of it get you down. It's definitely wrong, but I don't think it's beneficial for you to focus so much on that aspect right now."

Of course it is, she thought glumly to herself. *I'm never going to become a magician if I can't control something as simple as that.*

"And, you know," Jaremon continued, "now that I think about it, maybe it isn't such a big deal that your wallaroo is blue. They were creatures of the Old World. No one really knows exactly what they looked like."

"The Master Magician seemed to have a pretty clear vision."

"That doesn't mean that's really how they looked. All we know about them comes from a few bones in a museum. How can anyone—even the Master Magician—possibly know what color they were?"

"They say real magicians can see things ordinary people can't," she said.

"That's true, but a lot of what goes into a projection is up to the imagination of the magician."

"Yes," Kalaya locked her eyes on him, "and the right to imagine is earned . . ."

". . . after the student masters imitation," Jaremon finished the well-known saying. "Well said. You're right."

"Thank you," she replied. It wasn't often he said that to her.

Jaremon observed her quietly for a moment, then tilted his head ever so slightly toward her projection. "Maybe you should take a break. Why don't you try projecting something that's really easy for you. How about that funny walrus you used to make all the time. What was his name?"

Kalaya shuddered. "Ugh. Walter? No way. He's so depressing."

"I suppose he does come across a little bit sad," Jaremon admitted. "But I always thought that was part of his charm. The way you designed his mustache to droop and wiggle whenever he moved was really quite clever."

That was an accident. "Anyway," Kalaya said in hopes of changing the subject, "I need to learn how to do my wallaroo right. It's important to me."

"Yes, but she might not be ready for tomorrow—testing with her could be a big gamble. You should spend some time refreshing your skills with your other characters. Your walrus has really high levels of Kingdom. He's probably your best work."

"Yeah, but Walter is so simple for me to make. I'd rather spend the little time I have left working on what I care the most about."

"I understand," Jaremon said. "Well, if that's what you want to do, I think you should stop worrying about the color for now. It seems like it's taking all of your focus."

"Okay. I guess I could work on something else." Kalaya examined her wallaroo closely for flaws. "What about the ears? They should probably be a little longer, right?" she asked.

"Yeah, probably a little bit," Jaremon agreed.

All right. That should be easy. She started to wiggle her fingers at the wallaroo's ears, but as she did, they stretched out and were suddenly an extra three feet long. "Whoops!" She laughed nervously. *Yikes! I can't let that happen tomorrow.* She narrowed the gap between her fingers. This time, the ears shrank down to a more realistic size.

"Good," he affirmed, "much better."

Kalaya was nine-years-old when *The Roo and the Rower* was released to the islands, and ever since then, she'd wanted nothing more than to make a wallaroo dance for the Magician's Workshop. But she had always known it would take hard work. She pressed her feet into the sand and kept at it.

"It's coming along nicely," Jaremon said as the sun finally set and the Violet watch began. "I don't think you need to be worried."

"Easy for you to say." Kalaya needed a break, and so she plopped down next to him. "Everyone is moved to tears whenever you project anything. How many gold chips did you earn the first year you tested?"

"It's not important. Honestly, the best advice I was given before my first Festival tests was not to worry so much about the chips."

"What am I supposed to worry about then?"

"The simulacrum," he said.

"The what?" Kalaya had never heard the word before.

"Simulacrum. It's what the chroniclers call projections."

"Oh," Kalaya said. Jaremon had recently returned from a visit to the Island of the Infinite Wellspring, where he'd been studying in the Hall of Ancient Wisdom. Ever since his return, he couldn't stop expounding his knowledge to her. *He's so smart. I'm very fortunate to have someone as amazing as him preparing me.*

Jaremon turned his eyes away from her and stared out at the sea, where he made one of his dolphins do a graceful flip through the air. "The real trick is to know as much as you can about what you're trying to simulate and then go and make it happen. You're talented, and driven, and that'll take you far."

"You really think so?" She bit her lower lip. "But what if . . . what if all this work is for nothing? I mean . . . there's a chance I won't get a Color."

"Sure, anything can happen, but your odds are far better than the average person's."

"I still don't know how you can be so sure," Kalaya said. As much as she liked it when he said things like this, his reasons never really made sense to her.

"It's all based on the history of your clan, your natural skill and level of determination, and the exceptionally high percentage of Colors that come from our island. While the average kid has roughly an eighty-two percent chance of staying a commoner, you have only a thirty-two percent chance." Jaremon threw out the calculations casually, like he'd run them through his mind many times before. "The odds are way in your favor, so don't worry—you'll be fine."

Kalaya glanced down at the Green collar tied snugly around his neck. Although he was right—it did seem like people from the Island of the Golden Vale were more likely to get Colors—nothing was guaranteed. "But, if I can't figure out—"

"No more buts!" Jaremon faced her with a grin. "Tomorrow will bring what it will. Let's focus. I think it's time for you to add some smell to this little girl."

"Hmm, I haven't even thought of that yet," Kalaya admitted. "Do you remember what it was like in the Grand Projection?"

Jaremon stroked his chin. "Just make it smell like an animal."

"Make it smell like an animal? Wow. That's great. So specific. Thanks for the tip."

"Hey," Jaremon said and leaned forward, "that's what I'm here for, right?"

Kalaya scrunched up her nose at him and then focused back on the wallaroo. *Okay. Animal smell . . . maybe I can mix a cat with a . . .* But before she could finish her thought, a thick, foul stench wafted over them.

"Ugh!" Jaremon recoiled. "When I said 'like an animal,' I didn't mean a dead one!"

"That's not me!" Kalaya gasped for air and jerked her hand up to cover her nose. "Where's that coming from?"

Suddenly a piercing screech tore through the air. Both of them ducked down as an enormous black dragon materialized in the sky. Covered with sharp, blue-tipped scales, the dragon was at least twenty feet long and was shrouded in a thick cloud of ice crystals. It swooped down until it was right above them, then sent a freezing sensation across their skin. Kalaya and Jaremon watched as the dragon looped and shot straight back up into the air, soaring higher and higher. It flipped, tucked its wings close, and spiraled down toward Kalaya's wallaroo.

She could do nothing but watch helplessly; the dragon plunged down, snatched her wallaroo by the ears, and took it screaming into the sky.

"No!" Kalaya and Jaremon both scrambled to their feet. She flicked her wrists at the dragon and clapped her hands, but she didn't have near the level of Power needed to stop it.

"Ump. Thun. Ra!" Jaremon chanted in the old tongue—his newly adopted way of making projections—and a golden bow appeared in his hands. The bow glowed magnificently, and the sight of it sent a thrill of hope through Kalaya's heart.

He's going to take care of it.

"Doom-Ra!" he shouted, and a bronze, flaming arrow appeared in his hand. Jaremon loaded the arrow into the bow and shot it at the dragon. But to Kalaya's shock and dismay, the arrow deflected off the dragon's scales and did nothing to diminish the beast.

"Please, save her!" Kalaya pleaded.

Without looking, Jaremon sent out a touch projection to Kalaya's hand. She squeezed her hand tight and sent one back to him.

"Doom-Ra! Sargen-Ka!" Another arrow appeared for Jaremon. He shot it, and this time the arrow managed to sizzle a hole through the dragon's wing.

"There. Take that!" Kalaya cheered.

He shot four more arrows, one after the other, and each arrow cut another hole through the beast. It seemed to be weakening.

"Yes, yes, yes!" Kalaya squeezed her own hand, knowing that Jaremon would feel it.

But then she watched in horror as the holes in the dragon filled with solid chunks of ice and the frost dragon grew larger. *Oh no!* Kalaya shook with fear. *Whoever made this put a lot of Power into it.*

Jaremon did not waver. A look of determination burned in his eyes. "Doom-Ra! Sargen-Ka!" he chanted over and over. Each arrow made its mark for a moment, but Jaremon could not shoot fast enough to take down the monster. Kalaya's heart filled with despair as she watched her wallaroo dangling helplessly in the air.

"Ha ha! We got yer rabbit!" a pair of voices snickered. Kalaya and Jaremon shifted their focus from the sky to the brush further down the beach, where the voices came from.

"Come out, you cowards!" Jaremon shouted as he continued to shoot arrows.

Olan is-a Twig confidently stepped out.

What is he doing here? Olan was a nineteen-year-old Crimson mage with a spiky red and blue Mohawk and a thick, lightning-stylized goatee that was so precise it could only be a projection. His eyes were half closed and his hands stretched up to the dragon in the darkening sky above.

Behind him stood his two younger brothers, Grog and Grimes.

"Olan!" Jaremon growled the name of his cousin as he shot more arrows through the dragon. "Leave Kalaya alone!"

"Look at you, using those fancy old words to try and rescue your girlfriend's rabbit," Olan mocked. "How . . . cute."

"What babies!" Grog giggled.

Kalaya shook off and dissolved Jaremon's projected hand, clenched hers into a fist, and sprinted over to them. *They're going to regret that!* While still a few feet away from Olan, she thrust her hand in the air, sending out the most painful projection punch she could manage.

At least, she thought it was painful.

No way! Kalaya frowned. If Olan felt anything, he didn't show it. He kept his focus; Kalaya's touch projection did nothing to distract him from controlling his dragon.

"Nice try, weakling," Grimes laughed. He and Grog began to jump around her chanting, "We got yer rabbit! We got yer rabbit!"

"It's not a rabbit!" Kalaya snapped. "It's a wallaroo! Let her go!"

"A blue wallaroo?" Olan chuckled. "Tell me—what is it now?" he asked, and then he whistled sharply.

Kalaya looked up and watched in helpless horror as the

dragon opened its mouth and—*Please, no!*—blasted her creation with cold, icy air.

It was instantly frozen solid.

My wallaroo . . .

With wild laughter, Olan spread his fingers apart; his dragon released its prey. The wallaroo tumbled through the air—frozen in a block of ice—until Olan snapped his fingers and two bolts of lightning shot out of the dragon's eyes.

It didn't stand a chance. As soon as the lightning struck, the frozen wallaroo shattered into a thousand pieces and sprinkled into the ocean below. Kalaya slumped to her knees and watched her pitiful projection fade from existence.

"Pretty isn't it? Makes you want to cry, right Jaremon?" Olan teased as Jaremon dissolved his bow and stormed over to them.

So many watches of work, gone, just like that.

"That was easy," Grog laughed.

"Way too easy," Grimes agreed.

But it seemed that Olan wasn't finished. Kalaya watched with trepidation as he started to twirl his hands together, causing his dragon to follow the same motion. It descended like a corkscrew straight toward them.

What is he doing now? "Stop it! Haven't you done enough?"

The dragon opened its mouth, revealing its sharp, shimmering, ice-covered teeth. A ball of blue crystal began to form in its throat, and they all felt the temperature drop.

Calm and quiet, Jaremon stepped over to Olan, whose entire focus was on controlling the dragon as it shot a ball of ice directly at them. Kalaya half shut her eyes as her boyfriend pulled back his arm as if to hit the ice ball. But instead . . .

. . . he punched Olan in the jaw.

The ball of ice immediately exploded, sending crystal shards in every direction as Olan stumbled back and landed on the sand.

Did he really just do that? Kalaya could hardly believe her eyes.

Jaremon quickly turned to the now-vulnerable dragon and shouted, "Kala-Boon!" In an instant, his bow was back, loaded with a blazing arrow of fire. Jaremon wasted no time: he released the arrow into the sky. Kalaya watched as it soared gracefully up toward the dragon, piercing straight through its heart.

Now that Olan was on the ground and in a daze, his dragon didn't stand a chance. The arrow tore through the monster, exploding it into a ball of green fire that lit up the sky.

"Umala-Thawl-Zhou!" Jaremon's arrow turned in midair and spiraled back down toward his rivals. They tried to scramble away, but the arrow was too fast; it shot into Olan's chest and went out through his back, zagged, hit his two brothers, and returned to Jaremon, who caught it with his waiting hand.

"That was way too easy," Jaremon said smugly as the burning dragon disintegrated into the ocean behind him.

"Wha-a-a-at's yo-yo-your pro-o-oblem!?" Olan tried to yell, but he was overcome with emotion. Tears started streaming down his cheeks.

He's crying over that? What's going on?

"I've got no problem." Jaremon shrugged.

Olan tried to say something else, but he couldn't manage to get the words out because of his sudden, uncontrollable sobbing. Grog and Grimes were crying too, but they managed to ask, "Wha-wha-what's ha-a-a-ppening, O-o-olan?"

When Olan finally regained control of his emotions, he responded. "Stupid Jaremon loaded his moldy arrow with Glory!"

Oh, that makes sense. She had forgotten how good he had become at this sort of thing.

"Tavit!" Olan cursed. He stood up and brushed the sand off his legs. "That was a completely illegal move!"

"Making people cry is my gift," Jaremon replied.

"I'm not talking about that. You're not allowed to punch me!"

"And you're not allowed to destroy someone's simulacrum."

"Someone's what?!" Olan spit.

"Simulacrum."

"Whatever, library boy," Olan mocked. "Big words don't give you the right to hit me."

"You were the one who had no right to go after Kalaya's wallaroo. We're even."

"Not even close!" Olan's face was as dark as the Crimson collar around his neck. "You punched me! That's different!"

"So go cry to the elders about it."

"Maybe I should. You know what happens to people who bully."

"And you know what happens to people who use their projections to destroy," Jaremon said as he looked Olan straight in the eyes. "Or do you need your daddy to teach you another lesson on how things work?"

"Shove off! We destroy people's projections in the Competitions all the time, you mold brain."

"This wasn't the Competitions. This was practice!" Kalaya shouted. "And I was working on Kingdom—not Power!"

"Ha. You need to be strong in all three if you're going to compete. Stop whining and making excuses. All you're doing is making our island weak," Olan said. "I hope they don't find a Color in you tomorrow, because from the look of things, you won't even survive training camp."

Jaremon put his fist in Olan's face, but Olan didn't flinch.

"Oh, is the righteous Green mage going to bully me again?" Olan sneered. "I doubt it. Even you wouldn't put your chances to compete at risk." He paused and looked his cousin straight in the eye. "Just stay out of my way!"

Jaremon reluctantly lowered his fist. Part of Kalaya wished he would punch him again, but far off on the horizon, she could see a dim glow radiating from the Island of the Magician's Workshop. That was the prize. None of them wanted to put that at risk.

Ever since Kalaya was small, she'd dreamed of working there. But, would she? Olan's wallaroo-devouring dragon was just the latest in a long string of reminders that she wasn't good enough. *Maybe he's right. One of the first things babies learn is how to change colors, and I can't even manage to do that.*

"You'd be wise to stay out of her way," Jaremon said as the brothers turned to leave. "Kalaya has more experience with Kingdom than you'll ever have."

"Oh yeah?" Olan spun around. "I bet she's never experienced this kind of Kingdom—at least, not from you."

Kalaya reeled as a hot blast of air shot across her skin. She felt the sensation of invisible, wet, and sloppy lips kissing her cheek. Her eyes grew wide with shock and anger.

"Gross!" she cried as she clawed at her face and tried to wipe away the pink shimmer that she knew must be there. Olan and his brothers ran off into the forest, hooting and hollering as they went.

"Try that again and see what happens, you dumb weeds!" Kalaya shouted after them.

"You okay?" Jaremon asked. "Did he kiss you?! Want me to go after them?"

"No, there's no point. Crimson mages are used to doing whatever they want."

Kalaya looked up at Jaremon and felt her breath catch in her chest. Deep in his blue eyes, she saw how concerned he was.

Kalaya didn't hesitate. She leaned over and grabbed Jaremon's hand—his real, physical hand. "Thanks for defending me." There was a tremble in her voice; the thrill of holding his real hand in hers was greater than she expected. *I never imaged it would feel quite like this.*

Kalaya and Jaremon walked together across the beach in silence for uncountable moments, basking in the joy of physical touch. It was similar to what projected touch felt like, but at the same time, so very different. It felt warm, soft, and intimate in a way projections never were.

"Kind of gets sweaty after a while, doesn't it?" Jaremon mused.

"Oh, I'm sorry." Kalaya felt her face flush. "I'm—uh—not really sure what to do about that . . . should we stop?"

"No, it's fine."

She liked the way she could feel the warmth coming from him. She'd never done anything like this before. She found the whole experience to be quite exhilarating. *I'll have to remember this sensation next time I make a hand-holding projection.*

And then a wave of sadness washed over her; she remembered the sight of her wallaroo shattering apart, and she slid her hand out of his. *That wallaroo was the best thing I've ever made, and it was helpless when attacked. I'm so grateful I have Jaremon in my life.* She felt her stomach twist. *Will he still be so attentive to me if the puller doesn't find a Color?*

"What's wrong? You're shivering."

Kalaya turned away and faced the ocean. "He destroyed my wallaroo like it was nothing."

Jaremon thought for a moment, then shrugged. "It's not like she's dead. The wallaroo still exists inside you. It was your vision that made her. You can remake her just as easily as before."

Kalaya raised her eyebrows at him. "Are you kidding? It took me all day to get her where I wanted."

"Right, so now you know how to do it," Jaremon stated as if this would be easy. "Come on. I bet you can remake it in no time."

"I don't think so. It won't be the same." Seeing her work torn apart so easily was devastating; she had little desire to go through all that again.

"We can bring it back. Watch. Oomp. Cha. Za. Waze. Mon. Zaye!" Jaremon shouted the words.

"What are you doing?" Kalaya scowled when she looked back and saw that he'd started recreating her wallaroo projection. "Jaremon, stop," she said and flicked her wrist to dissolve it before he could finish. *Look how much faster he can make it than I can!*

"Come on, I'm not dating a quitter."

"But, what if Olan is right? What if I'm not balanced enough?"

Jaremon looked her right in the eye and said, "Don't listen to him. He's a judgmental coward who cares only about himself. He's just jealous of you."

"Jealous? Of me?" Kalaya raised her eyebrows. *I highly doubt that.*

"Seriously. Your grandmother was in the Workshop for years. She still has fans who visit her in the Garden of Heroes. You've heard what people say about you. Everyone knows how Color often skips a generation. You've got everything going for you. With your family history, talent, and drive, you're bound to earn high scores in the Competitions. You have everything Olan has ever dreamed of."

As he spoke, she felt a bit of hope awaken. "But . . . do you think it looked like a rabbit?"

"Of course not. They were just trying to upset you," Jaremon insisted. "Come on, remake the wallaroo. Show me you can do it again."

His encouragement brought a smile to her face. "Okay. Maybe you're right," she said, her resolve starting to return. "I really would like to perfect it before tomorrow."

Kalaya stood next to him and worked on recreating her original vision. It took them until the bottom of the Violet watch, but she was able to get the wallaroo to almost the same level of perfection that she had achieved before.

"Excellent work," Jaremon said as they stood back and looked at her wallaroo stumble around in its awkward way.

"It's not quite as good." *And it still can't dance.* She shut her eyes and tried to visualize it bounce and spin with joy. When she opened her eyes, she saw that it hadn't worked. The wallaroo just tilted its head and stared at her. "It's hopeless."

"No it's not. Close your eyes, focus, and try again."

She did, but not for long.

"Hey look!" Jaremon exclaimed. "You did it. She's brown!"

Huh? Kalaya opened her eyes and was shocked to see that the wallaroo was now, in fact, the correct brownish-red hue. "But I . . ." Kalaya narrowed her eyes and then turned and looked hard at him. "You did that, didn't you?"

"I'm supporting you."

"Jaremon!" Kalaya crossed her arms. "I have to be able to do it on my own."

"And you will, but you don't have to be alone." The way he said it was so tender and sweet, it took some of the weight off her. "You're my girlfriend. You don't need to worry about anything. I'll always be here for you."

She bit her lower lip and tried to hold back the wave of emotion that she felt stirring inside her. "Thanks."

"Of course." Jaremon took her hand into his once again, and her heart leapt.

As she stared back at him under the light of the moon, she pictured his hand holding hers for the rest of their lives. *That would be beautiful.*

The Dome

~Layauna~

This timeless masterpiece tells the story of a magician who labors to make projections real. After a lifetime of hard work and perseverance he finally achieves that goal. On his deathbed—and with his last breath—he whispers one word and a single coin appears in his hand. His body goes limp, color drains from his face, and the platinum Old World coin falls out of his hand and hits the floor with a loud clink. Triumph! It's real! He achieved his dream. It's a vital reminder to all of us living today that anything is possible if you just believe.

—Opinionator Alice is-a Moose, on *The Magician's Whisper*

"Layauna is-a Wind! Stop daydreaming by the window and come warm up by the fire," Mother shouted to her from the other side of the house.

"I wish it could warm me, Mom," Layauna replied. "But it's just a projection."

"Young lady, that's not the point. This is a family day."

"Okay, Mom," Layauna answered with a forced, cheerful smile.

She pulled herself away from the rain-streaked window and shuffled into the projection room. Her mother and little brother, Sorgan, lay sprawled out next to the flickering fire that Sorgan had projected in the center of the room.

"Everyone take your medicine," Mother ordered as she passed around pieces of namra. Sorgan snatched a piece of the violet root and immediately began to wiggle his nose and scrunch up his face in the way that he always did when making flavor projections. "Layauna, you too," her mother instructed as she passed the tray over.

Ugh. It tastes so much worse here. "Sure. Thanks, Mom." Layauna did her best to sound enthusiastic. *Just focus on something else. You have to stay positive.* The nasty, bitter taste of the namra root overpowered her tongue and she struggled to keep from vomiting—but somehow she managed to endure it.

"I made mine taste like blueberries this time!" Sorgan announced.

Layauna forced down the root. After she felt like she could safely speak without it coming back up, she tried to encourage her brother. "Good job, Sorgan."

Her brother stared at her with a blank expression and blinked several times. "What do you think of my fire? Do you like it?" he asked abruptly, and a mischievous smile crossed his face.

It's weird. I actually miss that smile. "Yeah, good work! It looks very real."

"Oh really? So you don't think it's too . . . SCARY!?" All of a sudden, Sorgan lifted up his right eyebrow, wiggled his nose, and puckered his lips. The fire flared up and the flames took on the appearance of a massive open mouth with long, sharp fangs. The fire-face leapt out and snapped at Layauna with a sharp hiss.

Although she knew it was coming, the fire still managed to startle her. "Ah!" she gasped.

"Ha ha ha!" Sorgan bent over laughing.

"Sorgan!" their mother scolded. "That was not very polite! Normal fires only, please."

"Aw, but Mom!"

"Sorgan." Mother narrowed her eyes.

"Yes, ma'am," Sorgan said, and then he rubbed his face with his two hands, causing the fire to shrink back to its original form.

The faces of both her brother and mom went blank again, and then they blinked in rapid succession.

"It's too easy." Sorgan shrugged. "She's a baby."

Layauna resisted the urge to project something back at her brother. *Stop. Remember, you want things to be different.* Instead of being upset, as she usually was, she lit up with enthusiasm and said, "We should do something! How about the story game?"

Sorgan stared intently at her, as if trying to process her enthusiasm. *Oh no, I think I clattered him.*

A few heartbeats passed before her brother spoke. "Nah, I don't really like that game."

"Sorgan's right," her mother agreed. "I don't think that's a good idea."

What? They love this game and have always wanted me to play it with them. Even though she was cold, Layauna felt her palms get sweaty. "Why not? It will be fun."

"You never like playing it," her mother reminded her.

"You always complain," Sorgan added. "Last time you ran away crying like a baby. A scared little baby!"

Uh-oh. This isn't good. We need to play the game. "No, please. I want to do it. I'm different now. Look, I'll start."

Layauna slowed her breathing and closed her eyes. *Don't think scary. Just stay calm. Remember what Samaal said about breathing techniques and nature.* She focused her thoughts on beautiful waterfalls, babbling brooks, and green forests. *There's nothing to be afraid of.* "Once upon a time, there was a scared little girl who hoped to one day be a mage and save her family from their suffering."

Layauna opened her eyes and breathed a sigh of relief when she saw that over the fire was a projection of a young girl with long, raven black hair and emerald green eyes. *Looks like me. That's fine. At least I didn't project a monster.*

"I don't want to play this game." Sorgan crossed his arms.

"Sorgan! We have to, it's the only way," Layauna said.

"Don't speak to your brother in that tone, young lady!" her mother chided.

Don't react. Don't react. Just be gentle. "I don't want to fight." She forced a smile. "I just want to finish the game."

"We said NO!" Sorgan shouted.

Layauna felt something like a dam burst inside her. The projection of the young girl started to grow bigger and bigger. *Uh-oh.*

"What's wrong, Little Brother?" the projected girl asked.

Layauna watched in alarm as the sweet, innocent look on the projected girl melted away in the flames. Her skin turned ghostly white, and her smile drooped into a dark, horrendous scowl. *No, please. It was going so well.*

"Layauna wants to play the story game," said an angry, deep voice coming out of the projected girl. "Why won't you play?"

Sorgan scrambled away from the fire, ran to his mother, and hid in her arms. "Mom," he whimpered. "She's doing it again."

"Children! Enough!"

Layauna stood up and thrust out her arms at the projection, but no matter how hard she tried, she could not dissolve it. "Ha ha ha ha!" The voice of the girl laughed as the flames leapt up around her and she swirled around and around.

Crack!

A cold blast of wind struck the house, and the front door flew open.

Stop it! Stop it! Layauna went to close the door but froze when she saw what stood in the doorway. "No. No. No." *Not you, again.*

The black, two-headed hell-dog with red eyes and sharp, bloody fangs growled at her. Although the hell-dog was standing outside in the pouring rain, the water had no effect on its flaming patches of fur. Both of its mouths barked and snapped as it slowly made its way into the house. *Why won't you just leave me alone!?*

"Ha ha ha! Crimson doggy wants to play!" the voice of the girl cooed. *He's not Crimson! He's black.* The little girl looked Layauna straight in the eyes and, as if she heard her thoughts, said, "He is Crimson. Let him play, little Layauna. Let the Crimson doggy play with your family!"

"Leave us alone!" Layauna shouted at the girl. But as soon as she spoke, the hell-dog locked its eyes on her mother. *It's too late.* Layauna was powerless to do anything as the monster leapt through the air and bit into her mother's leg with one head and clenched onto Sorgan's neck with the other. *Please, don't do this again!*

"Arg!" Sorgan screamed as the one head of the hell-dog flung him around like he was a rag doll, spewing blood in all directions.

"Help!" Layauna's mother screamed as the hell-dog tore into her flesh and ripped her leg apart. Layauna continued to try to destroy her projections, but she knew there was nothing she could do. *They're too strong, I can't—I can't stop it!*

"What have you done, little Layauna? You're killing them!" The projected girl burst out laughing as her brother's lifeless body was flung into the flames and immediately engulfed.

"NO!" She burst into tears and bolted away from them as fast as she could. She slid into the kitchen, ducked underneath the table, and covered her ears.

Don't look. Shut it out. It's not real. It's not really happening. She tried her best to hum and block out the sound, but it did little to muffle the cries of her mother as she was devoured.

Layauna squeezed her eyes shut and screamed as loud as she could, "NO MORE! I'M DONE! STOP IT, NOW!"

*   *   *

"Layauna is-a Wind! Stop brooding by the window and come warm up by the fire," Mother shouted to her from the other side of the house.

Layauna opened her eyes and found herself once again staring out the window at the rainstorm.

"It's a projection," she replied dimly. "It can't warm me." *And if it's a projection, it also can't harm me.*

"Young lady, that's not the point. This is a family day."

"Every day is family day." Layauna sighed. *Anger doesn't work. Staying silent is useless. Happiness doesn't stop it.* Nothing she tried worked. She felt miserable and defeated.

She pulled herself away from the rain-streaked window and shuffled into the projection room. Her mother and little brother lay sprawled out next to the flickering fire that Sorgan had projected in the center of the room.

"Everyone take your medicine," her mother ordered as she passed around several pieces of namra.

Sorgan snatched a piece and immediately began to wiggle his nose and scrunch his face together in the way he always did when making flavor projections.

"Layauna, you too," her mother instructed as she passed the tray over.

If I have to taste that again, I think I actually might die. "I really think I need a break from namra."

"Don't start this again, you know it's good for you," Mother commanded. "Your grandfather has always . . ."

". . . eaten a root every day and he was a great magician. I know," Layauna repeated the words she knew she should say.

Responding in disgust has never helped, and being good and eating it without complaint always fails. I wonder what would happen if I just didn't eat the bitter root at all? So she didn't, and went on to say, "Sorgan, that's a pretty nice fire you made!"

Both her mother and brother jolted in place, blinked several times, and gave her a startled look. *I clattered them. What's going to happen now?* Her mother blinked some more, uncertain, before she put the tray away. *Did that actually work?*

"What do you think of my fire? Do you like it?" Sorgan asked with a mischievous smile.

"Yes, I told you, I think it's good," Layauna said, distracted. *Did Mom really just let me get away with not eating the root?* She relaxed for a moment until she remembered what was about to happen next. *Don't let the fire scare you. It's only a projection.*

"Oh really? So you don't think it's too . . . SCARY!?" All of a sudden, Sorgan lifted up his right eyebrow, wiggled his nose, and puckered his lips. The fire flared up and the flames took on the appearance of a massive open mouth with long, sharp fangs. The fire-face leapt out and snapped at Layauna with a loud hiss.

She didn't scream. This time, the fire-face only caused her to squeeze her eyes half-shut and let out a tiny whimper. But it didn't change Sorgan. "Ha ha ha!" He bent over laughing, the same as always.

This is torture.

"Sorgan!" Mother scolded. "That was not very polite! Normal fires only, please."

"Aw, but Mom!"

"Sorgan." Mother narrowed her eyes.

"Yes, ma'am." Sorgan rubbed his face with his two hands, causing the fire to shrink back to its original form. "It's too easy. She's a baby."

I bet he wouldn't say that if he knew all I've been through. "You guys feel like playing the story game?" Layauna asked even though she knew what their answer would be.

"No I . . . I don't want to . . ." Sorgan's lower lip quivered as he spoke.

Huh. Is he afraid? That's different.

"I agree. I don't think that's a good idea," her mother said.

"Please? I'd really like to create something with you guys."

Sorgan looked at her in a way that indicated he did not trust her. "No, Layauna. We said no."

"Only bad things happen when you project things," her mother stated.

I know. That's why I have to keep doing this over and over until it changes. "Please—you need to work with me on this."

The sound of rain pelting against the roof of the house grew louder, and the wind started to pick up. Layauna slowed her breathing, shut her eyes, and tried to remain calm. But she trembled as she thought about what always happened next.

"I said . . ." Sorgan stood up. ". . . I don't want to play the story game!"

Crack!

A strong blast of wind struck the house and the front door burst open. *No, no, NO! Is this terror ever going to end?*

Layauna didn't need to look; she knew the hell-dog was there. The sound of growling rippled through the air and sent a shiver down her spine.

Maybe it won't attack if no one moves. "Mom. Sorgan. Be still. Don't move," she warned as she slowly stood up and turned to face the hell-dog. "It's me you want—you stupid monster. Leave my family alone!" Both heads of the hell-dog looked at her and snarled.

"Layauna, run!" Sorgan screamed.

Stay quiet.

Sorgan screamed the words again, even louder, and both of the monster's heads turned toward him. He took a step back. The hell-dog took a step forward. Sorgan let out a yelp, turned, and ran from the room, through the kitchen, and out the back door.

No!

The hell-dog bolted after him, but before it could get very far, Mother grabbed it from behind and tried to hold it back. "Save your brother!" she screamed as she wrestled with it.

Layauna sprinted toward the door but stopped right before she exited. "Mom!" she cried as she looked over her shoulder and saw her mother fighting the monster. Which way should she go? Back to save her mom, or out to her brother? She had tried to pull the hell-dog off the person it was attacking many times before. *It never works. It's hopeless.*

She couldn't watch. Not again. She covered her eyes and ran out the door and into the pouring rain. As soon as she stepped out, the house behind her faded away, and she was left standing in a dark, wild forest. Thunder boomed all around her and lightning flashed in the sky. It was always storming in the forest outside her house.

She despised this place even more than she despised namra.

"Help!" Sorgan's voice rang through the air, sending a bolt of fear through her heart.

Mom's gone, but maybe I can still save him. "Sorgan? Where are you?" She strained her eyes to see in the inky blackness of the forest. There he was: a dark blob, crouched a few feet away. When she got near, she realized that Sorgan was surrounded by hissing cobras. They slithered around him as he held his hands over his head.

How can all these things possibly be in me? I hate horror. I hate it! It's my least favorite kind of Grand Projection. I like funny and romantic stories. So why is everything I project so horrible?

"Leave him alone!" she screamed, but the snakes didn't listen. They took turns lashing out at him and piercing his skin with their fangs. She stood over them and kicked. Nothing happened. She swatted at them with her arms. It didn't destroy them. Her hands and feet went right through them like they were made of mist.

She reached down to take hold of her brother's hand, but there was nothing for her to grab on to. She couldn't push him away. She couldn't shelter him. She couldn't do anything. *My projections are eating him alive and there's nothing I can do.* Layauna dropped to her knees and waited helplessly as her screaming brother was devoured.

He's not real, she tried to remind herself over the sound of his screaming. *He's not real. The only real thing here is you.* But no matter how much she tried to convince herself of this, she couldn't believe it. *It's impossible to tell the difference between reality and projections in this awful dome.* The horror playing out around her was all too real.

✳   ✳   ✳

"Layauna is-a Wind! Stop whimpering by the window and come warm up by the fire," her mother shouted to her from the other side of the house.

Layauna opened her eyes and stared out at the rainstorm. *Over and over, always the same.* She'd experienced this countless times. *How often do I have to go through the same exact thing?* She was sick of it. "I'm done."

"What was that?" her mother called.

"I'm finished. This isn't doing anything. Do you hear me?" Layauna shouted up at the roof. "I'm not doing this anymore."

Her mother and Sorgan looked at her from the other room. "Young lady, come in here this instant. It's time for . . ."

"Leave me alone," she cried. "I can't help you!" Layauna left the kitchen, pushed open the back door with her shoulder, and was about to leave, when—

Crack!

She knew that sound; the front door had flung open. *The hell-dog is here, already?* Layauna hesitated.

No, she wouldn't go back and watch again.

She ran out into the rainstorm. As she sprinted across the grass, an army of venomous cobras lashed out at her. She ran around their pool-turned-swamp that was filled with ugly green goblins, then through a hedge that was home to a cluster of blood-thirsty bats. All of this would have horrified her before, but she was sixteen now—almost a young woman—and the monsters didn't scare her as much as they once did. She had experienced their horror over and over for countless weeks. It never seemed to end.

Layauna ran and ran until at last she came to a monstrous tree. She pounded on it. It sounded like metal. "Open up! Open up right now!" she shouted at the tree.

The sound of her family screaming echoed in her ears, so she banged on the tree harder. After what felt like an eternity, she heard a loud clank. A door—now cracked open and framed with light—appeared in the tree. Layauna didn't wait to see who was on the other side; she flung her body against the thick metal door over and over until it opened wide enough for her to squeeze through.

The Hell-Dog

~Layauna~

Projections give a very realistic impression of reality, but they are not material. They are made out of light and thus consist of nothing more than empty wavelengths. Everyone was taught this in school. But—due to some unfortunate mistruths that have been propagated in some so-called Grand Projections, like The Magician's Whisper—*there are many who actually believe it's possible to make projections real. But it's not. Get over it.*

—Magician Qyennta is-a Smooch, *Power, Kingdom, and Glory: The Gift of Projections*

"Layauna!" a voice called out after her.

Leave me alone! Instead of a forest, she was now in a long, dim hallway. *I never want to go back in there, and I don't want to live here anymore.* She struggled to see her way through the maze of rooms and corridors as she ran. It was easy to get turned around in this place due to the dim lighting. *Where am I? I want to go back home.*

She was lost inside the ancient-looking stone building that had been her training place for far too long. Its main room, where she spent most of her time, was called the dome. This was where the forest was, where her projected mother and brother got ripped apart by her other projections, and where her nightmares seemed to be reality.

I have to get out of here. She ran until she turned a corner and found herself outside a room filled with people. They were sitting around a table that was carved out of a massive, ancient tree. Strewn across it were charts and diagrams covered in numbers, symbols, and various markings that she didn't understand. She'd spent countless watches in this room. It was where they met to go over the results of the day and track her progress. *And it's where they observe me.* The long back wall of the room was made entirely of a special glass that provided a clear view of all the horror she had created inside the dome.

She didn't linger here long, but in the short time she stood there, she saw her grandfather sitting at the head of the table. They made eye contact. He didn't seem angry, but there was a look of disapproval on his face, as if he was disappointed to see her out of the dome.

No, don't go to Grandfather. He'll just send me back in there. I've tried and tried. It's not working. I don't want to do this anymore! Layauna spun away from the crowded room and ran farther down the hall until at last she found an exit. She slammed against it and broke out of the building, into a real forest with real trees and real grass in the middle of what she judged to be the actual afternoon.

It felt good to be outside, to breathe the fresh air, and to feel the warmth of the sun on her skin. She took in everything. She heard a bird chirp. She heard the wind rustle the leaves of the trees. She heard a low growl. *No!* She looked over her shoulder and saw that the two-headed hell-dog had followed her out of the dome. *No! No! No! It's supposed to stay in there! That's the whole point of all this!*

The hell-dog bound after her through the forest with a look of fury in its eyes. Layauna jolted and scrambled to get away, but her legs could last only so long. *It's useless to try and outrun a projection, so why do I keep trying?* Eventually, Layauna lost her breath and collapsed on the ground near a gentle, babbling creek. The hell-dog was on her as soon as she fell, growling, barking, and gnawing at her legs.

I'm glad you're a projection and not material, she thought as she endured the terrible monster attacking her flesh. Although the hell-dog couldn't actually devour her, she still felt a stabbing sensation whenever its teeth touched her skin. It would be enough to make most people scream and cry, but after three years of dealing with this monster, she'd grown accustomed to the pain it caused her. *I can't keep doing this. It's never going to work. Why can't anyone else see that?*

"I understand your frustration," a man said from somewhere in the forest.

Layauna felt her heart leap up into her chest; it wasn't a voice she recognized. "Who's there?" she called as she frantically scanned the area.

"Hello, Layauna," an elderly man said as he stepped over to her and held out both palms of his hands.

What's going on? Is this another lesson? The man had dark blue eyes, medium length black hair, and a thick beard that was flecked with grey. He looked vaguely familiar, but she wasn't sure why. "Are you real?" Layauna asked. *He can't be. He's not wearing a collar.*

"I sure hope I'm real. You can feel me to be certain, if you'd like."

Layauna hadn't touched an actual person in a long time, and she felt a little weird about interacting with a stranger in this way, but she decided it was better to know. So she crawled carefully over to him—dragging the hell-dog with her as she went—and touched his foot with her hand.

Solid. The relief she felt was immediate. "I'm sorry to have to touch you," she quavered. "It's just . . . when I'm in that place, it's so hard to know what's real and what's not." As she said this she noticed that, out here, in the sunlight, her hell-dog didn't look nearly as lifelike as the man did.

"That's perfectly all right. I'm familiar with the intensity experienced within the domes," the elderly man said. He glanced down at the hell-dog, which was still gnawing on Layauna's leg, and said, "That's quite the hellhound you've created."

The hell-dog looked up at him and growled ferociously.

"I think it finds that term offensive," Layauna explained.

"Hellhound?" As soon as the stranger spoke, the hell-dog snapped its teeth repeatedly at him.

"Yeah. It prefers hell-dog."

"I see." The man smiled.

What's there to smile about? Can't he see I'm being tortured? "Are you . . . are you a new trainer?"

"No, no."

"Why are you here?"

"Your grandfather and I are good friends. We used to work together."

"You worked in the Magician's Workshop?" she asked. "Then why aren't you wearing your collar?"

"My collar sometimes gets in the way. And yes, indeed, your grandfather and I had quite a time together there. But things are different now. I must say, I'm not a big fan of these new training techniques. They feel a bit—barbaric, wouldn't you agree?"

No, it's worse. "My grandfather just wants to help me."

"Yes, he does. More than you know. That's one reason I'm here. He wanted me to see firsthand what you could do and find out if there was any way I could help."

Although he sounded sincere, Layauna wasn't so sure he could do anything. Many people had told her similar things over the last three years. *Nothing works.*

"Oh, so you saw everything?" She turned her eyes away from him as she said this and pulled her knees up to her chest. The monster circled around behind her and began clawing her back.

"It's quite impressive. The forest you made, the monsters, the recreations of your family—you have some very strong abilities. Much of it appeared quite real."

"Good thing it's not." She grimaced at the thought.

"One day, if we get the right people together, it may be," he said. Layauna looked at him like he was crazy. He sat down next to her in the grass. "I know it seems absurd to you, but creating projections that become actual, tangible things is the ultimate dream of every magician."

Dream? Is he serious? "I hope that never happens."

"No, no, don't say that. It would be the greatest blessing to O'Ceea."

A blessing? Layauna shook her head. "How could anyone want that? Did you see what this monster did to my family? If it was a real, solid thing, my whole family would be dead right now."

"That's why, before we learn to make them solid, we must learn to love them," he said in a kind and gentle way. "Do you love your hell-dog?"

Layauna looked at him like he was a fool. "I think it's pretty obvious. No."

"Why not?"

"I don't see any reason to love something that only wants to destroy me and everyone I actually care about."

"All right, that's fair. So let me ask you a different question. What's your hell-dog doing—right now?"

"Eating me."

"Ever wonder why it's doing that?"

"Because it hates me," Layauna replied grimly.

The man worked to hold back a laugh. "Did you mean that to be funny?"

"Sort of."

"Good, I'm glad. You know, it may very well hate you. But have you ever considered it may also just be hungry? What do you think a hell-dog would like to eat?"

"I don't know. My family, apparently."

He let out another short laugh. "And what else? Something good for it, and you."

Layauna frowned. "Maybe . . . I don't know . . . steak?"

"Good! Can you project some steaks for him—over there?" The man pointed to the nearby brook. "On that flat rock there, the one just barely sticking out of the water."

"I . . . can try." Layauna closed her eyes and tried to imagine a pile of steaks stacked up on the rock. She hadn't had a steak for a long time, so it was a challenge to imagine, but she did her best. *Uncooked, probably. And bloody. Stupid monsters like blood.*

"Ah ha, see? Wonderful," he said.

Layauna opened her eyes and was surprised to see that the hell-dog had left her and was now gobbling up the pile of red, juicy steaks she'd projected by the creek. "Wow. It actually worked!"

Unfortunately, the hell-dog ate the steaks faster than she expected, and as soon as it was done, it turned and started growling at her. *Great! So much for that plan. It's not even thankful.* "See? It's still mean." She pointed at it.

"But it's not eating you anymore. That's a significant step, right?"

"Um, I guess."

"Now, what else do you think he might want? Put yourself in his place. What does he want now?"

Hmm. Probably to drag people down to the heart of Helldoro. It is a hell-dog, after all. "Maybe . . . it's scared?" she said out loud. The thought was absurd, and she wasn't sure why she said it.

"Hmm . . . what do you think it could be scared of?" he asked.

"I don't have any idea. It's a monster. Monsters shouldn't have anything to be scared of. Everyone is scared of them."

"Oh, I've worked with a lot of monsters, and they all have things they're scared of. Just think of something. It doesn't need to be right. What's the first thing you can think of?"

The image of a knight with a violet lightning bolt flashed

into her imagination, then disappeared as fast as it came. "Maybe . . . uh . . . what if there is some other creature out there that it's afraid of. Something it can't see."

"That's very possible. There always seems to be a bigger monster waiting to attack. So, if there's a big, hidden monster out there, what do you think might make your dog feel safe?"

"I have no idea."

"Were you ever scared of something when you were little? At night, perhaps?"

"Of course."

"Did anything help you then?"

"I don't know," Layauna said. "I guess. My dad used to sing me a song when I was little. I remember him doing that whenever I woke up from a bad dream. I think that made me feel better."

"Great. Do you remember how it goes?"

Layauna worked her mouth back and forth. *I guess I could try.* She thought about the song and shut her eyes. The sound of her father's singing voice surrounded them.

> *"There is a place I know and love,*
> *A place where rivers run.*
> *And in the water, there I find,*
> *The birthplace of the sun.*
>
> *Forevermore, I'll sleep in peace,*
> *Safe—and with my love.*
> *When light has faded from my eyes,*
> *I'm there, my precious dove."*

The hell-dog started to calm down. *What's going on?* It stopped snapping and snarling, and while there was still wild anger and fury in its eyes, it was no longer directed at her.

"Your father has a beautiful voice," the man said. "See, it's calmed the hell-dog. It feels like much of the Power has drained from it. See if you can dissolve him now."

Layauna kept the song going and locked her eyes on the monster. *I actually think this is going to work.* "Be gone!" She waved her hands at the hell-dog, now fully confident she would dissolve it.

But instead of the hell-dog dissolving, the hairs on its back stood up on end and it snarled at her. *Of course. Now, I've angered it again. Nothing's ever going to change.* "See? It's still angry!" Layauna sighed, and the singing stopped.

The man looked from her to the hell-dog, and then back to her again. "There's something else. What is it?" he said half to himself and paused to consider. "Could it be you don't really want it to go away?"

"Of course not. I hate it. It's horrible!"

"It feels like it's weakened quite a bit," the man said. "I could easily dissolve it."

"Then why don't you? Please, try for me."

"Layauna, do you know who I am?" the stranger asked. She stared up at his face, but she still couldn't figure out why he looked familiar. *I don't think I've ever met him before.* She said nothing in response, and so he said, "I'm the Master Magician."

"You are?!" Layauna felt her eyes grow wide. She'd never seen him in person before, but her trainers had spent a lot of time teaching her about all the magicians in the Workshop. *Why didn't I recognize him? He's their leader!* Then a wave of shame hit her. *Oh no! I touched the foot of the Master Magician!*

"I am, but please, don't think of me any differently."

How can I not? I've been whining to the most powerful man in all the islands! "I . . . uh . . ." Layauna stammered.

"I'm sharing with you who I am so you'll hear what I'm about to say." Master Magician Greydyn moved over to the hell-dog and knelt next to it. "I've created many projections in my lifetime—many of them I've loved dearly—and I've had to dissolve all of them. Until you've participated in the creation of a Grand Projection, you won't understand what it's like to see it end for the last time. I grieve them like old friends who've died and moved on from this life. This is the reason your grandfather and I share a vision to one day see projections made real. Wouldn't that be wonderful?

"We could build entire islands right from our imagination and fill them with the characters we love. There'd be no hunger. No slums. No poverty. Whatever the Workshop projected could exist. There's so much empty ocean in O'Ceea. Haven't you ever wondered why? I believe it's because Tav intended us to one day fill it with the land we've created."

Layauna tried to hide the look of disbelief on her face. She'd heard that, ever since people had first been able to project, they had been trying to make projections real. But no one had ever been able to do it, and there was very little evidence that those who claimed it was possible—like Tav—could. *Just stories to give hope to those who wish they could live forever.* But this was the Master Magician speaking. *Maybe the rumors about Greydyn are true. He actually might be losing his grasp on reality.*

"But, until that day, projections need to be dissolved," Master Magician Greydyn said. "That can be hard, even when it's something you hate. But you have to do it."

"Trust me, I want to," Layauna said.

"Are you sure you actually do want your hell-dog to go away—forever?"

"Of course I do. My grandfather has repeatedly said that I need to learn how to dissolve it and to make sure that it never comes back. This has been the primary focus of all of my training over the last three years."

"Yes, your grandfather has told me a lot about it. Your trainers have also given me a lengthy report on how their techniques haven't been working."

Great. Even the Master Magician knows. Layauna lowered her head and looked down at her toes. "I do everything they say but it seems like I'm never going to learn how to dissolve my unconscious monster projections—they have more Power than I do."

"Unconscious projections aren't all that different from conscious ones," the Master Magician explained. "All projections come from within us. They are little parts of our soul that have come out. Conscious projections are the parts that we knowingly share. Unconscious ones are those that are so desperate to be expressed that they come out without thought or effort."

"They're horrible. I wish they'd just go away, forever," Layauna said.

"Personally, I don't find using the dome in this way has done much good. It hasn't seemed to work for you, has it? Your hell-dog keeps coming out."

It's never going to stop. It's going to be with me forever, she despaired. Then she cried out inside her mind, *Can you help me?* She didn't know why she couldn't say the words out loud. A part of her longed for the Master Magician to save her, but another part of her knew that even he wasn't strong enough.

"My belief," he continued, "is that your hell-dog keeps bursting out because it's very much a part of you."

How could this monster be a part of me? Layauna felt her hand tremble. The idea shocked her, but on some level she knew it was true, and so she didn't question the Master Magician. "I don't know what to do."

"It's not easy to get rid of a part of you. By dissolving it, you're saying goodbye to it. But you have to—you've seen how much it's torturing you and your family."

"But I don't know how."

"Say goodbye to him, Layauna. Grieve it and let it go. It doesn't need to torture you anymore."

Layauna pulled her knees up to her chest and stared at the hell-dog. It wasn't growling at her anymore. It didn't even look angry. For the first time, she looked in its eyes—truly looked—and saw within those blazing red orbs something of herself.

It is me! She saw it. Then the memory of her father's last meal with them flashed before her eyes. They were at Nosy's. She'd tried to make a pleasant flavor projection on a piece of namra, failed, and vomited all over everything. Although she knew that wasn't the reason her dad had left, deep down, she feared his mysterious disappearance soon after this was somehow her fault.

Since the hell-dog is me, maybe I really am the reason he left. She broke down crying.

"Good, Layauna. Let it out," the Master Magician said.

And she did. She cried harder and longer than she had in her entire life. It felt good to cry—to really cry—and to rid herself of all the pent-up emotions that were swirling around inside her. And as the hot tears streamed down her face, she looked up at the hell-dog and—for a moment—all of her hatred of it was gone. Somehow, she actually felt sorry for it.

As if responding to her emotion, the hell-dog stood up, raised its heads to the sky, and let out two lonely howls. Something had changed—Layauna knew it in her gut. *It's time.* She reached out her hand to the monster and—as effortlessly as a wave washing away footsteps in the sand—dissolved it.

I did it? . . . Yes, I finally did it!

"Congratulations, Layauna." The Master Magician grinned.

"I can't believe it!" She leapt to her feet, feeling like a giant weight had just been lifted off her shoulders. *I don't need to be tormented by my projections anymore!*

If she hadn't been in the presence of the most significant person in the whole islands, she might have jumped up and started to dance around. Instead, she pressed her hands together and tried to bow respectfully to him. "Thank you so much for helping me, Master Magician."

"It was my pleasure." He returned her bow. "Now, how do you feel about me taking you back? I'm sure your grandfather is quite worried about you right now."

"Do I need to go?" Layauna pressed her lips together. The thought of returning to the horrors she'd created in the dome caused her heart to beat faster, but she felt better knowing that she could dissolve them now.

"Yes, but don't worry. I have a feeling your grandfather will project some wonderful tastes on your meal tonight after we report your accomplishment here today."

Layauna felt her mouth water. The thought was too good to be true. "Do you think . . . Would he really do that?"

"I don't see why not. You deserve a reward. You defeated a monster."

"He's not a monster—" *Oh no!* Layauna stopped. *What have I done?* She said the words with bitter feelings, and they came out of her thoughtlessly. *I've just dishonored the Master Magician, after all he's done to help me. Why do I keep having these angry outbursts?* "I'm so sorry. I didn't mean it. I don't know why I said that." She couldn't look Greydyn in the face anymore.

"Don't be afraid, Layauna," Greydyn said. "I'm not upset. I've grown quite used to being told I'm wrong—especially after this past year."

"You aren't wrong, though. He really is a monster. A terrible, terrible beast."

"Yes, but there's something significant in what you said. You just called your projection a 'he.' That means something."

"Really?"

"Of course. When people stop calling a monster they project 'it' and start using 'he' or 'she' without thinking, it means the projection has become a character. This is something we are always watching out for in the Workshop."

Great, I've done something else wrong. "So, what do I need to do to fix it?"

A kind smile spread across Greydyn's face. "No, no. You're hearing me wrong. You haven't done anything that needs fixing. You've done a good thing. Grand Projections are full of characters. People care about characters. Creating one out of a monster isn't easy, and look, you—a girl who's not yet stood before a puller—have done it."

I did something good? With that monster? Even though it was the Master Magician who said it, it didn't seem right.

"The characters we project are often surprises—at least mine are to me. Sometimes the surprise is how horrifying they appear." At this he paused, as if for dramatic effect, before he said, "You do realize the most popular character I've created is a monster also—a terrible, terrible beast."

"Who?" Layauna couldn't imagine anything like her hell-dog coming out of this great man.

"Devos Rektor, of course."

The name hit Layauna with a force she could not have anticipated. How could that villain exist within the gentle, kind man who stood before her? This unexpected, troubling thought filled her with dread and she stumbled backward and fell to the ground. For the first time, she understood that Devos Rektor was a projection that came out of a person—this person, who now loomed over her. *If the Master Magician came up with a villain like that, then maybe he's not as safe as he seems.*

That horrible, ethereal presence—known throughout the islands—overwhelmed her, and a crippling terror stole her breath away and left her feeling naked and alone. She didn't know how to respond.

The Master Magician squatted down next to her and her dread disappeared as quickly as it had come upon her. When he spoke, his words now somehow brought comfort. "We all have villains inside of us that come out as projections—just like I did. Congratulations, you've now turned one of yours into a character."

Greydyn motioned for her to stand up, and as she did, her strength returned and she found herself able to trust him again. She turned to head back but stopped when she noticed that the Master Magician hadn't moved. He was staring intently at the nearby creek as if lost in thought. After a long moment, he turned and said to her, "You've fed him, sung to him, and cried for him. But there is still something else he needs from you." Layauna gave the Master Magician a look that said she had no idea what this could be, so he continued. "He needs you to give him a name."

"A name? Like what?"

"He's your character—look for a word that fits him. You'll know when you find it."

I will? Layauna worried she would never be able to find one. But her doubt lasted only a heartbeat, as a name for her hell-dog fell into her mind as if Tav himself had stepped out of history and dropped it there.

Blaze. His name is Blaze. From the moment it came to her, she knew it was right.

The Market

~Weston~

Oa'ka been forever used for prohibitions. Dey pops quite a bang-bang, right maum? Everyone gets a different hit from da precious drops. Dat's why it's such a mega love, special plant. Course, I'm guilty for lovin' da stuff, maum. But, I'm innocent of all dem crimes you're shoving on ta me, right maum. I've never been involved in selling or smuggling. I'm just a commoner, maum, just lookin' for a lil' excitement.

—Master Horatio is-a House, testimony under oath, *Elders of the Penta-Islands* v. *Horatio is-a House*

"Hot mildew! You mean they punished you, too?" Weston exclaimed to Luge as the two friends stood next to their bikes outside the Stone clan's lumber yard. It was the first time they'd been together since the King King they created had terrorized their island, and Weston had been looking forward to seeing Luge and all of the buds throughout his entire prohibition.

"Yeah, they put drops in my eyes," Luge said. He waved goodbye to his dad and the two boys started to bike toward Market Street.

"But you didn't make any projections that day."

"They told me I needed to be taught a lesson for participating with all of you."

Luge was innocent. Weston shook his head in disbelief. "That's soooo drench!"

Luge said, "My prohibition lasted only one day. Yours was, what? Eighteen?"

"Yeah, and every day was torture." *But all that's over now.*

"I can't imagine. Just one day was unbearable for me."

"I'm sorry," Weston said.

"For what? It wasn't your fault!"

"That's what all the buds keep saying, but I'm the one that put so much Power into that beast. If I hadn't, Kai would've been able to dissolve it, and no one would have ever known."

"I don't think that was the problem. We all played a part in it. We shouldn't have left before all of the projections were dissolved. I could have said something, but I got carried away with excitement about the Glimmering. So, I was part of the problem too—the IP were right to give me a prohibition."

"Yeah, that's why you're such a good bud—but it wasn't your fault. There wouldn't have been any problem at all without my Power."

"It could have been a really good day. We were all having so much fun. I actually kinda liked running away from King King."

"Yeah, Talia totally kissed the rainbow with it. But we did break the rules. Projections cause a lot of trouble when the wrong people make them." Weston took some comfort in knowing that on the same day they were all sentenced to their prohibitions, Gromer, Glender, Gropher, and Tiepan were also given prohibitions for what they did to Kai on that fancy yacht. "Projections are powerful things. I learned my lesson. I'm not going to make them anymore."

Luge stared at him like he'd just said he was about to sail away to Region 5 and never return. "What? What do you mean?"

"We weren't certified to make a projection like that," Weston explained.

"Yeah, but you're not going to totally stop projecting, are you? You're so talented."

"No, of course not. I'm going to be making them all the time—after I get my Color. Once I'm a mage, I'll be able to make all the projections I want. Kai, Tal, and I will be able to make a hundred King Kings and nobody can stop us."

"Yeah, that'll be mega! But, it'll be even better when all three of you get into the Workshop. No one on this island will be able to place you under a prohibition then. People will clap and cheer over the stuff you make instead of punishing you. And you'll each have a huge mansion in Little Hills."

"And the Workshop will pay you a whisper to build them for us. We'll all be rich and swim in pools filled with lykes," Weston said. A smile formed on his face. "Hey, I just had an idea. Follow me."

The two boys biked toward Waterton. It was the top of the Green watch. The sun was high, bright, and warm. It felt good paired with the cool ocean breeze. Ever since his arrest, Weston had refused to leave his room because of the destabilizing effects of his prohibition.

But that's all over now. I'm free! Weston delighted in his liberation. He'd always loved being outside, and as he peddled his bike, he took everything in as if with new senses. He didn't generally like biking, but after his prohibition was lifted, he found himself wanting to bike everywhere.

His heart was glad to be together with his friend. They weaved in and out among the people doing business on Market Street before turning toward the marina.

"Where are you leading me?" Luge asked.

"To a taste of our future, Budtastico."

They jumped their bikes over some fishing buoys, rode around a huge pile of nets, and then traveled down one of the docks. There, in a little shed, was Captain Cakes.

"Can you smell that?" Weston took in a deep sniff as he parked his bike. "The scents of glory!"

"Well, that's what his advertisement says." Luge pointed to the projection standing on top of the shack. A short, stocky pirate queen affectionately named Gale waved her hooked hand at them. "Yar! Welc'm t' Capt'n Cakes, where ye be tastin' th' scents o' glory!"

To Weston, Captain Cakes was the best cake stand in all of the islands, even though he'd traveled to only one other island before, the Island of the Red Tower—the place that hosted the Festival of Stars, the Color Ceremony, and the Intra-Regional Competitions. But nothing he saw there could alter his opinion of this run-down shack.

Ahhhh. It's been too long since I had one of these. "Let's get some cake! My treat."

"Are you sure?" Luge asked as they approached the grimy storefront window. "I mean . . . buying cakes . . . isn't that pretty expensive?"

"You budder believe it," Weston said. Luge looked at him with a blank expression. Weston thought he had used every imaginable variation of 'bud' before, but 'budder' was new. It just stumbled out of his mouth, and he liked it. *'Budder.' That's good. I need to remember that.*

The Captain was a Red mage from Luge's clan named Sammy is-a Stone. The two guild pins fastened to his Color collar glistened in the sunlight. Weston remembered attending the huge celebration the Stone clan had thrown for Sammy when he was admitted into the guilds and could finally pursue his passion for concocting flavors. He had opened this cake stand on the pier to satisfy the hunger of fishermen who'd spent all morning out at sea. Sammy set his prices at what a fisherman could afford, but even then, one of his cakes was an extravagant expense for Weston's family. They were simple makers of threadbare and could rarely afford to eat here.

"You know, I'm actually not very hungry. You go ahead and get one for yourself—you don't need to buy one for me," Luge said.

"Nah, there's always room for cake, eh Captain?"

"Weston an' Luge! Hello! I haven't seen either of you around for a long time."

"Yeah," Weston said, "we've been out of commission for a bit."

"I bet! Prohibitions can be quite harsh," the Captain said while feeding a piece of projected cake to the projection of a chubby penguin that sat on his shoulder. The penguin was dressed in attire identical to the Captain's, and it peeped happily as it nibbled the cake.

"Yeah, but it's over and I'd like two cakes—to celebrate!"

"Are you sure 'bout that, Weston?" the Captain asked.

"It's fine, I have plenty of gryns saved up. I've been keeping them for a rainy patch, but my life hasn't flooded out yet. So I don't see any reason to hold on to them any longer since I'll have a Color in a little more than a week. Once I'm a mage, I won't have to worry about silly things like budgeting."

"I don't know 'bout that, but it sure is an exciting time," the Captain said. "The whole island will be there cheering you boys on!"

When he was a young man, Sammy had scored higher in taste and smell projections than anyone in Luge's clan for the last two generations. *Now look at him!* Weston marveled at how far Color had taken this Stone.

"I want banana-mango-strawberry with chocolate ice cream," Weston said.

"I'll just have one—plain. Hold the projections, please," Luge said.

"Plain! Bud, come on. Plain ones are only two and a half gryns."

"They've got real whipped cream."

"Budalicious, there's no flavor in plain," Weston exclaimed. "What's the point of cake without flavoring? Go on, order something yummy."

"All right, fine. How about . . . coconut and persimmon? With a few sour bombs. And pako ice cream."

Weston didn't hide his disgust. "Are you serious? Maybe you should stick with plain. That combo is going to taste awful."

"Hey—I like mixing stuff up."

"All right, Budino. At least you'll never have to worry about people stealing your snacks."

"Okay, comin' right up," the Captain said. Then he rang a bell two times, shouted, "All aboard!" and got to work making their order while the penguin peeped out a little joyful melody. The Captain grabbed two pre-made pieces of thin, flat, round cake from a package in the cupboard and slathered some whipped cream overtop. Then he reached for one of the little glass bottles that filled an enormous rack on the wall behind him. Each bottle was labeled with the name of a flavor and was filled with a fine crystalline substance that the Captain had projected that flavor into.

He began sprinkling the small particles onto the whipped cream: banana, mango, strawberry, and chocolate ice cream flavors for one cake, then coconut, persimmon, and pako ice cream for the other. Then he pulled down a medium-sized jar labeled Sour Bombs and took out five pearl-sized balls, which he placed evenly throughout Luge's cake. Last, he rolled the cakes up and folded the bottom so the whipped cream wouldn't squeeze out.

Whoa! This is going to come out to thirty gryns! Weston realized. *The Captain must be rich! It's so simple for a mage to make big money.*

Weston held out the coins to pay for the cakes, but the Captain waved them off. "It's on the house today, boys."

Buds alive! I feel like I'm chewin' stars! "Thanks, Captain!" Weston and Luge said together.

"There's just one condition," the Captain said as he handed out the two cakes. "Be careful around Kai is-a Shield, yeah? I'd hate for some of his troublesome nature to wear off on you boys and cause some irreparable consequences. That King King he made threw a fireball that hit my shack and completely wiped Gale out. Guess how long it took me to restore her?"

"Uh, I wouldn't know," Luge said.

"Three days. Three whole days!"

A wave of guilt hit Weston. He knew it was his level of Power in the fireballs that had defeated the Captain's advertisement. *He should be mad at me.* "Did you lose much business?" Weston asked.

"Of course not. But Gale, me ol' wench—Tav bless her— she's never been the same."

"I'm really very sorry about that," Weston said. "I'm not sure if you heard but . . . I was part of making that King King."

"Yes, I heard. No one blames you, Weston. You boys have to practice making projections if you're going to get into the Workshop. It's Kai who is the problem. These kinds of things happen in his family. Just be careful. You don't want to jeopardize your chances of getting a Color," the Captain said with a wink.

Weston and Luge both refrained from saying anything in response to that—neither was going to betray their friend. So with a simple "thank you," they took their cakes and walked away from the shack.

I can't wait until Kai gets a Color and everyone starts treating him with the respect he deserves. Weston and Luge went to the end of the dock, sat down, and hung their feet over the edge. They bit into the cakes and reveled in the flavors as they stared out over the sea.

With Weston's first bite, he felt an explosion of flavor overwhelm his tongue and his eyes rolled into the back of his head. It was as if the cake itself were overflowing with juicy mangos, ripe strawberries, and sweet, creamy bananas, all rolled together in rich, chocolatey ice cream. *This. Is. Paradise.*

Luge, on the other hand, looked like he was having a seizure as he ate his cake. Every few bites he let out a loud "Eeeeek!" and twitched like crazy.

It's those sour bombs. I don't know how he can handle five in there!

"Do you ever wonder what these cakes would taste like if they had real fruit and ice cream inside?" Luge asked right before taking his final bite.

"Real fruit? Are you serious? Everyone knows sticking real stuff into a cake ruins the cake. First it makes them too full—you wouldn't be able to roll them up or fold the bottom. Second, actual fruit makes cakes get really soggy. My cousin tried doing that once, and it turned into a sticky mess."

"Really?" Luge frowned. "I'm sure there's got to be a way for it to work."

"He said it was impossible to eat. It dripped all over his threadbare and was a disaster. Afterward, he started calling food like that 'the Lord of Chaos,'" Weston said with a laugh.

"My uncle took me to an orchard once—the place the Captain goes to in order to make sure his flavors are accurate. Real fruit's actually pretty good, when it's ripe. Most people just haven't ever tasted it."

"I tasted ripe fruit once. It was pretty mushy. I still think projected fruit tastes better. Plus, projected fruit is ripe year round."

After they finished their cakes, they dipped their hands into the water to wash them clean, then got up and walked along the dock, back toward land. Even though Weston was feeling great after eating the delicious snack, he remembered the Captain's warning as they passed by the cake shack. When they were far away—and Weston was sure the Captain couldn't hear him—he said, "I hate how people always treat Kai like he's cursed or something."

"Me too. My dad has told me stories from back when they were building Kai's father's mansion—you know, that big house Mistress Jade keeps calling hers. My dad said all the workers acted like the S. Shields were gods or something. And then, after . . . well you know what, everyone changed how they saw them. Now they're treated like they have some disease. It's weird how people do that. I've always felt bad for Kai with all that he's had to live through."

"How's he doing, anyway? Have you seen him lately?" Weston asked as they walked their bikes through the island's outdoor market.

"I stopped in to visit him this morning," Luge answered. "He's Kai. He's acting like everything's okay, but I'm pretty sure he's having a hard time."

They were close to Nosy's, the restaurant known for having some of the greatest smell and taste combinations imaginable. Weston longed to eat there, so he paused to look at the menu posted outside. It was written in dark black ink on an old brown piece of paper. *It's so mega that Nosy's still uses paper and ink. They're such a classy place.*

"Whoa, they raised their prices again," Luge said. "I don't know how they can get away with it. It's now two hundred and forty-nine gryns for their seven-flavor sampler. Business must be good."

That's not so expensive for a mage.

"Anyway, those eye drops are really messing with his sight." Luge continued sharing about Kai. "Nothing's in focus, so he can't recognize anything or anyone. He's only seeing yellow and blue. It's pretty freaky to think he sees reality only in Conflicting

Colors. Everything was red for me—something about that made it really hard to look at people's faces."

"Yeah, I couldn't really see expressions on faces either." Weston shuddered at the memory. Color had been messed up for him too, but in a different way than either Kai or Luge experienced. For him, they were all mixed up, and each Color appeared as another.

"He has three more days left on his prohibition, but his grandmother is freaking out that he won't have enough time to recover before the Color Ceremony," Luge said.

"She's not going to let Kai rest until he gets into the Workshop, is she?"

"Of course not. That's why Kai's gotta be the only kid on O'Ceea who'd actually hate having a Color."

"And you—you don't want a Color, right?"

"I wouldn't hate it—at least not in the way Kai would," Luge responded. "I just don't need it. It's not likely to happen anyway. Remember what they said in school? Less than a quarter of people get a Color."

Poor Luge, he thinks something as magical and mysterious as Color can be reduced to something as boring as a number. "Well, you never know, it could happen. Maybe that'll finally be the thing that convinces you to make a projection." Weston laughed.

Luge shrugged. "Color would be wasted on me. Even if one was found, it wouldn't change much about my life. I'd rather Color be found in someone who actually wants it, like you."

This made Weston laugh again. "We have to be the strangest group of friends in all the islands."

"Yup. We can thank Kai for that!" Luge smiled.

That's true. Kai and Luge had become friends as seven-year-olds when Luge's dad was building Kai's family's mansion. But when Kai was forced to move from the wealthiest neighborhood on the island to the poorest when he was eight, he met Weston there. And even though they had vastly different upbringings, Kai was eager to play with him, and the two formed a tight bond.

It was thanks to Kai that Weston got to know Luge. The three of them hung out a lot together, but it wasn't long before Weston's cousin Snap demanded she be allowed to play with them too—and as she was a year older than all of them, she got her way. Shortly after that, Kai surprised them all when he brought Talia into the group. Weston and Snap were suspicious of her at first, because her family owned a lot of the most valuable properties on their island, but she never acted like she was better than anyone else. In the time that followed Kai's misfortune, the five of them quickly became inseparable.

"It's pretty mega, right?" Weston said.

"Hey, didn't Talia just finish her prohibition too? What's she doing today?" Luge asked as they approached the advertisement booth at the center of town. "I'd like to see how she's doing."

"Maybe. Snap declared it a girls' day, though. There's a foreign tailor in town and she wanted to take Talia. You know how she loves to make fun of the ridiculous outfits they project. We could probably try and join them."

"Nah, my mom will be there. Probably looking at clothes for me."

"You really have to stop her from dressing you like this." Weston pointed to Luge's skin-tight pants and deep V-necked shirt covered in sparkly gems. "She's devastating any hope you have of dating anyone."

"I don't know. I heard Daeya thinks I'm high-spun."

"She does not. She's just being nice because she feels bad for you," Weston teased.

"That may be a good strategy to get a date." Luge grinned.

A projection of a young woman inside the advertisement booth caught Weston's attention. She was announcing a traveling group of mages who were conducting a re-projection of *The Tragedy of Nic and Nalia*.

"Do you even like Daeya?"

Luge answered, "I think we're well matched."

"Then you should ask her out on a date! You could take her with you to this." Weston pointed to the advertisement of the re-projection.

"Nah. *Nic and Nalia* wouldn't be good for a first date. It's such a sad story."

"Quit being such a banana. There's no King King chasing you now."

"I'm not a banana. It's just that, after my prohibition, I'd like to take a break from sad things. Plus, I've heard rumors that they've twisted the story. There's probably stuff in it that would be weird or awkward—you know—to experience on a date."

"Yup, you're a banana."

"A person should know what a projection is like before taking a date to it," Luge argued.

"Fine. Then let's go to it." Weston turned to the woman in the advertisement. "Excuse me, when is the next showing?"

"During the middle of the Cyan watch! You'd better go now. You won't want to miss it!" she exclaimed cheerfully.

Weston looked up at the communication tower and saw there was only one beam of Green light shining up in the sky. It wouldn't be long before the Cyan watch began. "Okay, Luge. I've still got all those gryns I was going to use to buy the cakes. We can see it today, and then you won't have any more excuses. You can ask her to go with you tomorrow. That, or you can stay a banana."

The look in Luge's eyes said it all. "Okay, sure. Lead the way, Budster."

The Fear

~Weston~

There's something profoundly moving about the most recent retelling of The Tragedy of Nic and Nalia, *specifically in the way the tale ends: a moment of profound love in a story traditionally seen as a tragedy. If one is not careful, one is bound to miss the beauty of what happens amidst the archaic and sometimes confusing language.*

—Opinionator Mage Ziah is-a Tree, on *The Tragedy of Nic and Nalia—with a twist!*

The re-projection was being conducted at Latika's Lagoon. Weston and Luge arrived at the top of the Cyan watch, but there were not many spots available on the large crescent of beach that served as the seating area. Just about every inch of the sand was covered with people—mostly young adults on dates.

Look how many people are here! Weston was surprised; most people took a nap during the Cyan watch. *This must be a really good re-projection!*

The ten performing mages positioned themselves out on the water. They stood on four floating platforms that were connected by narrow bridges. From there, they would weave their projections and transform the lagoon into another world.

"Remember when we saw *Neckies and Nobodies* here? That one Indigo mage was so totally dissolved in his work that he fell into the lagoon while performing," Weston said to Luge. "That was hilarious."

"Yeah, and his character didn't even flicker! The mage kept on casting like nothing happened."

"Remember how he was doing everything he could to keep his head above water? I can still picture him raising both arms up in order to stay in control of his projections."

Weston and Luge managed to squeeze into an open space close to the shore. It wasn't the best spot—all those were in the back, where you could better experience everything—but it was the perfect spot if you wanted to watch the mages and study how they performed. *I bet I'll learn something mega that I can use to get more chips.*

The Tragedy of Nic and Nalia came from a time before they were even called Grand Projections, so the language was difficult for modern ears to understand. This was normally enough to keep kids away, but judging from the large number of young people here, the mages had found a way to make the old story popular again.

Mages who perform classical projections like this are seriously talented. It should be good.

Weston was curious about how they chose to twist the story, and whether it would be good or not. But as soon as the re-projection started, his mouth dropped open; the mages had turned Nic into a living corpse, Nalia had the ability to project dragons that were somehow real enough for her to ride on, and the enemy of their love was a vast hoard of death walkers. And, much to Weston's delight and Luge's surprise, it was excellent.

Weston had experienced *Nic and Nalia* once before, in its original version without the twist. But this time the story actually made sense to him. It was a romantic tragedy about a boy named Nic and a girl named Nalia, two lovers who made a pact the night before the Color Ceremony to stay together no matter what happened. The next day, Nic was found void and Nalia had Yellow pulled from her.

Weston didn't feel anything when Nic walked away empty. However, when Nalia's Yellow burst out and shot into the sky, he felt a deep pain in his gut. He tried his best to ignore it.

As soon as Nalia was revealed to have Color, she proclaimed it to be a sign that the Color gods had determined she and Nic should no longer be together. So she broke her vow and devoted herself to training to become a magician. Nic, however, kept his promise and refused to let his love die, pursuing Nalia faithfully to the end.

"I must forth go!" The projected voice of Nalia rang out across the lagoon. The story was close to being finished, and while the pain in Weston's stomach still burned, all of his attention was focused on the unfolding action. "I now—a mage of Yellow be—make hope to see one day projections solid true. Responsibility, like breath itself, I find compels my spirit. See? Pray, understand? And so my choice forever force me flee."

At this, Nalia jumped onto the back of her dragon.

"I know, but see," the projected voice of Nic quivered as he paced back and forth across a burnt field of grain, "you have but one true heart to give, and that—indeed—surrendered to another. I rest my feet upon scorched land and waste—for you! Repent. I beg. Turn—it's me! Your one unvarnished love."

"I wish—oh for things that could untwine," she cried and pulled out a sword of fire.

"Indeed, thereby, so as do I. Now, please—be quick! Make haste your choice for me. See? The dead do rise."

"Forevermore your love, shall it be lost to me? A fool, am I, to ever know a face divine? I must but flee from such tragedy." Nalia prodded the dragon with her heel and it took flight with her astride.

As she flew away from him, Nic cried out, "True love remains to fight and die. And so, too I, will stay and scorch these weeds, and sing this song. The song—of yours and mine."

And then, in the most heartbreaking moment of the story, Nalia turned her dragon around and hovered high above him in the blue sky. It appeared that she'd had a change of heart, and the triumphant music made Weston feel strong. *Do it. Go back for him!* He wanted to shout out.

With a look of sorrow, Nalia stared down at the death walkers circling Nic. *Why won't you do something?* Weston screamed inside. *You can go back and fight! It would be easy. You have a dragon and a sword of fire!* Unable to keep his feelings inside, Weston shouted, "Go on. Do it!"

It felt good to shout, and as soon as he did, the pain in his gut started to fade. But his cry did nothing to alter the story. Nalia did not go back. She pulled her dragon away, and the death walkers fell upon Nic. He did everything he could to destroy them, but there were too many. They overpowered him, took his body, and threshed it like wheat.

Luge closed his eyes tight.

"Come on, bud," Weston told him. "I know it's really gory, but you should watch this."

"I don't need to watch. I can feel it all."

Wow. He really does have sensitive skin.

Nalia spiraled up and away from her former love and sang out, "When fools remain to fight—they die. My love cannot be won. I flee from you—oh isle of fire—to know that I'm alive. With love you get one taste of life, but not true life itself, and miss the wisdom in the song, this song of yours and mine."

Overall, it was one of the strangest re-projections Weston had ever seen. But now that his eighteen days of punishment were over, he drank in all the rich and stormy emotions that the

Glory in this projection had triggered in him. *This is what life is all about. I hope I never experience a prohibition again.*

Then, as tradition dictated for the end of such performances, the mages thrust their arms in the air to dissolve their projections. As the world they had created started to fade from existence, they gradually brought their arms back down to their sides. There was wild clapping as the crowd clamored for more.

But no more was coming. The ten mages bowed, and just like that, it was over. Luge and Weston got back on their bikes and left.

"Wow," Luge said after a pause. "That was . . . something else."

"Yeah—wasn't it mega!?"

"Do you think Nic really dies at the end?"

"Of course he dies. Didn't you see what happened to him?"

"Sure. But living corpses can't die—right?" Luge asked. "They just keep coming back to life. So, what if Nic does come back? He vowed to keep loving Nalia. That means he'd keep fighting. He'd probably have to do it a bunch of times, but eventually he'd defeat them all."

"Uhhh . . ." Weston wasn't sure what to say. "I think it would have been easier if Nalia just went back."

Luge was caught up in his train of thought. "I can't figure it out. The twist they made is either super profound or utterly drench."

"Hey, Budaloo? Stop thinking so much. Here's a tip: you should keep all that pantsy-fancy stuff to yourself on your date with Daeya, okay?"

"What do you mean? What should I say instead?"

"'How about, 'Wow, that was totally mega? Hey, I'm hungry, do you want to go and get something at Captain Cakes?'"

"I like talking about projections after they're over."

"Not on a date," Weston said. "Now, what's next for us? I feel like riding somewhere." Weston looked up and saw one Blue beam shining from the tower. *We spent the whole Cyan watch and most of the Blue watch already? Whoa, cake-filled Zango! Time's flying!* "I know! Let's head over to Daeya's house and you can tell her you want to invite her to the re-projection tomorrow. Afterward, you can take her to a playground and make her a rose, like Nic did for Nalia—I was watching the Green mage when he did that. He flicked his wrist in a wacky way. I can't wait to try it when I get tested for Glory." *Maybe that'll help me not crunch when I test in small form, romantic.*

"Nah. You know that's not really my thing."

"What? Romance or making projections?"

"Both."

"Come on, girls always like stuff like that," Weston said with a grin.

But when it came to making projections, Luge was stone-willed. He had been this way for as long as Weston had known him. "I know, I know, not your thing." Weston sighed. "I've just never understood it. There's gotta be some crazy stuff going on in that head of yours. Right? Something that you want to get out."

"Not really." Luge made a fist and knocked it against his head. "It's pretty straightforward in here."

"You don't make any projections—like ever?"

"Nope."

"You have to at least have dream projections. Everyone has those, right?"

"I don't think so. I never see flickers of any when I wake up, and no one's ever told me I do."

"What about unconscious projections, like Kai's fire?" Weston probed. "I bet you have some little vole that scampers out of you at night, or some weird smell that fills your nose when you laugh too hard—hey, that's it, that's why you never laugh very much!"

"Nope."

"Really? You have to make some unconscious sounds. Everyone makes those once in a while," Weston said. He was sure Luge had to be hiding something.

"Not that anyone's told me."

"Whoa, you're stranger than Kai," Weston teased.

"I don't know, I just don't think that way. I really enjoy projections but I just don't think it's valuable for me to get all tangled up about making them. My family has always been focused on building material things. I know people don't value that kind of stuff very much, but it seems really important to us. You have to live in an actual house, after all."

"Yeah, material stuff's important, I guess." *But I'm sure glad there's a whole lot more to life than just that.*

"It is. I don't know if you know this, but I always get kind of down whenever I see projections take over someone. Sometimes it seems like they're the only things people in the islands care about. It's all kind of crazy to me."

"Yeah, I've actually felt like that a couple times," Weston said. "I bet it happens to people when they don't experience projections for a while. I mean, they're so amazing, and when someone goes a few days without them, it's natural to start feeling a little bit sad. That's why people spend so many coins on cakes and re-projections like we just did. Projections really do cheer people up. Reality's not all that spectacular, you know. Most of it is pretty boring."

"I don't know. I think there's a lot of beauty on O'Ceea—natural, real beauty—but people miss it. Why make a projection of a secret fortress when you can go and play in an actual one?"

"Oh Luge. Sometimes, I feel bad for you, Buderooski. You're missing out."

"Hey, I enjoy playing with all the projections you buds make."

"But it's so much more fun when you make them."

At this point they were riding through a thick stretch of forest. Luge glided to a stop next to a big avocado tree and pointed right at it. "Look at this tree. What do you see?"

"Uh—a tree," Weston said with a laugh. "Fruit. Leaves. Tree stuff."

"But really look at it. Focus on the intricate details of the bark, or the way this vine grows up and around the trunk. Can you see the patterns? Or—here, look at this, do you see how all the little ants are weaving in and around one another on this rotten piece of fruit?"

"Oh yeah, I've seen stuff like that before," Weston said. "I've studied lots of things to learn how to increase my Kingdom."

Luge scrunched up his nose and thought about something for a moment, then rubbed his fingers against the back of his neck in the way he sometimes did when he was nervous. "I wasn't going to do this until after the Festival . . . but . . . I think I'd like to show you something . . . uh, something I've been working on."

"Something you've been working on?" Weston said with a smile. *Ah ha! So he has been making projections after all.*

"Yeah. It's kind of a surprise."

"Luge, Luge, Luge—I always knew you could do more than you let on. Let's see it!"

"Well—okay, but please understand I haven't quite finished it yet. It needs more work."

Aw, poor guy. He's nervous to project in front of me. "Don't worry, Buderoni. I won't give it a score. I'm just excited to see you make something!"

"It's already made—or I mean, I started it a while ago . . . just don't tell the others yet. You promise? You can't tell anyone else, especially not the buds."

"Sure, I promise."

"All right. Follow me." Luge turned off the main road and biked in the direction of Kanaka Falls.

✳   ✳   ✳

After traveling through some of the thickest undergrowth Weston had ever traversed on a bike, they came at last to a small clearing in the forest. *Luge found the most remote spot possible. I never even knew this part of the island existed.*

"Okay. We're here," Luge said.

"We are?" Weston scanned the trees and brush around him, but there was nothing out of the ordinary. "I don't see anything."

"I made it hard to spot."

Is that the trick? Did he project a realistic-looking tree and hide it amongst the real ones? Kind of boring, but that would mean he's got some mega abilities with Kingdom.

"Look up," Luge said.

Weston, feeling quite confused, followed his friend's gaze straight up. It took a long bit, but then he realized what he was looking at. "A tree fort? That's incredible!"

Suspended above them in the treetops was an impressive network of platforms connected by rope bridges and ladders. The first platform was built with a tall railing, the second supported a little hut with a thatched roof, and the third was extremely high up and resembled a communication tower. *It seems so real. How did he manage to do that?*

"Do you like it?" Luge asked.

"It's great! I can't believe you made this!" Weston exclaimed as he projected some Old World soldiers onto the lower platform. The soldiers held swords and looked out into the forest like they were expecting an attack. "Now we just need to add something to attack them . . ." Weston considered his options. "Maybe evil tree frogs, or an army of tribal cannibals?"

"Hey!" Luge shouted as soon as he spotted the soldiers. "Take those out."

"Huh? You don't like them?"

"No, no. There's nothing wrong with them. It's just, right now I want us to use the fort without any projections. And besides, I thought you weren't going to make anything until after the Color Ceremony."

Oops. "Oh yeah. I guess got carried away by what you did. It's a good thing we're way out here in the middle of nowhere."

"Do you mind dissolving your soldiers?"

"Sure, but . . . if I don't add my projections to it, how can we use it?"

"We climb up. I built a ladder," Luge said.

"Okay, I guess." Weston dissolved the soldiers, and then he exclaimed, "Wait—an actual ladder?"

"Yeah, over here. See?" Luge went over to a nearby tree and pointed to a few planks of wood that were nailed to the side.

"Why would you build a material ladder up to a projection of a tree fort?"

"Aw, come on, are you truly not getting it?"

And then it all made sense. "Ohhhh, right. I get it. Having an actual ladder makes the tree fort look more real. That's a great idea. I think they do that kind of thing in Region 3."

"Bud." Luge pressed his palm into his face. "You're such a bloomer. None of it is a projection."

Weston stared up, completely perplexed. "Say again?"

"It's solid. It's a material tree fort. I made it with actual wood, with my physical hands. Look. Watch." Luge climbed all the way up the ladder, stepped out onto the first platform, and started walking around on it.

Seriously? Weston was stunned. "That's an actual tree fort?! But . . . but, I thought you . . ."

"Nope, I didn't make a projection. Sorry. This is solid," Luge called down to him. "Come on up!"

Weston felt his throat constrict. He hesitated at the foot of the ladder. *Whoa, be careful, bud.* He'd never climbed up something like this before. "I'll just admire it from down here," Weston said, not wanting to face the fear of heights he'd never quite managed to overcome.

"Come on! To truly experience it, you have to climb up all the way. There's something mega at the very top I want you to experience."

All the way? To the top? Weston tried to swallow, but his mouth had gone dry. "You sure it's safe?"

"Absolutely. Look!" Luge started to jump up and down on the platform. "Sturdy as a mountain."

Okay. You can do this. Weston gritted his teeth and placed his hands on the planks of wood. He kept his eyes focused straight ahead and climbed without looking down. Rung after rung, Weston climbed up, until at last—

"You made it!" Luge reached out his hand and helped his friend onto the first platform.

Weston let out a breath he didn't realize he'd been holding, dropped to his knees, and crawled over to the nearby railing. He grasped it tight and knelt for a long time as he waited, in vain, for his heartbeat to slow. "I can't believe this is real," he said once he could speak.

"See? There's nothing drench about real things."

"This must have taken you years to build."

"Not years. I started building it about a year ago. I haven't finished yet. I'm planning to add a few more things to make it even better—like a rope swing!"

"Don't expect me to use that," Weston said with a nervous laugh.

"Come on! There's more to see on the other levels."

He wants me to go higher? "Aw, bud."

Weston was thankful that climbing up to the next level was easier. This platform contained the thatch-roofed hut, and Luge showed him all the things he had built in it: a table, three chairs, and two hammocks. *Wow, Luge put a lot of thought into this. It's nice enough to live in—if it were on the ground.* Luge had carefully and masterfully crafted every aspect of this structure to hold the weight of people. *This is incredible.*

After how easy it had been to climb up to the second platform, Weston didn't think it would be hard to climb up to the third and top one. He was wrong; it was remarkably high up.

A voice in his head started to scream at him to stop and go back down. But Luge was behind him, urging him on, so he went forward. When Weston finally pulled himself onto the third landing, he gripped the railing so tightly that he feared he might break it. He looked down for a short moment before vertigo struck him and he had to turn away. *I don't know how I'm ever going to be able to climb back down from here.*

They were high up in the canopy of the forest. From this vantage point, it felt like they were in a completely different world, hidden in the middle of an ocean of leaves that the wind brushed back and forth against the fort like waves. "Why'd you have to build it so high?"

"I wanted it to be a place where we could all come and hang out without fear of being caught," Luge explained. "So I built it high enough that it wouldn't be easy to spot unless you knew where to look. My hope was we could come here and be ourselves, no matter what happens at the Color Ceremony next week."

"I'm sorry, bud, but I don't think I'll ever be able to be myself this high up," Weston said as he tried not to look down. "You should have made it a lot lower."

Luge furrowed his brow. "You said you wouldn't score it."

"I'm just kidding," Weston said.

"No you're not."

"Well, I would be if I weren't so afraid. You did an incredible job. It's mega on every level. One problem, though . . ." Weston glanced back at the ladder. "If someone does see us up here, it would be super easy to catch us. All they have to do is stand at the bottom of the ladder and wait. Eventually, we'll have to go down."

"Ah, I thought of that. So I built an emergency escape."

"A what?"

"A mega quick way out. It's what I wanted you to come up here to experience. But we have to go up even higher to get to it."

Weston had a bad feeling about what was coming next.

✳ ✳ ✳

I should have stayed in town for the Indigo performance of the Nic and Nalia re-projection. Weston trembled as he stood on the roof of the lookout tower. There was no ladder to get here. They had scrambled up the thick beams of wood that the tower was built from. Every move he made had been dangerous, and now that he was on top, it felt even more perilous.

There was no safety railing, only a short metal bar that Weston now clung on to and loved more than all the cakes in Captain Sammy's shack. He tried not to look down because every time he did he couldn't help but imagine his body falling—as if in slow motion—to the ground. No one could survive a fall from this height. *I'm going to die up here. Luge brought me up here to die a week before the Color Ceremony.*

Without thinking, Weston projected a thick brick wall around himself.

"Who's the banana now?" Luge laughed. "Come on. Don't be scared. I've used this a bunch."

"I don't think this is going to hold me."

"Don't worry, it's safe. I reinforced it. Trust me—I know what I'm doing."

Weston's palms were sweatier than they'd ever been. "You know, the ladder will be fine. I should just crawl back to the ground."

"Sure. But didn't some famous trainer say great projections allow us to lose our connection with the ground and fly off to wonderful new realities? How will you ever be a good mage if you don't know the thrill of actually flying?"

"I have a powerful imagination."

"Come on—just try it. It's way more exciting than even you can imagine."

"You're sure it's safe?" Weston asked hesitantly.

"Positive."

"Shouldn't you go first? The person who builds something should always be the first person to die from it. Right?"

Luge shook his head. "I need to hook you up properly so you don't get hurt."

You can do this. Be brave. How bad can it be? Weston took a deep breath. "Okay. Let's get this over with." He dissolved his brick wall with trepidation.

"Great," Luge said as he secured a rope around Weston's waist. "Now all you need to do is jump off the edge. Whenever you're ready."

"Jump? You expect me to jump off that edge?" Weston gripped the metal bar even tighter. "Why don't you just push me off? I mean, you're already trying to kill me."

"Just enjoy the ride," Luge said with a laugh.

Enjoy the ride? Luge is crazy. He is legitimately crazy. Weston clenched his fists as tightly as he could around the metal bar and tried not to think too hard about what he was about to do. "Okay."

"I'll count you down," Luge said. "Three . . ."

Weston tried to think about something else—anything else.

Color.

"Two . . ."

He struggled to catch his breath. *The Competitions.*

"One . . ."

His heart pounded so fast he thought it might explode. *The Workshop.*

"Go!" Luge shouted.

Before he could talk himself out of it, Weston screamed at the top of his lungs and leapt off the roof of the lookout tower. The metal bar he clung to was attached to a thick red wire that was connected higher up in the tree and ran down through the forest. As soon as he stepped off the solid surface, he started to glide effortlessly through the air.

"AHHHHH!" Weston screamed louder and more shrilly than he thought physically possible.

He soared like a bird in flight and felt the cool, brisk air whisk across his skin. He was completely aware of his body in a way he'd never been before. Every single muscle was tensed, and he could feel his blood pumping through his veins.

Then, to Weston's surprise, the absolute terror that came with jumping dissolved and was replaced with a feeling of pure joy. His screams became shouts of delight. "WOOOOO HOOOOOOOO!"

This!

Is!

Incredible!

Weston began to laugh uncontrollably. He whooped and woohooed and woooted with unscorable emotion as he whooooooooshed through the treetops, descending deeper and deeper into the forest.

As he flew through the trees, he realized what Luge had done. He'd managed to produce the very thing that every great magician strove for. He had created something that produced authentic and overwhelming feelings.

Luge, you crazy genius! The buds are going to flip when they experience this!

The Elders' Meeting
~Kai~

There's no question that Mage Malroy is an exceptional trainer. I've grown more in my short time as his apprentice than in all my years of training. However, he willfully turned a blind eye to the sudden and unusual spikes in his son's abilities—people just don't improve that fast—and for that, he must be held accountable. If he had only listened to my concerns, I feel we would not be where we are today.

—Trainer Mage Lemmet is-a Stone, testimony under oath, *Elders of Four Kings v. Malroy is-a Shield*

"Kids!? What do you mean 'they're just kids'? This island knew nothing but growth and prosperity from the time of the Flood because every citizen—adults and children—knew their place and kept to it," a condemning voice said.

Yes, as we've so often been told. Kai couldn't help but recite the old nursery rhyme in his head:

Waves in the ocean,
Stones on the shore.
Leafs do the growing,
Shields for war.

This was the way the people on the Island of the Four Kings functioned to restore their society after the devastation caused by the Flood. The Waves were responsible for shipbuilding and fishing, while the Stones were the builders. The Leafs farmed and harvested food, while the Shields provided military and island patrol.

But that was a long time ago; the old roles no longer had as much meaning today, though some in the older generations still held to their traditional place.

"For countless generations, the order has remained unbroken," the condemning voice continued.

That's not true. Nastium was-a Stone fell out of place. Harad was-a Leaf was shunned and sent away when he got Green and Red. Jamick was-a Wave cut many others off from the magic.

"Our ancestors suffered to build this great island. They sacrificed to win our reputation and honor. Then everything we hold dear was knocked down eight years ago. Everyone in this room knows it—everyone on this island has suffered because of it—and you're justifying their actions because they're just kids. I can't believe this! We've been too lenient too long."

How much longer will I have to endure this? Kai sat crosslegged on the cold floor in the center of the island's large council room. It was dark except for a bright array of projected light that shone on Kai—the accused. While this made it impossible for him to see, he still knew who was there.

Before him stood the island elders, one from each of the four clans. They faced him, shoulder to shoulder, like an impenetrable wall. Then, hidden in the dark of the room, just about everyone else on the island crowded in and surrounded him. They came because they could watch and voice their concerns from the safety of the shadows. This was by design, so no one would know who said what, allowing people to speak freely without fear of being judged. *The judgment is all reserved for me,* Kai thought glumly as he shut his eyes and tried his best to block out their voices.

Twenty-seven days earlier, Kai and his friends had run through the forest with fear and delight in the shadow of their illegal monster projection. *No one understands it was an accident. We didn't mean any harm.* But Kai knew their actions had caused harm, and so they had to be punished.

He'd only recently recovered from his prohibition. His friends had suffered to lesser degrees, but he had spent three weeks under the influence of the drops.

Kai unconsciously squirmed when he remembered how the cold liquid that Captain Markus squirted into his eyes had refashioned his perception of reality. For three weeks, he couldn't discern color accurately. Everything became hues of yellow and blue. *Why did it have to be Conflicting Colors?* After seeing nothing but these two colors everywhere he looked, he understood why his grandmother said, "There aren't Conflicting Colors in nature for a reason."

He wondered why the eye drops affected him in this way. The liquid had a unique effect on everyone. For Snap, color disappeared altogether, leaving her in a reality with only shades of grey. She found it intolerable. Fortunately, her prohibition lasted only five days.

Luge had to endure his reality being taken over by one color: red. Everything he saw was some shade of it. However, because he had not made the projection but had only participated with it, his prohibition concluded after one day.

For eighteen days, Weston experienced color shifting. Nothing retained its proper color, so grass become violet and the sun green. He said it had been terribly disturbing to look out at a blood-red ocean, but he joked about how much fun it was to eat blue yams and green bananas.

Talia faced what was known as the Color Flow. For her eighteen-day prohibition, color was no longer dependable.

According to how she described it to Weston, the natural yellow of a lemon would flow out and be replaced with blue, but only for a time. After a few moments, the blue would flow away and make room for red to have its turn. Nothing kept its color for long. With everything she experienced so unstable, Talia could no longer stand up without feeling as if the ground under her was moving. Apparently, she had found this fascinating, even inspiring. But it caused her to lose her balance and fall whenever she went out, so she spent most of her prohibition in bed.

The liquid did not affect only color. A person's sense of distance could also be altered. Something across the room could appear within hand's reach. A long hallway might be seen as very short, a small room perceived to be vast. People under a sight prohibition were always bumping into things and falling. When the prohibition was lifted, most people were battered and bruised as a result of their inability to perceive reality as it actually was.

For Kai, one of the most disturbing aspects was the way the drops impaired his ability to see detail. Texture and fine lines disappeared. Contours and intricate features vanished. One leaf of a fig tree looked exactly the same as any other, all songbirds were identical, and all oranges were alike. But that wasn't the most distressing part.

Without the ability to discern details, Kai was unable to recognize the minute differences in human faces. Each time she approached him, his mother had to say, "Kai, this is your mother," so that he would not mistake her for his grandmother.

The eye drops were administered so that the offender would learn that the power to project is a privilege, not a right. The hope was that if a criminal spent enough time afflicted by perceptions they could not control or stop, they would learn to take projections seriously—and thus no longer commit crimes.

But it seldom worked. Thus other forms of punishment were devised: solutions to numb each of the five senses were created to punish lawbreakers. The one Kai received on his fingers and hands was a touch prohibition. Wearing special gloves to protect himself, Captain Markus had rubbed a gel into the skin that completely covered Kai's hands up to the wrist. The effect—and purpose—was straightforward: the gel numbed all sensation of touch wherever it was applied. Talia and Weston had received a touch prohibition for two weeks, Kai for three.

Kai knew that the senses were essential for creating realistic projections. One of his grandmother's cousins had been born blind, and she had to undergo extensive training in order to make sight projections that looked in any way real. There were some elderly citizens of the island who lost their ability to hear, and after this their sound projections grew more and more distorted.

The inability to feel touch affected Kai the most. It was as if some vital part of his body had been severed off and placed just beyond his reach.

Where would I have been without Mom? She had made all the difference; what could have been three weeks of misery became one of the sweetest times of his youth. His mother had cared for him every day. She sang to him for watches, like she did when he was a baby. This comforted him, as did the food she made for him. Food had never tasted as good as it did when sight and touch were taken away.

Together, Kai and his mother had created all manner of sound, taste, and smell projections. He had never appreciated the power of the senses to impart energy and zest to life. They laughed for several watches at the strange projections they concocted together. Kai had forgotten how much he had loved doing this with his mother when he was little. And it was fitting that now, on the very cusp of the Color Ceremony—when boys and girls were declared young men and women—he got three weeks of uninterrupted childhood time with his mother.

Because of her loving service, Kai had thrived in the face of his punishment. It irritated those who came to re-administer the drops. "He should be suffering, yet there he is—smiling."

"Laughter is not for those under a prohibition."

"There really is something wrong with him. No one enjoys being cut off from their senses."

Kai had ignored the disapproving voices then, and he was attempting to ignore the ones speaking now. It was going fairly well, but then one voice broke through and shocked him into full attention. ". . . and that's why Kai is-a Shield should not be allowed to participate in the Color Ceremony tomorrow!"

Wait!—What?

"Three weeks is not enough time to learn the responsible use of projections!"

"Agreed!" a proud voice shouted.

"Hang on. Kai has paid the price required for his crimes. There is no legal reason his prohibition should continue," one of the elders said.

"That's not true! The IP didn't convict him on everything he did."

Could they really prevent me from standing before a puller?

"Let us—your island elders—remind you, the focus of this meeting is to come to an agreement as an entire island about setting Kai free so he can stand tomorrow with honor."

"He shouldn't be allowed to test!" an angry voice from the back shouted.

Kai couldn't believe it. *Everything about the rest of my life depends on what happens tomorrow.* It had never occurred to him that they could prevent him from going. *All I want to do is stand before a puller and be found void. Please, don't deny me that.* No

Color meant no pressure to help the Shields regain their reputation. No Color meant liberation from the responsibility of undoing what his father had done. No Color would mark the beginning of a new, better life.

"The eyes of every island will be on Kai tomorrow. He's sure to be the feature spectacle at the Ceremony."

"Which is why it's so dangerous to let him stand alongside Talia!" a hateful voice insisted.

"It is a good point. How can we be sure he understands?" a fearful voice asked. "Our island can't take another blow to its honor."

"I have warned Kai and I assure you he understands all that's at stake for our island."

You've all been warning me my entire life. Don't worry. I'll be on good behavior. The last thing I want is more attention on me. Kai wished he could speak and defend himself, but he didn't dare break another rule. He, along with his mother and grandmother, were required to remain silent.

"If he didn't understand that before, I highly doubt he understands it now," the hateful voice said.

"Are you suggesting his punishment was insufficient?"

"Yes. He must be made to miss the Ceremony. It's the only way he'll learn."

"Kai is-a Shield is not yet ready to progress past childhood," a critical voice spoke out. "This boy could single-handedly ruin our only two real chances of getting a talented mage this year. What more proof do we need than his actions four weeks ago? He has been spreading disorder and chaos for years, infecting the children of parents who aren't smart enough to keep them away from him."

Talia's mom isn't going to like that.

"Out of order," someone who sounded like Weston's dad called out.

"Island elders!" the unmistakable voice of Talia's mom's spoke out. "I would like to request an inquiry into the accusation spoken just now. Is said reference of 'infected children' referring to my daughter, Talia is-a Leaf?"

"Come on, Serena, you don't need to invoke such formalities," the critical voice said. "Yes, I'm referring to Talia. Wake up! She was influenced to place the ethereal presence of Devos Rektor into a towering projection that ravaged Market Street!"

"I believe you are failing to give credit where it's due," the voice of Terra, Talia's father, said. "My daughter created the projection—minus the sundress and earrings, which were the work of another talented citizen of our island. My understanding is that Kai was responsible only for the projected fire."

"Great, so she projected the entire thing—under Kai's influence. It wasn't her place to project it without supervision, let alone to combine it with such terrible feelings. They should have been in a playground."

I never wanted any of that to happen. Please, why can't everyone just stop and let me go?

"But, it was so flipping incredible!" the voice of Limmick rang out. "Come on! Has everyone been rubbing prohibition drops in their eyes? Is that why no one can see the obvious? Together, these children of our very own island projected something as grand as anything that has come out of the Workshop. No, that's wrong. They did it better. Think about that. Come on! Think about it. Last year's so-called 'Grand Projection' was a spectacular flop because its King King was a wimp. Sure he was magnificent at ripping everything to shreds, but he didn't evoke any feeling."

"This isn't the place to express your views on the Master Magician's last performance," the ruling elder said. "And I must remind you all, this is a time for the anonymous sharing of opinions. No using given names, please."

Limmick ignored this and kept on ranting. "But, King King combined with the Lord of Chaos? Brilliant! That was brilliant."

Yes! Finally someone's defending us. Kai listened for the sound of others agreeing, but he heard nothing. *Please, please! Tell me it's not only Snap's dad who understands.*

"Why am I the only one flipping out about this?" Limmick asked.

"Whether or not it was an impressive feat does not change the fact that Kai is-a Shield is clearly not ready to represent our island before a puller," the condemning voice said.

"It is too dangerous a risk," the hateful voice agreed. "What if his presence there negatively affects the chances of Weston and Talia?"

"You've already said that," Terra said.

"We cannot let that happen!" the fearful voice said.

Loud murmurs of agreement echoed through the room.

"Nonsense," a reasonable voice said. "Color is either in someone or it's not—no one can control that. Kai's presence won't make a difference."

Exactly. That's an excellent point.

"Pulling Color is a great mystery," the hateful voice said. "You can't be sure that he won't negatively affect them."

"Come on people, don't give up hope!" Limmick exclaimed. "We used to be the envy of all the islands. Everyone with the means to pay wanted their son or daughter to come and train here—with us. I still remember how we were then: positive, enthusiastic, encouraging. We really did live on the best island. But look at us now. No wonder no one wants to send their kids here for training anymore."

"That's not the reason," a sad voice said.

"Then what is?"

"You know. Everyone knows what happened."

"Aw, come on. Didn't Flint do more than enough already? What everyone needs to do is stop blaming him and Malroy for what's happened to us. The real problem is we've never recovered after the cheating scandal. Why can't we just forgive the S. Shields and move on? Then we can focus all our attention on rebuilding our reputation and proving to everyone that the Island of the Four Kings is still the best place—anywhere—to receive training."

"We know, we know," an annoyed voice said.

"No, actually, we don't. Because if we did, we'd see that we have three kids who have the potential to prove to all the islands that we're still great. And one of them is seated right here in front of us. But all we seem to be able to do is judge him and his family. Kai didn't do anything wrong. Look, within a few years, this island has a great chance of producing a magician—maybe even two! Three, if the gods are good to us. Then we'll all be back in business!"

"Only if Weston, Talia, and Kai all have Color inside them, which is a pretty big if," a whiner said.

"Oh, come on, did any of you actually see their King King?"

"That doesn't matter. Nobody can control Color. You either have it or you don't," the critical voice said.

"Those kids have something special and everyone here knows it. They've grown up together. They're a team. Keeping Kai away will only hurt them."

"No," the condemning voice said, re-entering the argument, "letting Kai go could be disastrous. That fire in his hand is evidence enough that he is not in control of himself. Our citizens can't afford to be shamed again. We all know it, and that's why everyone, deep down, understands we'll all be better off once we banish the Shields from our island forever."

That brought a startled gasp from many in the room. *He can't be serious?*

"Think about it! What need have we of shields when O'Ceea is without war? Kai and that infernal ball of fire in his hand are all the evidence we need that the Shields are a serious danger to us all!"

"Grendul is-a Wave!" a voice boomed from the back of the room. "You are out of order and you will be silent."

Everyone in the room stood stunned; in this meeting that cloaked people in darkness, someone dared to speak out against another person, by name. And Kai recognized that voice—it was one that wasn't easily forgotten. *Could Master Forecastle really be defending me?*

Any doubt was erased when Kai saw the shadow of an imposing figure moving toward him. Forecastle navigated his large frame through the crowd of people. As the others in the room began to recognize him, a low rumble arose, and several voices mumbled, "He's named someone from his own clan."

A simple man dressed in the traditional clothing of ancient shipbuilders stepped into the light, and stood right next to Kai. This was Forecastle is-a Wave. He was a shipwright and lived a simple, quiet life on the far side of the island. He rarely spoke publicly, but when he did, people listened, as they did now.

"To all the citizens of this island, I humbly apologize for this young, impetuous voice from my clan. And to Mistress Jade and Widow Declarious is-a Shield, I ask your forgiveness."

Whoa, is he really doing this?

"Master Flint was-a Shield brought great honor to this island in becoming a magician. This is our past, and it is an honorable one. Let me remind all who are within the sound of my voice that there has never been any credible evidence that this citizen of our island ever engaged in any illegal actions. He lost his position in the Workshop because his score dropped below the admitting threshold and he was displaced—the same thing happens to many magicians every year. He was never convicted of cheating."

No one dared speak openly against Master Forecastle, but Kai could hear the murmured rebuttals.

"If that were true, why did he cut himself off from the magic?"

"Exactly! His reaction was proof enough."

"Kai," Forecastle continued as if he didn't hear them, "the condemning words from my clansmen were most of all directed against you. So, on behalf of my entire clan, I ask your forgiveness."

Is this really happening? Is he really saying these things out loud, at an elders' meeting? As Kai was forbidden to speak, he nodded his head. *This is too perfect to be real.* Then something inside him stirred, and he knew he needed to listen—to truly listen—to what this man was about to say.

"Tomorrow you will stand before a puller. It is a time to look forward to. I am not part of your family, and we are not of the same clan, but I will lower my honor in order to bless you as you begin your transformation from child to adult." Forecastle placed his hand on Kai's shoulder.

"May Täv fill you with the grace you need to face and forgive those who've heaped judgment on you. Go—and no matter what happens tomorrow—take the talents Täv has granted you and use them to increase life—in whatever part of the islands you may find yourself."

Kai let the words sink in. He didn't really understand what Forecastle meant, but he expected he would, someday. When most people spoke of Tav, they didn't speak with the weight that Kai thought Tav really deserved. This was not the case with this shipbuilder; he did not use the name lightly.

"Well said, Master Forecastle," the ruling elder agreed. "Is there anything else that must be spoken about the accused?"

Silence. No one was about to say anything after Forecastle just publicly validated Kai.

"Once. Twice. Third call. Four," one voice cried out. All four elders waved a hand from right to left and the sound of four bells rang out through the room.

"The matter is finished," the ruling elder proclaimed. "Kai, now that your fellow citizens have had their voices heard, we, your elders of the Island of the Four Kings, release you from your accusers. You have paid your debts and are free to test tomorrow and represent our island at the Color Ceremony."

Wooo hooo!

"This gathering of the island elders is concluded. Luge is-a Stone, Weston is-a Wave, Snap is-a Wave, Talia is-a Leaf, and Kai is-a Shield have each been released from their prohibitions. They have paid their debts. Citizens, go forth and treat them with peace."

As the meeting broke, the light that was focused solely on Kai spread and illuminated everyone in the room. Kai remained on the floor. He looked up and saw the reassuring face of his mother. Seeing her smile brought him joy. *My punishment is over!* He'd never been so excited to get home and go to bed in his entire life.

Now all I have to do is make it through tomorrow. After that— after it's made clear to all the islands that I don't have a Color—I can finally see my friends again and leave all this judgment behind me once and for all.

18

The Festival of Stars
~Kalaya~

Characters in all stories need someone or something to rescue them. Thus, I like to think of stories like little magic bottles that contain some kind of savior inside. By the end, something will have saved the day. The reason a good story grabs hold of our hearts and doesn't let go is that we long to know if the characters we've come to care about will be rescued.

—Magician Tophious was-a Lamp, 25 years in the Magician's Workshop: What I Learned About the Grand Story in Grand Projections

"Isn't it wonderful!" Kalaya's mom exclaimed as their ferry docked in the bay of the Island of the Red Tower. "Today my little girl becomes a young woman!"

"Uh-huh." Kalaya swallowed hard. *I suppose that also means today is my last day being a kid.*

Beyond the docks, at the top of a hill, sat Granada Royce—the town made famous for hosting the Festival of Stars and the three nights of the Region 2 Color Ceremony. Even from here, she could see the enormous, brightly colored decorations that adorned each rooftop and street in town. She'd come here almost every year for as long as she could remember, and it always made her feel like she was a part of something much bigger than herself. It was an exciting, magical four-day holiday and she always looked forward to it. But this year was different; she was no longer just a spectator—it was her turn to be on stage.

"Aw. Looks like they've already started," said Aliva, Kalaya's eleven-year-old, freckle-faced sister.

"I knew this would happen." Kalaya felt her palms grow sweaty as they disembarked from the ferry. "We're late."

"Nah, it's fine," Jaremon said with a suppressed yawn. "Some people just get here early to beat the lines. We have lots of time yet."

If it had been up to her, Kalaya would have been one of those who arrived early. She'd wanted to take the Crimson ferry with her dad, who had to work at the Festival all day, but her mom insisted she stay in bed until the top of the Red watch because she'd been up past third nightmark. Not that it helped. Kalaya still felt like she hadn't slept at all. Her mind raced through the night with thoughts of what was going to happen. Her dream projections were far worse than normal; her room kept filling up with black collars that had little mouths that cackled with cruel laughter before morphing into Jaremon's disappointed face. When she was finally allowed out of her room, she looked so awful that her mom insisted on projecting a strong layer of makeup on her to hide the bags under her eyes.

"Okay, well, I'm off to find my friends!" Aliva said. She sped away toward town as soon as her feet touched the dock. "Have fun testing, Kay!"

"Oh! Wait!" their mother called out. "We need to set a time and place to meet!"

"Don't worry, I'll find you." Aliva turned back and said with a wry smile, "I'll just look for the weird blue projections."

Ha ha, very funny.

After they stepped away from the ferry and started up the avenue that led to town, they came to a section of pastel-colored cobblestones that emitted an assortment of pleasant and soothing aromas. These stones usually excited her, but today each step triggered a pang of uncertainty. *I might not actually have Color.*

"I feel sick to my stomach," Kalaya projected to Jaremon's ear.

"Oh, really? That's odd. The stones smell accurate to me. Nosy's sponsors them, after all," he projected back.

"No, that's not what I meant." Kalaya found herself once again frustrated by the limitations of voice projections. They served as a great way to communicate private information, but it was really difficult to project tone and emotion accurately. She decided to be blunt. "I feel nervous."

"Don't be. You'll be fine. You only need four gold chips to dramatically increase the likelihood of getting a Color."

"Hang on—last night you said I wasn't supposed to worry about the chips," she reminded him.

"Yeah, you shouldn't worry, but you still need to do your best to get them. It's very rare for someone to get four gold chips and not receive a Color," Jaremon projected. He then threw out a long string of statistics explaining his theory. It didn't help Kalaya, who remembered a different time—not long after they had started dating—when Jaremon spouted off a long list of depressing statistics about all the highly talented kids who turned out to be void even after earning a lot of chips.

"Trust me," Jaremon projected, "you have what it takes to get four. Probably more. I'll help you find the right booths."

"Okay. Thanks." She felt a little nervous about testing in front of him, but she was grateful for his support. Although he'd been a Green mage for only two years, Jaremon possessed an enormous amount of insider knowledge that she knew would be beneficial to her.

"Don't you just love these homes? They look better and better each year," her mother observed as they approached the town.

"Yeah," Kalaya quietly agreed. The houses on the Island of the Red Tower were renowned for their unique and creative styles. No two were the same; each was carefully structured and shaped to resemble something. One looked like a dark and scary castle, another appeared to be an impenetrable fortress. Kalaya's favorite was a mansion that was designed to look like a mountain with waterfalls splashing down its walls.

High up to her left, there was a grove of giant fig trees. Inside the canopy of leaves, Kalaya saw one of the more exotic neighborhoods in Granada Royce. The small homes built among the branches were bright yellow and were constructed to resemble beehives. Each treehouse was connected to the others by ropes, wooden bridges, and tall, twisting stairways. Flapping around this network were some sort of human-like creatures covered in feathers. *Are they projections of birds that look like humans? Or humans projecting bird outfits on themselves?* Kalaya didn't know. Their chubby, feathered bodies and beaked faces made it hard to discern. *People here are so weird.*

As Kalaya walked the avenue leading from the docks to the enormous, golden gates that marked the entrance into the town, she became aware of triumphant chanting rising up all around her: a choral arrangement of voices that blended together in perfect harmony. *That's really beautiful,* she thought to herself, until—

"Ah!" Her mother screamed and pointed straight up.

The beautiful choral music was coming from the top of the gate, where an intricate web of ancient-looking men and women hung. Their bodies were stretched out and woven together like a tapestry, and their heads lolled back and forth as they sung for all who entered. Kalaya was horrified.

"That's new," Jaremon observed.

And creepy. Their pale, blank, expressionless faces sent an eerie chill through Kalaya. *What's that about? Are they supposed to look like Dy'Mageio?*

"Come along, dear," said her mother, who lowered her eyes and picked up the pace as they passed under the gate. "We've got to get you registered."

Inside Granada Royce things became even crazier; people of all ages and from every island in the region gathered around to watch or participate in the numerous challenges that the testing booths provided. Kalaya was quickly overwhelmed by the cacophony of sounds, sights, smells, and tastes that bombarded her as the tests were taking place. The booths were scattered everywhere throughout the town. At each booth was a tester, a person being tested, and a line of others waiting their turn. This caused the streets to fill with crowds so thick that it was a struggle to get anywhere. *Is it busier this year?*

"How do you feel?" Jaremon yelled over the roar of the crowd.

"Oh, good—great!" Kalaya had to shout to be heard. She wished they could keep speaking through projections, but that form of communication was never a good idea in a crowd. It almost always caused problems, as it was next to impossible to avoid accidently projecting the message into a stranger's ear. No one liked having someone else's privately projected message cast into their ears—it was invasive, confusing, and sometimes embarrassing—so voice projecting was rarely done in public places like this.

As they moved through the center of town, Kalaya noticed all the other hopefuls who were being tested at each booth. It wasn't just teens who were trying for chips; men and women of all ages traveled here to have their skills graded. Kalaya couldn't help but stop and watch as a balding, middle-aged man stepped up to one of the testing booths and desperately tried to project a rope dangling from a tree. The rope looked real, but no matter how much he strained, it did not sway like a real rope would.

"What's this test for?" Kalaya asked Jaremon as the man turned and left with a look of misery.

"Kingdom. Rope motion."

"Huh. That's really specific."

"Yeah, it does seem odd," Jaremon said, "but rope motion is tricky, and important for certain jobs. For example, it's an essential chip if you want to get into the Ship Designers Guild."

"Really? Hmm. Do you think that's what he wants to do?"

"Sure, look at him," he said as the middle-aged man drooped like a wilted leaf. "It would make sense."

"Aw, that's so sad," Kalaya said. "What if that's the last chip he needed?"

"I'm certain it would be disappointing." Jaremon paused. "But, at the same time, if he's not skilled enough to make a realistic looking rope, how can he be trusted to project the intricate designs ships require?"

"But he's so old. I bet he's been working for years to get that chip. Maybe ship design has been his lifelong dream, and now he'll never be allowed to do it just because he can't make a dumb rope swing back and forth."

"Unfortunately, many people lack the skills required to perform to the set standards. That's why guilds are so important. Before guilds, there was no way to regulate who was qualified to make certain projections, and that caused a lot of problems. Guilds were formed to ensure that people were qualified to do—"

"I know how it works, Jaremon. I live on O'Ceea, too. I'm just thinking about that man. He looked so sad."

"Well, we can't really know if that's what he wants to do, right? But, if you're correct, then there's nothing for us to be sad about. It's hard to get into some guilds, but this is for our protection. You wouldn't want a chef preparing your meal if he wasn't certified in spice control. I know a guy who ordered rice from some unregulated floating restaurant. It was so spicy that he said it felt like his head was going to explode. It took several watches before his mouth was back to feeling normal."

"I understand why the islands are the way they are. But it's still sad," Kalaya insisted. *How many people come here each year only to have their dreams shattered?*

"You have a very kind heart," Jaremon said with a restrained smile. Before she could respond, he took her hand and linked their fingers together.

The sudden touch shocked her, and as she glanced up at him, she felt her pulse quicken and her cheeks flush. *This hand-holding thing is pretty great.*

"Oh my!" her mother exclaimed as she quickly motioned them to pull their hands apart. "None of that!"

"Apologies, Mistress Kathy," Jaremon said with a respectful bow.

They continued to make their way through the town in silence until Kalaya said, "Hey, Jaremon, I don't understand why you aren't going to do any tests today."

"I'm here to support you this year."

"But . . . I'm still confused about why you don't want to get into any guilds."

"Because I'm a Green mage," he replied.

"I know that. But most mages are in guilds, especially ones as good as you."

"True. However, I can't afford any distractions right now. I need to focus all of my attention on training, competing, and getting my scores up."

"And dating me, right?"

"Well, yeah. Of course that. It's going to be so great after you get your Color and we can be on the same team. We'll be able to spend all of our time together then."

"Yeah, that will be mega." *But what will happen if I don't have a Color?*

"As for guilds, I'll be able to join whichever ones I want if I can increase my score high enough to get into the Championship Games." Jaremon paused. "I really liked my time in the Hall of Ancient Wisdom. Maybe, in a few years, if I find I've peaked and can't compete anymore, I'll work to get credentialed for the Guild of Chroniclers or something like that."

"If you peak?" she said with a laugh. "That's not going to happen. You're going straight to the Workshop, and you know it." Kalaya admired his clear vision. *I can't imagine anything better than us working there together one day.*

"Welcome, welcome!" an overly energetic nine-foot man crooned at the entrance to the registration area. "Step right in and make yourself knoooown!"

Kalaya took a deep breath and moved forward. "Hello, it's nice to meet you. My name's Kalaya. Where do I go to register for the Color Ceremony?"

"Woooohoooo. Doooo yooooou believe yooooou have a Color?" The man's whole body slithered down until he was short enough to stare her right in the face.

"I . . . I hope so."

"Yoooooooou'd better be prepared! It all happens"—he paused—"at the tooooop of the Violet watch! Woooohoooo!" At this his eyes grew a few inches in diameter and shifted through all the Nine Colors. *What's going on?* He then shot back up to his original height and his face returned to normal. "Welcome, welcome! Step right in and make yourself knoooown!"

"It's a projection," Jaremon informed her.

"Oh." Kalaya felt her face burn red. *How embarrassing.* She reached out as if to touch the character, and sure enough, her hand passed right through. "It looks so real."

"Just remember, if you see anyone that looks or acts really strange, or starts repeating, they're probably not corporeal."

"If everyone used that logic," Kalaya said, "then they would think I was dating a projection."

"Har har. Nice one."

Inside the registration area there were several lines, and Jaremon led her to the one filled with eager, yet tense, young faces. Although Kalaya knew she shouldn't worry, she couldn't seem to shake the feeling that she was in over her head. *Just remember what Jaremon said. You have a . . . wait, what was it? A sixty-seven percent chance of getting a Color?* She thought about asking him but didn't want to sound even more insecure than she already felt. *Whatever it was, it's a high percentage. I need to stay positive! All I have to do is get four gold chips. How hard can that be?*

"Name?" the big-nosed woman behind the desk asked as soon as they made it to the front of the line. Although she had an Indigo collar, her eyes looked lifeless, and Kalaya had a hard time imagining that she could make any kind of projection at all.

"I'm Kalaya," she answered.

The woman placed her elbows on the desk, clasped her hands together, and locked eyes on Kalaya. "Clan?"

"Oh. Cloud. Kalaya is-a Cloud."

"Clan verification?" the woman's monotone voice droned.

"I'm Kathy, her mother," she said as she handed the registration fee to the mage.

"How wonderful for you. Collar please."

"Oh, that's right. Sorry," her mother stammered as she fumbled to take her collar off. "It's been so long since I've removed it."

She handed over her collar, and the registration woman handed back a temporary collar embroidered with all Nine

Colors. This would indicate to everyone who saw her today that she had a child who would stand before the puller this evening. "Oh, thank you so very much. Isn't this so exciting?"

"Thrilling. Do you vow to take full and complete responsibility should anything go wrong today?" the woman continued to drone on.

"I do, but you don't need to worry about that. My daughter is quite—"

"You understand the consequences of cheating, stealing, transferring chips, false identity, and any illegal or inappropriate use of projections?"

"We do," Jaremon answered for Kalaya's mother.

At this the woman glanced up at Jaremon. She stopped at his collar before giving his face a long look. "I recognize you. You're that Twig who got within a hundred points of making it into the Championships. Nobody expected projections like that could come out of a young mage from the Island of the Golden Vale!" she said.

"Thank you. I have high hopes of improving my score enough to make the cut this year."

"Spoken like a true Twig. Good luck. You're going to need it with that trainer," she said, and then she reverted back to her monotone. "Mistress Kathy, I need verbal confirmation that you, as the clan verifier, understand and agree to the rules."

"I do," Kalaya's mother said.

The woman reached under the desk and pulled out a colored glass buoy. *They made them yellow this year. It's really pretty.* The glass buoys, commonly called globes, were used exclusively for testing and were tinted a different color each year. On top of the sphere was a little slot just the right size for a testing chip; once a chip was placed inside, it was impossible to get out.

The Indigo mage placed her hand on the globe, projected a grey blob onto the glass, and then spent a moment creating another projection inside of it. Then she handed the globe to Kalaya. "May all the radiance of the rainbow shine on you today. Next!"

After they got outside, Kalaya held it up, and all three of them leaned in to look at the projection the mage had placed inside. Kalaya cringed when she saw it, but her mom said, "I think you look nice."

"Yes, it definitely captures your good looks," said Jaremon.

"Thanks," Kalaya said, but she didn't agree. *I look so short and insignificant.* She held the globe up to her face. *Are my cheeks really that chubby?* Inside the globe, the mage had created a projection that looked just like her. The Inter-Island Regional Patrol had established this procedure as a security measure to prevent people from cheating. Kalaya found it unsettling to see a version of herself trapped inside a little glass ball. She handed it off to her mom to hold.

"Hey," Kalaya said to Jaremon, "how could that Indigo mage capture so many details about me so fast when she only gave me a quick glance? She must have amazing Kingdom. Why isn't she in the Workshop?"

"You have to be a lot better than that to get into the Workshop," Jaremon said.

Kalaya frowned as she thought about how long it took her to build a realistic-looking projection for the first time. *It usually takes me all day to make something so detailed, and this woman did it in a few heartbeats. What hope do I have of ever getting into the Workshop?*

"Don't get me wrong. She is really talented. Just look at your clan symbol." Jaremon pointed at the grey blob the woman had projected onto the glass. Peering close , Kalaya saw it was the symbol of her clan: a puffy grey rain cloud moving about in a figure eight pattern. "See how much precision it has? It's perfect, and I bet she can do the same with every clan symbol for Region 2."

Seeing the noble, ancient symbol filled her with a mix of pride and fear. *I can't let my family down.* "Hey, Jaremon," Kalaya whispered, "I'm feeling pretty nervous."

"I did too. You'll be fine," Jaremon insisted. "Your skill with Kingdom is incredible. You have range, depth, clarity, detail, and definition. So, let's find a Kingdom booth to start with."

"Okay," she replied as Jaremon scanned the various booths for one that would be a good fit. Now, more than ever, she was grateful to have him in her life.

19

The Test

~Kalaya~

One of the most wonderful and peculiar things I've come to learn about magicians is that they always do their best work when they project characters that they sincerely love.

—Master Magician Evette was-a Hand, *Words of Wisdom from Former Master Magicians*

It didn't take long before Jaremon found a booth with a short line for Kalaya to start at. The tester was a short, plump, and extremely hairy man with a thick moustache that curled around his face in three wide loops. *There's no way this guy's from our region.* Above him, the sign on the booth had a thin-lined representation of a slice of bread followed by a "greater than" sign followed by a thick-lined representation of a slice of bread. She recognized this to mean it was a Kingdom test in masking food tastes.

Kalaya turned her attention to the young Blue mage who was currently being tested. He sweated profusely as he stared at a tiny white mushroom on a table in front of him. Then, taking a deep breath, he snarled like a wild animal and scratched his head—apparently his way of making a projection. Gradually, the image of a thick, juicy steak covered the mushroom.

"I'm done," the young man said after one final snarl.

The plump tester picked it up and took a bite. "Ugh!" he exclaimed as he spit the mushroom into a container and tried to wipe the taste off his tongue with the hair on his arms. "It look like steak but taste like mushroom!"

The young man hung his head and slumped away.

"Don't worry," Jaremon whispered. "This is Haal is-a Swish. He's grumpy, but easy to please. He likes strong tastes that mask the flavor of his least favorite food: mushrooms. If you can disguise the mushroom, and make it taste good, you're guaranteed a chip."

"Thanks for the tip," Kalaya said. *Hmm, this might not be so hard. As long as I don't have to project any fruit.* Kalaya hated projecting fruit. She always focused too much on getting the texture right and usually missed the mark on taste.

The next person to be tested was a very tall blonde woman, a commoner with bright blue eyes and rosy pink cheeks. Though she had a collar, and therefore must have been older than Kalaya, she dressed and acted like a little girl. "Hi there! My name's Melody, but everyone just calls me Bell! Would you like me to make you some steak?"

"No steak!" Haal vigorously shook his head and slid another mushroom onto the table. "From you, I want marshmallow!"

Bell worked her mouth back and forth as she considered his request. "Marshmallow? Oh. All right." She raised a finger to her mouth and began to chew on the end of her nail. As she did, the image of a fluffy, golden-brown toasted marshmallow concealed the mushroom. "Okay. I think it's ready!"

Haal's eyes watered as he lifted the marshmallow and gobbled it up. "Ow!" he exclaimed, but he did not spit it out.

"Are you okay?" Bell asked.

"Of course no okay! Did you no hear me say, 'ow'?" Haal removed the marshmallow from his mouth and tossed it into the container. "You make it too sweet for marshmallow! Good thing it projection, or I rot all my teeth! How then would I eat anything, hmmmm?"

Bell's shoulders sagged.

"But!" Haal held up his hand. "Too sweet is still taste good! So, bronze chip for you!"

Wow, Jaremon was right. This guy is easy to please. Bell looked like she was about to fall over.

"Are you serious? Oh wow!" she said as she held out her globe and Haal slipped a bronze chip inside.

"Congratulations!" Jaremon smiled at her.

"Wow! Bronze! Thanks so much! Dad, Dad, look!" Bell ran from the booth to a grinning, elderly man who stood watching nearby.

Okay. You got this! Kalaya took an uneasy step forward. "Hello, I'm Kalaya, how are you doing today?" she asked.

Haal eyed her suspiciously and then held out his hand and said, "Payment, please."

"Oh, yes." Kalaya's mom handed Haal the testing fee. "How silly of me to forget."

The hairy man pocketed the coins and then pulled out another little mushroom. "From you," he said, "I want starberry."

Kalaya felt her heart skip a beat. "Oh. Um, is there a chance I could do something else?"

"No! I crave starberry after marshmallow! That the way it go in my new favorite song: steak, marshmallow, starberry!"

Great timing. Kalaya exchanged a nervous look with Jaremon.

"Just do your best, sweetheart," her mom said.

Kalaya nodded and started to fiddle with her fingers. She tried to envision the perfect starberry: not too sweet, but plump and juicy. *Just like those ones I found with Dad on my fourteenth birthday.* As she pulled up the memory, a realistic yellow starberry began to form overtop the mushroom. *Good thing it didn't come out blue.*

When she felt she was done, she lowered her hands and waited. Haal picked it up, examined it with one eye shut, then tossed it into his mouth. He chewed three times, said, "Hmm," then stuck out his tongue, plucked it off, and threw it away. "No. Taste is strange."

Kalaya felt like she'd just been punched. *That's it?* "Can I try again? I'm good at making steak."

"No more steak. New favorite song all finished. Now all over."

"I can project something else then."

"Yes, that's a good idea Kay-Kay," her mom said. "No one in the family is any good with fruits and berries. Let's try something else."

"You have ears, no?" Haal asked. "I say all over."

Kalaya's mom reached into her coin purse and said, "We can pay you another testing fee."

"You leave, pay fee next year," Haal said and turned to the next person in line.

"It's fine," her mom said encouragingly as they stepped away from the booth. "You just got some bad luck with him asking you to make a fruit. I'm sure the next booth will work out better."

Jaremon said this was an easy booth. If that's true, this is going to be much harder than I expected. How am I possibly going to get four gold chips? she thought as Jaremon led them to the next testing station. On the sign above it were three squiggly lines over a dog's face.

"What's that the symbol for again?" Kalaya couldn't remember exactly, but she knew the squiggly lines represented smell. She couldn't focus. Part of her mind seemed to have run away after her failed attempt to make a starberry. *I would have earned a chip if he'd asked me to make a marshmallow like he did that other girl.*

Jaremon gave her a critical look. "Bad smells."

"Right, I knew that. I'm so glad you're here to help me."

The tester was a skinny Crimson mage who was dressed like a potato farmer. Next to her was a fat, dirty pig in a cage. *Okay, it must be a Kingdom test in making animals smell better.* There was no one in line, so she went straight up to the booth.

"Pig. Stink," the tester said after Kalaya's mom paid the testing fee.

Kalaya was confused. "Um. It sure does."

"No." The tester sighed. "Change stink."

Oh. Kalaya realized this was going to be easy. *I can do that.* She tightened her lips and focused all her attention on the caged pig. *What takes away stink? Flowers?* She concentrated on projecting the fragrance of a rose in bloom.

A moment later, the pig stink was overpowered by the pleasant aroma of roses. The pig gave her a look that seemed to indicate it was pleased with the smell, but the tester's face didn't change one bit. Kalaya didn't understand. She was pretty sure she'd done a good job.

"Not rose petal," the tester said.

"Was it not good?" Kalaya asked.

"I hate flowers." The tester shook her head. "Change stink."

Okay. Kalaya tried again. This time, she perfumed the pig with freshly ground cinnamon.

"No." The tester was getting irritated. "Change stink!"

I don't understand. Kalaya shot Jaremon a confused look.

"She wants you to make it smell bad," Jaremon whispered.

"No helping, Green mage!"

Oh. She wants me to make something that already smells bad smell—bad? Kalaya ran her fingers through her hair and tried to think of something. *Maybe that dead animal smell that Olan projected last night?* Although she'd never purposefully tried to make a bad smell, she wrung her fingers together and did her best to replicate it. As soon as she started, the pig began to squeal, run in circles, and press his snout against the cage.

"Pig's angry. Good," the farmer mage said. She crouched down, took in three deep breaths, and then said, "You've made carcass," with a huge smile on her face. She popped back up, reached into a bag, and pulled out a bronze chip.

"Oh—Thank you! Thank you!" Kalaya said.

"Dead pig is good, but could be worse," the tester said. "Practice garbage. If smell worse next year, I'll give you better chip."

"This is my daughter's first one. Can we look at it before you put it in?"

"Fine. Globe first," the tester said.

Kalaya's mom took the globe out of her bag and handed it to the tester. After the mage verified that the projected image inside matched Kalaya, she handed them the bronze chip. Kalaya and her mother examined it carefully. It was the size of a large coin and was engraved with three squiggly lines over a dog's face. The round chip of polished metal was heavy in Kalaya's hand. When she rubbed it, she found she liked how its intricate lines felt against her fingers. After they were done examining it, they handed the chip back, and the tester slid it through the slot and into the globe. The chip clinked against the glass so loudly that it sounded like it might break. Kalaya winced.

"It's all right," Jaremon said. "The glass is made by a special process in Region 1. It would take a whole a lot more than that to break it. Good job."

Kalaya looked inside the globe at the little projection of herself next to the prize. *My first chip! It's only bronze, but that's okay. It's a start.*

*   *   *

"Okay, there he is. Perfect," Jaremon said after doing a quick scan of the area. "C'mon, I think you'll like this one."

Jaremon led Kalaya and her mom to the next booth, one with a symbol comprised of three white slashes inside a circle. She knew the circle represented character, but she didn't know what the three slashes were for. After the look Jaremon had given her when she inquired about the bad smell symbol, she didn't dare ask him, even though she thought knowing what every symbol meant was an unrealistic expectation. *There must be hundreds of them.*

The tester stationed at this booth was a middle-aged, fuzzy-bearded Yellow-Violet mage with a monocle over one eye. He watched them intently as they approached. "Is that . . . ? Can it be? Jaremon is-a Twig!"

"Hey, Tego." Jaremon leaned against the booth. "I'd like to introduce you to Kalaya is-a Cloud, the granddaughter of Agatha was-a Cloud—and my girlfriend."

"Magician Agatha's granddaughter, you say? What a treat! Very well met, darling! Tell me, how did you fall in love with this Twig? Did he weep you off your feet?"

"Did he . . . what?" Kalaya wasn't sure how to respond.

"Weep you off your feet. Get it? Weep?"

"Oh. Ha. Yeah. I guess." *Why are all the testers here so weird?*

"Ha ha! Don't pretend like he doesn't bring tears to your sweet little eyes. I'll never forget how he made me bawl like a baby when he tested here two years ago. Takes a special kind of crazy to make a tester cry during a Kingdom test! But seriously, how's the day going?"

"My daughter is doing quite well," Kalaya's mom answered.

"That's great! Way to go!"

Maybe this guy isn't so bad after all. "Thanks. So, what's the test here, exactly?" Kalaya asked.

"Oh, it's a tricky one: character details," Tego said.

"Excellent," Kalaya's mom said as she handed him the fee. "My daughter is quite skilled in Kingdom."

"Is she? Well, then this should be a breeze." Tego took the coins and then motioned to a roped-off space next to him.

"What do I do?" Kalaya asked.

"Project a character in the space within the ropes."

"That's it?" her mother asked.

"For now."

Kalaya looked at the roped-off section, hesitated, then turned to Jaremon and whispered, "Should I make the wallaroo?"

"No, I don't think so," Jaremon whispered back. "It's not ready. What if it comes out blue? I'd make Walter. He's your sure thing."

Ugh. Not that dumb walrus. Kalaya knew that she could make Walter without any difficulty. But he was depressing, and more than anything, she wanted to make her wallaroo dance in the Workshop. *Maybe, if I make her dance here, and I get a gold chip, the Master Magician might hear about it. But . . . Jaremon's probably right.*

Kalaya stepped away from Jaremon and her mother and positioned herself in front of the open space. *All right, what am I going to make?* She struggled until she considered her dad, and what she knew he would advise her to do in this situation. *Okay, I'll do it. It's what I've been training for.*

She squeezed her fingers together, then, ever so gently, started to wiggle them in the air. She trusted, with all the practice from last night, that she would be able to project it fast enough for the test. *Just don't you dare come out blue!* She focused all her mental energy on the character she chose to create. It was like the character was standing right in front of her. Kalaya could see her so clearly in her mind's eye. And then everyone else could see her, too.

The wallaroo that materialized in the space before them was perfect in every way—but it was, of course, completely blue. *Ugh!*

"She likes that color," her mother said to Tego. "Always has."

I hate that color.

"Uh-huh. But, please, remain quiet."

"Oops, sorry. I will," Kalaya's mother said. "Quiet as a mouse. I'm just so excited." She stepped back and started to fidget.

"So, blue, huh?" Tego sounded disappointed as he stepped out of the booth. "Make it smaller, please," he ordered as he approached the wallaroo.

"All right." Taking a deep breath, Kalaya clasped her hands and rubbed them together in a circular motion. As she did, the wallaroo shrank down until it was no higher than Tego's knee.

"Smaller. Smaller!" he shouted.

Kalaya rubbed her hands more, and the wallaroo shrank in half.

"Smaller!"

Really? I've never shrunk a projection this small before. She wanted to speak her concerns, but she knew that she might make things worse if she did. She moved her hands again, and the wallaroo shrank some more.

"Keep going. Smaller. Smaller still. There! Stop! Stop! Stop!" he screeched.

Kalaya pulled her hands apart, and the wallaroo stopped shrinking. She was now as small as a blade of grass.

"Wow! Good work, Kalaya," Jaremon affirmed.

"Quiet please," Tego said.

It was difficult to tell, but it looked like she'd managed to keep its proportions accurate. Tego lay down and pressed his face right against the ground as he examined the wallaroo up close with his monocle. *Wait . . . that's not a monocle. That's a magnifying glass!*

"Alrighty," he stated as he stood back up and dusted himself off. "Now I want you to make the wallaroo as big as the tallest tree in town."

Big means everyone will see it. Kalaya trembled. *"We got yer rabbit!"* the mocking voices of Grog and Grimes rang through her mind. "Oh . . . sure." She pressed her hands together once again and rubbed them, reversing the direction. *Focus. You might be able to salvage a chip out of this if you're careful.*

This time, the wallaroo grew and grew and grew, until she loomed over the buildings. Kalaya didn't dare look behind her, but she knew many people could now see it and were almost certainly criticizing the blue tint.

"Interesting," Tego said while circling the wallaroo.

"Interesting is good, right?" her mother whispered to Jaremon as she shifted her weight from one foot to the other. "That has to be a good thing."

Jaremon raised his finger to his lips and whispered, "Let him focus."

What's taking so long? Kalaya felt sure that the eyes of everyone in the whole region were on her projection. She wanted to dissolve the wallaroo as quickly as possible.

After what felt like several watches, Tego finally stepped away from the wallaroo. "You can dissolve it now."

Kalaya wasted no time. She thrust her hand out and wiped the blue wallaroo out of existence. Tego moved back behind the booth and mumbled some inaudible things to himself as he dug around. "Was it okay?" Kalaya asked nervously.

"You did well," Jaremon said with a smile and a wink.

But what did the tester think? She'd never been more nervous about anything in her entire life.

Tego popped up from behind the booth and stretched out his hand. "Your globe?"

"Oh, right!" Kalaya's mother took the globe out of the bag.

Tego held his closed fist over it, paused, and then slowly opened it to reveal a bright gold chip marked with three white slashes inside a circle.

No way! Kalaya's eyes nearly popped out of her head. "Are you serious?"

"You earned it," Tego said as he tossed the chip at Jaremon, who caught it out of the air and rolled it between his fingers.

"Kalaya is-a Cloud!" Jaremon announced as he held the chip up in the air to show the crowd.

Until now, Kalaya had not fully realized just how large the crowd was that had gathered at the booth. When they saw the gold chip, they let out amazed gasps.

"A gold chip!" one woman exclaimed.

"But her wallaroo was blue," another murmured.

"Keep an eye on that one," a third said.

"Well done." Tego smiled. "I don't give out many of these."

"That's my girl!" Her mom's proud grin spread from ear to ear. "I knew you could do it!"

"I . . ." Kalaya was speechless.

"Careful, now, don't let this get to your head," Tego warned as he took the chip and pushed it through the slot in the globe.

"Thank you," was all she could manage to say. *I did it . . . I earned a gold chip! Maybe I can get four after all!*

As they stepped away from the booth and made their way through the cheering crowd, Kalaya heard Tego mumbling to himself. "Giant blue wallaroo. Huh. There could be something to that . . ."

Tego liked that it was blue. He actually liked it!

"I kept saying you had nothing to worry about, didn't I?" Jaremon said. "One down, three to go."

The Poozers Proclaim
Their Presence

~Kaso~

I do not believe Color should be a requirement for entrance into the Magician's Workshop. I've trained many individuals who are just as talented as any mage or magician. Everyone has worth by the very fact that they are alive. Since we are all born with the ability to project, we should all have equal opportunities to earn a spot in the Workshop.

—Senior Trainer Mage Aaro is-a Tree, "Eye-Opening Interviews and Outlooks," *The Weekly Word*

I thought places like this existed only in Grand Projections. Kaso could hardly believe what he was seeing when he caught his first glimpse of the Island of the Red Tower. Quint had explained that Region 2 was much wealthier than Region 3, but Kaso didn't fully understand what that meant until he saw it with his own eyes.

The Island of the Red Tower glistened in the sunlight like a rare gem, beckoning all to come, see, and experience its wonders. It didn't matter that this island was small. This place had somehow found a way to entice people to flock to it and spend their wealth on the luxuries it offered.

With its high hill, the island loomed before them, like some city of the gods. And there—crowning the very top—was the colossal white stadium where all the glory of Color would be revealed over the next three nights.

"Wow!" Coby gasped when he saw it. "That's mega-mega!"

"Just wait until you see it up close!" Quint said with a wink.

Kaso wanted to say so many things, but seeing the stadium shut his mouth. *Could people actually build something as enormous as that?* It looked like it came from the Old World, lifted out of the sea and set on top of this island by a giant. It was overwhelming. *That's where I'll stand tonight—if everything goes well. That shining white stadium is my destination. Everything about my future will be decided there.*

"I can't wait to see that whole place fill up with your Color," Coby said.

"There's nowhere better in all the islands to have your stars seen," Quint said.

Kaso remained in a state of awestruck wonder as Quint and the others tacked their ship back and forth up the channel toward the island's main harbor.

How can a place like this exist? he thought as the ship pulled into a slip and up to the dock. He couldn't believe he was actually here. He'd left his home at the orphanage; lived, sailed, and trained with this ensemble of poozers for six days; and traveled all this way so he could officially know whether there was a Color in him. The entire time, Kaso had been confident he'd made the right choice.

But now that he had finally arrived, he suddenly realized that he did not belong here. *Why did I believe that I would be accepted by these people and allowed to participate in their Ceremony? I'm an orphan—a Blank—and a foreign one at that. My pockets are empty, and everything here will have a high price.*

"I don't think we should draw any attention to ourselves," Kaso said.

"Tell that to our captain," Treau said as Quint came out of the wheelhouse, transformed.

Quint was now the terrible barbarian known as Migo the Marauder. Projections of gigantic muscles, bold tattoos, and multiple scars covered his body. He wore tattered pants, no shirt, and a thick leather belt. A warrior ready for battle, he looked nothing like himself, and this seemed to please him.

"Tell what to your barbarian captain?" Quint asked.

"Kaso thinks we should slip onto the island unawares."

"Nonsense! Unnecessary and unwarranted attention is the only attention that's ever really necessary! Now stand still so I can make all of you necessarily unnecessary."

"I'm dressed fine as I am," Kaso said.

"We can't have you stand before a puller in your threadbare, now can we? You're a poozer now. It's time for you to pooze."

"Pooze or lose!" shouted Forcemore.

"Pooze or lose!" the others echoed back.

"I'm not a poozer. I'd prefer to enter the festival as myself."

"Sorry to break this to you, Big Brother, but 'myself' is boring, especially if the 'myself' is 'yourself.'"

A small group had already gathered to gawk at Quint's ship, *Castor's Choice*. The large golden schooner with black-and-yellow striped sails was stylized to resemble the grand exploration ship from *The Adventures of Wolly and Wog*.

As Kaso looked up at the big sails, he thought for the hundredth time, *I still would like to know how Quint really came to own a ship like this.* He'd asked Quint about it as soon as he first laid eyes on *Castor's Choice*. In response, Quint spoke at length about how "the islands are full of enigmas!" while saying nothing at all about how he actually came to own such a vessel and maintain its small crew. When Kaso kept pressing, Quint said, "It's a mystery, even to me, and I'm the only one who knows how fortune fortuitously fell upon a humble soul such as myself," and "Poor creatures such as I can't reveal all their secrets, now can they?" When Kaso insisted, Quint insisted back, "You will come into the glorious light in due time—you'll see I'm nothing more than a poor erstwhile orphan, same as you."

The crowd on the dock grew as people gathered to watch Quint cast projections on his crew: Forcemore, Treau, Bankfort, Kaso, and Coby. The audience watched in absolute silence as he fashioned the costumes.

Quint insisted that they all dress as characters from *The Epics of the Cursed* in order to "make the most impressive impression imaginable." When he finished placing the final elements onto Kaso, he exclaimed, "There we go, my fair-hearted squiggler! Now you're a perfectized poozer!" The people watching clapped their approval.

"Kaso! You look just like the Crimson Blade!" Coby exclaimed.

I certainly do. Kaso looked at the costume Quint had projected onto him. His entire body was covered with a kind of red armor that looked like it was made from the scales of a dragon. It was quite a feat, requiring masterful Kingdom skill. Few ever tried to attempt it. Of course, it wasn't nearly as good as what the Workshop had created, but it was nonetheless remarkable.

Treau, who also hoped to stand before the puller tonight, was now dressed as Redden the Hunter. His costume was equally impressive. On his head was the iconic ram's horn helmet, his face was covered by a full red beard, and over his shoulders was draped a thick cloak of fox fur.

Bankfort and Forcemore, while not as glamorous, were dressed as temple watchmen. They each held a shiny white staff in one hand and wore long, flowing robes that pulsated with the Nine Colors.

"Me next!" Coby shouted.

"But of course, my dear Cobalee." Quint spun and faced the young boy. "You're the most important of all."

"I am?"

"Absolutely. We can't show up as characters from *The Epics* without one of us becoming the Lord of Chaos himself!" As Quint spoke, he covered Coby with black armor. Next, he weaved together an intricate replica of the famous black-and-white cloak. Then he fashioned the iconic white mask and projected it over the boy's face. As Coby was much too short—and far too excitable—to appear anything like the real Devos Rektor, Kaso thought the outfit looked ridiculous. But this didn't stop his little brother from being the happiest kid on the island.

"Whoa!" Coby exclaimed as he looked at the black gloves woven with silver strands that appeared on his hands. "I really look like him. I really do."

"Yes indeed, my Lord," Kaso said as he knelt down before his little brother. *He's loving this. Even if things don't go well today, at least this will be a good, lifelong memory for him.*

Kaso smiled at Quint. Although he was far from the ideal travel companion, he'd remained true to his word and caused them no difficulties on their journey. And, like now, he always treated Coby well.

"Ah ha! Most excellent, indeed!" Quint clasped his hands together. "Now our posse of poozers is complete!"

"Indeed it is," an unknown voice called out in response, "but I trust you are more than just some ancient warlord."

Kaso looked over and saw two older, cloaked men staring at them from a neighboring boat. They stood on the deck of a cutter, a vessel much smaller than *Castor's Choice*. The sailboat appeared to be quite old. The paint was peeling, and years of grime had soaked deep into the hull. *No one sails on things that old anymore.* Kaso suspected it was actually a modern boat, stylized with a vintage look. *It must have cost a lot to get such detailed work done.*

"I may look wild and untamed," Quint called back, "but you may place all your fears to rest. I am Migo the Marauder, leader of the free, come to wage a holy war against this very short and very giggly infidel named Rektor."

"Well, I wish you both victory. May you lead civilization to higher ground when the waters rise, and may your small friend grow to wreak havoc upon the Color gods."

"You can be certain we will," Quint called back, "but before I enter the battlefield, may I ask your name?"

"Magpie is-a Boot, at your service. If you ever need a strengthening hand, do not forget my name."

Quint bowed his head and said, "I will not forget the name of Magpie if you tell me what business you have on such a fair island."

"Unfortunately, our mission must remain a mystery. We're here on our own dangerous quest. I bid you farewell in Täv's name—we have much to do before the day is out." Magpie hesitated and clenched his lips together before finishing with, "May you break from your marauding ways, Migo of old, and return home to the love that awaits you there with open arms." And with that, the two men left their boat and disappeared into the crowd on the dock.

That was a good man. He gave strangers a blessing and spoke of Tav the way Auntie does—as if he was real and acts in the islands today. I will remember his name.

After this encounter, Quint could not contain his excitement. He leapt onto the dock and swung his arms about in large triumphant circles. The four poozers, Kaso, and Coby made their way up the hill and passed through the giant gates of Granada Royce, the Island of the Red Tower's main town. The town itself was split down the middle by a wide cobblestone street that wound its way up from the docks to the big hill, on top of which the enormous stadium towered over everything.

Quint had kept quiet until now, but once they began traveling up the hill toward the festivities, he turned to them and exclaimed, "Do you realize who that was?"

Kaso didn't have any idea.

"That was none other than Mage Malroy!"

Kaso and the others continued to stare back at him.

"I'm seeing a lot of blank faces on Blank faces." Quint sighed. "Let me clarify, my squires of squalor. That was Mage Malroy, famous trainer and master of disguise!"

"He said his name was Magpie," Kaso stated.

Quint shook his head as he paced back and forth and said, "Have none of you heard of Mage Malroy?"

"How can he be a master of disguise if you recognized him?" Forcemore asked.

"I've seen him before—lots." Quint said. "We used to be friends."

"Then why didn't he recognize you?" asked Bankfort.

"Because I'm in disguise too!" Quint started shaking his hands in a way that made Kaso think he was trying to project his knowledge into their heads, to force them to understand.

"Meh, your costume was a lot better than his. His only disguise was a basic cloak. Anyone can project one of those," Forcemore said with an indifferent shrug.

"But the cloak wasn't the disguise," Quint exclaimed. "He's not really a decrepit old man."

"No, that's impossible," Bankfort said. "I've seen a lot of people project themselves into old men and none of them looked anything like that."

"Yeah, there's no way that guy was young like us. He looked really old—like ancient, almost-dead old," Forcemore said.

Quint took a deep breath—Kaso assumed it was an attempt

to calm himself down—and then resumed walking toward the town in silence. After a short distance, he stopped again and said to the others, "He is seriously famous, though. Everyone knows about him."

"Yeah, everyone, like all of us," Treau said with a laugh.

"No, I'm sure you know who he is," Quint insisted. "His son was a magician who got kicked out of the Workshop due to conduct of dishonor."

"Due to what?"

Quint looked away and said, "His son cheated to get in."

"Really?" Treau asked. "That guy is Flint was-a Shield's dad? He's really famous."

Quint raised up his hands, triumphant. "Indeed, o' faithful watchkeep! I'm glad the Nine Colors have finally illuminated your eyes."

"Why would you want to be his friend?" Bankfort asked. "What his son did was terrible."

"Yeah. Cheating to get into the Workshop is worse than a restaurant projecting delicious smells and taste onto rotten food," Forcemore insisted.

"No, it's way worse than that," said Treau. "It's like an old hag disguising herself as a beautiful young mage to trick a wealthy magician into marrying her!"

"Gross!" Bankfort made a gagging sound. "I can't believe you just said that out loud. Now I'm not going to be able to get that idea out of my head."

"Good thing you aren't a wealthy magician, then. Ha ha!" Treau laughed.

"No, my squigglers," Quint insisted, "Malroy is a most honorable man."

Treau, Bankfort, and Forcemore could not be convinced, and a vicious debate erupted amongst them. Quint attributed most of the foundations of high poozery to techniques Malroy taught when he was a trainer. The others judged him as a fraud, proven by his son's crimes against the Workshop. *How could such a good man have such a terrible reputation?* Kaso thought as the debate raged on.

As they got higher up the hill, the crowd grew thick and loud. The whole way, Kaso felt everyone's eyes turn to them as they passed; their costumes made them an attraction wherever they went. *At least all the attention seems positive.* It was odd to hear a stranger shout words of approval and to have random passersby burst out in applause. He didn't know what to do when people came up and started talking to him as if he were the actual Crimson Blade, so most of the time he tried to ignore them and not say anything. The crowd seemed to like this, as this cold reaction fit with their understanding of the character.

But when one little boy came over and asked for his projectograph, Kaso felt he had to say something. "I'm sorry, I can't. I'm not the real Crimson Blade, you know."

Coby, however, loved the attention. "Isn't this amazing?"

"It's sure something," Kaso responded.

"It's what your whole life is going to be like after you become a magician." Quint flashed a toothy grin at some kids.

A life like this would be awful. Kaso was relieved to find that the attention did not last. As they got near the top of the hill, the wonders of the town around them increased. There was much more to look at, so people paid less attention to them. *Fame really is fickle and fleeting*, Kaso judged inside his head.

"Look at that!" Coby pointed at a four-headed giraffe. When it started singing in perfect four-part harmony, everyone in the crowd turned their attention to it. As soon as the giraffe finished its song, the crowd burst into cheers and demanded a gold chip for the older lady who had projected it.

Crowds here sure do have a short attention span. Kaso had heard rumors of the fantastic projections on this island, but since he'd spent so much of his life poor or in the orphanage, he hadn't traveled much. Now that he was here, he realized that he'd never be able to take it all in. *I could spend weeks here and not see everything.* He wanted to stop and take good long looks at the exotic neighborhoods, unique stores, and various restaurants, but Quint kept them moving forward.

When they crested the hill, Kaso had to stop.

Across from him, up on a further, higher hill, was the stadium. It loomed over the town of Granada Royce with a presence that was both beautiful and frightening. Giant marble columns lined its long, arched colonnades. Stout towers rose up out of the massive stone buttresses and were topped with elegant spires that seemed to pierce the heavens.

That's where it's going to happen. Tonight, I'll know.

The Poozers Prove Their Prowess

~Kaso~

The work done in the Magician's Workshop is about so much more than entertainment. Think. There can only be two hundred eighty-eight magicians. Do you believe for a moment that number is random? Not many know this, but two hundred eighty-eight is the number of actual Color gods who created the universe. Each active magician is a reflection of one of them. What else are magicians but glorious numbers in the grand cosmos of existence? Add them all together, and like the Color gods before them, they create a Grand Projected universe every year.

—Mistress Mazannda is-a Moon, *Spooky Signs in Wicked Times*

What a prodigal place, Kaso thought as they made their way through the crowds and toward the registration tent. Quint had told him that very few people actually lived on the Island of the Red Tower and had described it as a deserted wasteland most of the year. Kaso struggled to believe this as he looked around at all the shops packed with customers.

It sure looks like the entire population of Region 2 has gathered here. If that's true, then all the other islands in the region must be deserted right now. He tried to picture this place after the Festival, when everyone went home. *It doesn't seem right for a whole island to sit empty when there are so many orphans without a place to live.*

Although Granada Royce had many stores and restaurants to serve as distractions along the way, Kaso's eyes kept inspecting the simple wooden testing booths that had been set up along the cobblestone streets. There were several hundred of them scattered around Granada Royce, and each had a unique symbol etched across the top that identified the type of test performed there. Kaso scanned the lines of people at the booths, young and old, waiting to have their projections graded by the mage inside.

"There are far more older people testing here than I would have expected," Kaso observed. *Most of them are commoners.*

"Rather wearisome for them, isn't it? It may take a poor, pitiful, non-poozerific person years to earn all the horrific, glorific chips necessary to be proclaimed worthy," Quint said and then projected to Kaso, "Isn't it a tremendous relief that mages like you and me don't have to put up with all the tedious restrictions placed upon commoners before they're allowed to proudly project publicly in the presence of the poor public?"

"I'm not a mage," Kaso answered out loud.

"You are. Just not yet."

How can he be so certain? No one can know for sure.

"Yeah!" Coby exclaimed as he danced around Kaso. "You are. And as soon as just one of these testers experiences the warmth you can make, everyone will know you've got Color inside!"

"Right he is, Big Brother. Gold chips will bury you like the Flood waters on our ancient homeland."

Kaso didn't know how to take this. Should he laugh or be offended? In the six days he'd spent with Quint, Kaso had grown to like him. He still didn't trust him—plenty of mystery remained about the real Quint—but even though there was a lot Kaso wasn't certain about, one thing was clear: Quint wasn't cruel or mean-spirited.

"Nothing at all will happen unless they allow me to register,"

Kaso reminded him. "I'd like you to take me there."

"At your service, oh humble apprentice," Quint said, referring to the fact that the Crimson Blade was a servant and apprentice to Devos Rektor.

"I don't understand something," Coby said.

"And what might that be, oh dreaded Lord of Chaos?"

"You said that gold chips would rain on Kaso. But I thought we came here for the Color Ceremony," Coby said as they passed by a booth where a teenage girl had just received a gold chip for projecting a giant wallaroo.

Impressive. It looks just like the one from The Roo and the Rower. *Odd color choice, though.* Kaso looked at the girl who had made it. *She has sad eyes. Uncertain about her future, probably. I bet that's why she made it blue.*

"We did. But chips are still important," Treau explained. "They're a way to grade someone's skill with projections."

"So how many chips does Kaso need to get a Color?"

"Zero all the way to the blessed infinity of the heavens," Quint chimed in.

"What?" Coby looked confused.

Come on, you understand this. "The number of chips a person gets doesn't seem to have any connection to having a Color," Kaso explained.

"If it did, then my dear, sweet Bankfort would be blessed with a Color as fine as my own," Quint said. Bankfort said nothing, but the look on his face indicated he was not pleased with Quint's comment.

"Well, that's stupid," Coby said. "What's the point of all these tests then?"

"Auntie taught us about this," Kaso reminded.

"Pretend you wanted a job doing something with projections," Bankfort said. "Well, the guilds make it impossible for you to do it, unless you have the right credentials and do every little thing they say."

That's not true. Lots of people work outside of a guild. Father did.

"Oh, I remember!" Coby said, "You have to pass a lot of tests to get into a guild, right?"

"Yes, and they're all corrupt," Bankfort replied.

"No they're not," Kaso said.

"Of course they are. They're strangling O'Ceea. To do anything, you have to be certified by a guild."

"That's not true either," Kaso said, frustrated.

"Coby," Bankfort said, ignoring Kaso, "before you can be admitted into a guild you have to earn chips in all the categories that the guild deems necessary. Some people come here every year of their life trying to earn all the chips they need to get into a specific guild. The pressure to get in can be so great, it causes people to do horrible things. That's why I joined Quint after I was void. I wasn't about to waste my life trying to win chips. The community of poozers is the only honorable guild."

"Don't listen to him, Coby," Kaso cautioned. "Poozing isn't a real guild."

Coby looked back and forth between Kaso and Bankfort, then asked, "Does every job making projections require you to be in a guild?"

"Most of them," Bankfort said at the same time that Kaso said, "No, there are a lot that don't."

"What about the Magician's Workshop?" Coby asked. "What guild is it a part of?"

"The Workshop is its own kind of guild," Kaso said, "but you can't get into it with chips. You need to have a Color and get a high enough score in the Championships."

"And don't forget to vanquish all your foes, now," Quint added.

Coby frowned. "Hmm. I don't like it. If someone is

really, really good at projections—like really, really good—and earns lots and lots of gold chips and gets a really high score in the competitions, they should still be allowed to get into the Workshop. It shouldn't matter if they have a Color in them."

He's worried I'm going to be found void, Kaso realized. "Unfortunately, that's not the way the islands work."

Treau broke his silence and said with passion, "There are lots of people who want things to be different, though."

"Color, no Color," Quint droned. "Come on! Let's start a revolution. Right now. I'm dressed for it. Ahrra, ha, ra!" he growled.

"Don't joke. There are plenty of commoners who are upset about it," Treau said.

"And plenty of IIRP who would love to stop us," Bankfort said, pointing to an Inter-Island Regional Patrol officer standing guard nearby.

Coby started trembling. "Captain Quint, do you think Kaso will get a Color?"

"Cobalicious," Quint said, "Violet courses through his veins like pure namra."

Did he just compare me to the most disgusting root on the planet? "But I have to register first. So let's go."

Quint seemed to know everything about this place. He led them swiftly through the streets until they came at last to a large white tent that housed the registration booths.

When they arrived at the front of the long, slow-moving line, the big-nosed woman behind the desk eyed Kaso's red dragon-scale armor and Treau's horned helmet with suspicion. "Name?" she droned.

Quint, crouching behind Kaso, popped his head up and said, "Why, this is the Crimson Blade and Redden the Hunter, can't you tell?" He then ducked back down.

The woman stared blankly at them.

"I'm Kaso is-a Blank." He shifted his feet as he spoke. *This is it. This is the moment.*

"And I'm Treau is-a Blank."

"Who's your sponsor?"

"Sponsor?" Treau asked.

"We're orphans," Kaso explained.

The woman shook her head in disapproval. "Blanks are no longer allowed to test or register for the Color Ceremony without a sponsor."

Quint jumped up, pushed Kaso and Treau aside, and faced the woman. "What? Since when?"

"Rules just changed."

"No! That's wrong!" he shouted.

"Next," the woman said.

Quint held his hand up in the air. "I apologize. You must understand, there is a bit of a barbarian in me. When you say the rules changed, what meaning do you intend to bestow upon us?"

"I mean exactly what I said," the woman grumbled. "You and your pretentious poozers are no longer welcome to test in Region 2. You can inquire about the rules in Region 5, if you so desire."

It's over. Kaso knew that all the Festivals and Color Ceremonies in Region 5 were completed for the year. *Unless I can manage to get all the way there next year, I'll have to wait until I'm nineteen.*

"If you'll allow me one more moment of your precious time, my faithful Queen." As Quint spoke, he leaned forward and kissed his own fingers. All at once, a sparkling red rose with white-tipped petals and an enchanting scent appeared in his hand. It was impressive, but not to this woman. "You see," he continued, "my dear collarless compatriots, Kaso and Treau, are poor, helpless orphans from Region 5. Twins—but not the identical kind."

What's Quint up to now?

"The impoverishment on their island was a bone-sucking curse. It cut their father off from the magic, then their brothers, and finally their mother. But before she died and left these two boys all alone, she cried out, 'My beloved sons, you will become great magicians one day. The prophecy of Violet and Blue spoken over you will come true. You will join the Workshop. You will be the final two members of the two hundred eighty-eight, and with all the holy sparks Tav used to create O'Ceea gathered together, all the effects of the Flood will be undone. The waters of judgment will drain away, the islands will be no more, and all of humanity will be set free.'

"Then their precious mother paused, and with her dying breath, she said, 'But, you must leave this region. Do not be tempted to test here. Only evil will come if your Colors are exposed in this wicked, backward place. I love you. Do not fail me. Do not fail the islands.' She closed her weary eyes and all the magic left her. That was three years ago, and now they're here, eligible to test. Can you deny them their chance? Can you deny every citizen of the islands their right to salvation?"

The woman looked straight into his eyes and scrutinized them.

She's trying to figure him out. Good luck.

"Next."

"But—but their poor mother," Quint said.

The woman narrowed her eyes. "Rules are rules. Next."

Quint cleared his throat, then said in a deeper, more fervent tone, "These are orphans, after all. I'm certain a fine, upstanding mage such as yourself would relish the opportunity to be the blessed hands and feet of Tav. Will you heed his voice and make an exception?"

The woman did not blink and continued to stare straight at him.

Quint looked away before he tried again. "See my collar?" He waved his finger near his neck and revealed the Yellow fabric hidden under his barbarian projection. "I myself am a Yellow mage. I will be their sponsor."

"Unless you can prove you are a registered member of a clan of Region 2, Masters Kaso and Treau will be unable to test today. Now, if you'll step aside, there are others waiting."

Coby rushed forward and slammed his fists down against the desk. "I am the fearful Lord Devos, and I command you to allow my brother to stand before the puller tonight!"

Before Coby could make a bigger fool of them, Kaso grabbed his little brother, said, "Thank you, Mage," and dragged him away.

Coby was kicking and screaming at the top of his lungs. "It's not fair!"

"You heard her," Kaso said. "That's the rule. No point fighting about it."

Treau kicked the ground. "Stupid Region 2. Let's get out of here."

All of them except Quint left the tent. When they were outside, Kaso turned to Treau and said, "What was that all about? The holy sparks of Tav? The two hundred eighty-eight? All humanity being saved?"

"Who knows. But I have few fancy words of my own I'd like to give him," Treau said.

"But . . . we're not brothers from Region 5. Everything in that story was a lie. What was he doing?"

"I don't think anyone understands Quint," Forcemore responded.

"Especially the registration lady," Bankfort laughed.

Kaso scanned the crowd for mages. *There's still one other way. I need to find a sponsor.*

"Ah, there you are!" Quint exclaimed as he stepped out of the tent and joined them on the street.

As soon as Treau spotted him, he swung his fist. "You told me I would get my Color here!" Treau growled as Quint stumbled back from the force of the projected punch.

Quint took a few heartbeats to recover. "Indeed I did, and indeed you shall." He flashed a grin at his gang. "True brothers, hear me! A minor setback is no cause to jump ship."

Treau stepped close to Quint and stared at him with fury in his eyes. "A minor setback?" He punched Quint again in the stomach, but this time he used his actual fist.

Coby gasped as Quint bent over in pain, then fell.

At the same moment, Kaso spotted a young Green mage exiting the registration tent. Without wasting a moment, he went right up to him and said, "Excuse me, I'm an orphan from Region 3 in need of a sponsor in order to be allowed to stand before a puller. Would you be willing to vouch for my good character?"

The Green mage did not stop or even appear to hear his words. *Huh. This might be more difficult than I expected.*

When Kaso returned to the others, Bankfort was helping Quint stand. Although he'd just been knocked down, Quint maintained a look of confidence as he said, "Aye, Redden the Hunter never trusted Migo, did he? Rivals to the end, wasn't it? We're living *The Epics* at last." Quint stood up straight and faced Treau. "But when you hold the truth in your hand, nothing in life can be more than a minor setback. For what is registration, but the giving of . . . a globe?" Quint projected a glass testing buoy into his upraised hand.

"Whoa!" Coby and Forcemore both exclaimed.

"One of your illusions isn't going to work here, Captain Quink!" Treau said.

"Oh my fragile heart! You had to remind me of that precious

orphan girl, my favorite squiggler. What was her name, Big Brother?"

"Macea."

"Indeed. Macea, my love. Things would have worked out so differently if she had joined us."

"Get off it, Quint," Treau said. "You promised me I could test. We could have gone to Region 5 earlier. We would have had time if you hadn't insisted we go to the Island of the First Watch. Now I have to wait a whole year."

"I admit I made a grievous error. But I promise—I'll make it up to you. Just wait. Don't leave this spot. I will return," Quint said, and he sprinted away.

The entire Yellow watch passed before Quint returned. In that time, Kaso tried—without success—to find a mage who would be his sponsor. Treau, Bankfort, and Forcemore sat in the shade of a tree and grumbled about their predicament.

When Quint reappeared, it was as if from nowhere. "We may be on land, but I'm still the captain of our destiny," he declared.

"What have you been doing? You should have told us you were going to be gone so long," Bankfort grumbled.

"Yeah," agreed Forcemore. "I've been really hungry."

"Some miracles take a wee more heartbeats than others," Quint said as he held up two yellow glass testing buoys.

"You did it! You really did it!" Treau said.

"I did, and now it's time to go kersplunking. Are you ready, boys?"

Kaso took a step toward him and looked at the globes with suspicion. "Where did you get those? Did you steal them?"

Quint put his barbarian hand to his chest and said, "Mercy, you've given my poor heart the death quakes at the very whisper of a stain upon my incorruptible nature."

"Come on, Quint, are they stolen or not?" Kaso asked.

"Stolen is such a primitive word. I'm a poozer, not a prowler!"

"It will work, right? I mean, they have the right security features?" Treau asked.

"Must I verbalize all my doings? Is there no love of mystery left in the islands? Behold, look into your wondrous globes." He handed the globes to them, and sure enough, when they looked closely, they saw little projections of themselves inside. "And look, you even have a clan symbol."

Kaso saw, moving on the surface of the glass, a symbol of a blue, crashing wave. He didn't recognize it, but that didn't surprise him as it was obviously a Region 2 clan. *This is bad. I need to break away from them if I'm going to find a sponsor.*

"Whoa, that's our symbol? It's so mega!" Coby clapped his hands.

"Indeed it is! Now, let's begin our conquest!" Quint said.

"No. I'm not going to cheat," Kaso stated. He didn't know what the rules were in Region 2, but in Region 3, those caught cheating were not allowed to test for chips again, and to make sure they learned their lesson, they were sent to the Island of the Howling Jackals for a long, long time.

"You know, Big Brother, I've always admired your admiration for truth-ology. So I humbly suggest you might perchance be looking out the porthole of life sideways," Quint said. "There will be no cheating. No squigglers will be shooting off projections for you. The plethora of chips that will fill your precious globe will be acquired—"

"Quint," Kaso interrupted, "I appreciate all you have done for me. I don't know how I would have gotten here without you. But right now, I need to find a sponsor."

"You have a sponsor, Big Brother, from the Wave clan. I foresaw that calamity might arise to thwart our path to glory. So long before we reached these illustrious shores, I found it prudent to acquire some globes. The Waves are a backwater clan with more branches than they can account for."

"How does this help us?" Treau asked.

"The backwater branches of some Waves have lost their faith in their Colored comrades. They're isolated and rarely come here, and this presents us with this fine opportunity to pooze our way into the Ceremony as some of their kin."

Kaso saw flashes of disdain on Quint's face as he spoke. *I bet he's from the Wave clan. I wonder what caused him to separate from them?*

"But we aren't really Waves. What if we're caught?" Coby asked.

Quint waved his hand like he was dissolving a bad projection. "Improbable."

"But it's highly illegal to buy or sell globes," Kaso said. "If you bought these ahead of time, how did you know what color glass they would be using today? No one outside the Workshop knows that sort of thing until the first day of the Festival."

"Oh, my treasured Big Brother of little faith. Haven't you by now realized I have friends in high places? Trust me, they are authentic globes. Can't you see, I'm wearing a sponsor's collar." He pointed to his neck, where he now wore the ceremonial collar given to those who had handed over their own in exchange for their sponsored child's globe.

"I'll be right back," Kaso said. He turned and, taking his globe, headed for the registration tent.

"Wait, where are you going?" Quint called after him.

"If this is legitimate, I'm sure you'll have no problem with me asking the IIRP to validate it." *How he responds to this will tell me everything.*

"You know, you're right. I may have presented our predicament with a bit more optimism than is warranted."

Knew it. "These are stolen, aren't they?"

"I prefer to look at things from a more Yellow point of view," Quint said. "I suppose it's just my nature, but I'm inclined to promote the idea that I'm their current owner."

"That's good enough for me," Treau said.

Kaso knew he couldn't be part of this. "Treau, you can do whatever you like, but Coby and I are going to go look for a sponsor."

"It's honorable of you, Big Brother. I don't envy your future and I fear your dreams may be vanquished. It's no small thing to sponsor one such as yourself! The cost is higher than any sane mage will be willing to count!"

"He just needs a sponsor for the day," Coby said.

"Oh, no, no, no, my dear friends. Sponsorship is akin to adoption and thusly far beyond the reach of such trifles. Your good and most noble sponsor must take your Blank-ness and replace it with their name, and that means they will bear the burden and be responsible for all your dumb-witted deeds and dilemmas until your self-righteous clock turns nineteen—or they find a way to dump you on someone else."

"That long?" *I had no idea.*

"Indeed, I'm afraid so. With such short notice, you'll have more luck finding a Cee'dragon in the waters of the Crystal Lake than you will a sponsor who'll take in a foreigner like yourself," Quint exclaimed. "Come with us, and that Violet will be yours tonight!"

Although this new information made Kaso realize that finding a sponsor would be infinitely more difficult than he had thought, he was resolved not to cheat. "Come on, Coby." He turned away from Quint.

"All right, so be it. I wish you well as you test your luck on the stormy seas of human generosity!" Quint's voice faded into the noise of the crowd as Kaso moved away.

The IIRP

~Kaso~

Tav chose to be born into an age when Dy'Mageio were at the height of their power. They worshiped the Color gods and believed projections were for only a small select few whom they deemed worthy. But Tav said that the Color gods were created to serve us, to be the gems that scatter his light throughout O'Ceea and upon every person, so that all would have the means to project. Tav proclaimed that projections were for everyone, and he died as a result.

—Historian Magician Michelle was-a Rain, *The Story of Tav*

"I'm sorry, you look honest enough, but my clan doesn't allow us to sponsor foreigners. Now, please excuse me while I go eat." Kaso and Coby stood still as the Violet mage walked away from them and over to his family seated at a nearby table.

They were standing on the street, just outside a restaurant that had a large patio. It seemed like a desirable place to eat. It was full of flowers and sky lanterns, delicious smells, and laughing, smiling faces. There was even a band of highly skilled mages who stood on a little stage and cast relaxing music into the air. The two dozen dining tables on the patio were completely full and a line of people waited to get a seat. Kaso thought this was unusual for the Cyan watch, which was normally the quietest time of the day.

The Green watch had passed and Kaso still hadn't found anyone with even the slightest interest in helping him. *We don't belong here. We shouldn't have even come.*

"Aw, this isn't working, Big Brother," Coby whined.

"Please don't call me that," Kaso said.

"Okay, but what are we going to do?"

"Nothing."

"Nothing?" Coby scrunched up his face. "I don't understand. When things aren't working, you always know how to fix it."

"Not this time, Coby," Kaso admitted. "I've talked to—what—over thirty mages?"

Kaso stood next to the patio wearing nothing but his threadbare. He had dissolved the costume of the Crimson Blade as soon as they left Quint because he believed it would be unlikely to find anyone comfortable sponsoring someone hidden under scales of red armor. He wanted to dissolve Coby's costume, too, but there was no way to separate him from his imagined identity as Lord Devos without causing him to break out into a fit of tears.

"You can ask some more, can't you?" Coby asked. "We just need to find one mage who'll say yes."

No one is going to sponsor a foreigner. "No, Coby. There's nothing left to do."

"That's not true. We can find Quint and you can use the globe he got you."

Kaso shushed him. "I'm not going to use a stolen globe," he whispered. "Even if there were a guarantee we wouldn't get caught."

"But there has to be a way. You always figure things out. What about Tav? Maybe we should pray to him. Auntie taught us that he's real and he acts in the islands today. Remember? She always says that, and Auntie doesn't lie."

"Oh Coby, I want that to be true, but I just don't know how it can be. I don't see how some guy who died hundreds of years ago can do anything to help us now. We've done everything we can. It's time to let go."

"I know what that means. It means you're g-g-giving up," Coby stuttered. He was on the verge of crying. "I don't want it to be over! I want you to get your Color—tonight! Then we'll be with Dad again soon."

"Oh, Coby." Kaso pressed his lips together and sighed deeply as he saw just how much pain Coby was still enduring. *If only revealing a Color would make all that go away. But who in all of O'Ceea would want to sponsor me—an orphan with a little brother to take care of?* Kaso watched as the Violet mage he'd talked to earlier started eating with his family.

"Hey, I know what your problem is! You need to eat something!" Coby said after he followed Kaso's eyes to the mage's family. "We haven't had anything since those seaweed cakes this morning. I've been starving, but I haven't complained—not even once. But maybe some food will help you think of a new plan."

"We don't have any gryns, Coby, and even if we did, we certainly couldn't afford to eat here."

"I know. We can head down to *Castor's Choice* and find something to eat," Coby said. "I bet Quint and the others are back, taking a nap."

"I don't think it's wise for us to spend too much time with them," Kaso said under his breath after seeing a patrol officer who was seated two tables away. He didn't remember seeing this man before. *Did he just sit down?* Although the man's back was turned to them, Kaso had the strong sense he was observing them. *There's nothing to be worried about. Neither of us has done anything wrong*, Kaso tried to reassure himself, but it didn't work.

It was impossible to ignore this man. He wore the distinctive uniform of the IIRP: a crimson-colored chainmail shirt over a deep indigo tunic suit. *Was he here when we were talking about the globes?*

Kaso thought about walking away, but then hesitated. There was something about this officer that caused him to take a closer look. *There's something odd about him. What is it?* Kaso stared intently at the man.

And then Kaso realized what was so strange. *He doesn't have a Color collar.* The fabric tied around the neck of the officer was black. It did display a star pattern, however, which indicated that he had reached the highest privilege level available for commoners. Most of the IIRP were mages. Kaso had never seen a non-mage officer before. *I guess they must have sent every rank of officer here to patrol the Festival.*

But no, there was something else unusual about him. Kaso took a closer look and noticed that instead of wearing a thick belt, heavy-laden with a wide assortment of weapons, as was common for IIRP, this officer wore a thin belt that held only a single item: a strange-looking baton.

"Aw, Kaso! If we're not going to eat, why are we just standing here doing nothing?" Coby asked. "Smelling all this food has made me really, really hungry."

Kaso looked at the wide variety of grilled, lettuce-wrapped meats and seasoned rice those seated at the tables were eating. *I'm hungry too, Coby, but there's nothing we can do.* "You're right. We don't belong here. Let's get going."

As soon as Kaso spoke these words, the IIRP officer placed his hand on the handle of his baton, turned, and said to them, "Excuse me—you two boys—can you both come over here please?"

Coby looked up at his brother. Kaso felt a surge of adrenaline and his heart started beating furiously. *We haven't done anything wrong,* he said to himself as he obeyed the officer's call and stepped through the gate onto the patio. Kaso could feel the attention of several of the diners turn to them. They grew quiet, as if to hear what the officer would say.

"A fine Cyan watch, wouldn't you agree?" the officer said as soon as they were next to him.

Kaso looked down at the officer's face and immediately saw that there was something else unusual about him. *He's blind!* A thick, white film covered the brown of his eyes, almost like a cloud. "Yes, Officer," Kaso replied and bowed his head respectfully. *How could a blind man work for the IIRP?*

"Would you be able to do me a favor?" the officer asked as he took his hand off his baton and began untying his coin pouch. "Could you count out a hundred and eighty gryns for me?"

Kaso was stunned; he didn't know what to do when the officer held out the pouch full of coins.

"The fifty gryn coin is remarkably similar to a lyke, if you can't see the color," the officer said with a smile.

Is this some kind of trick? Kaso wondered, but he felt it would be unwise to refuse, so he said, "Sure. It would be my pleasure." He took the bag and carefully counted out the correct amount. "Here's your pouch back," Kaso said as he placed it back in the officer's hand.

The officer began retying it, but when Kaso went to give him the handful of coins, the officer said, "Could you take that into the restaurant? I need to pay for my order. And could you also take in my flask and have them refill it with pako juice? It's been a long morning."

"Yes, Officer," Kaso said, and then he and Coby went into the restaurant. Kaso carefully thought through his every move. *There's no reason he needs us to do this. He could just as easily given the waiter his money. This has to be some kind of a test—that is, assuming he really is IIRP and not someone trying to pull a scam.*

"Whoa," Coby said when they were far enough away to not be heard. "A hundred and eighty gryns for a single meal? Captain Quint wasn't lying when he said people are really rich here."

Kaso paid one of the waiters, had the flask filled, and returned to the officer as quickly as he could. "I've done as you've instructed," he said as he returned the flask. "May we go now?"

"Oh, yes, you're certainly free to go wherever you please. You're not in any trouble, at least not with me—are you?"

"No, Officer."

"Well, that's certainly good news. Why don't you both have a seat, then. That way you can keep me company. I'd certainly love to hear you tell me some stories about your life in Region 3."

What? How could he possibly know that?

"You are from Region 3, right?" the man continued. He asked it in a way that said he knew the answer.

"Yes, Officer."

"Then take a seat. I love meeting people from different parts of the islands. And technically I'm a detective, not an officer."

Kaso did not feel comfortable with the idea of sitting in this fancy restaurant and watching the detective eat his expensive meal— *but do we have a choice?* He and Coby reluctantly sat down.

The conversation felt awkward and shallow, and even though the detective seemed to be nice enough, Kaso couldn't shake the idea they were caught in some trap. *I need to find a way to get us out of this.* It didn't help that Coby was—of course—sharing far more than he ought to.

"It was nice to meet you, Master Detective," Kaso said after what felt like an appropriate amount of time to be considered polite. "But my brother and I really ought to get going. There's lots of the Festival we haven't seen."

"Going so soon? But Anteen is just arriving with our meals. Please stay. I've already paid for them, after all—or actually, I suppose you have."

What? Kaso looked up and saw a waiter approaching them, carrying three plates of food. *How did he know he was coming?*

And wait. The money we paid was for our meal?

Anteen, the waiter, placed three steaming plates of chicken pineapple fried rice in front of them, saying, "I trust these will be to your liking, Detective."

So he really is IIRP. Some of Kaso's fears eased. Still, he felt some uncertainty about what was going on. He said, "I'm sorry, Master Detective, but I'm afraid we must leave. We can't pay for these meals."

"Of course you can't. That's why I bought them for you," the detective said. "It's my gift. Please consider it my way of welcoming you to our region."

Kaso wasn't sure what to make of this, but now that the food was in front of him—and the delicious fragrance of juicy chicken, cooked pineapple, and creamy coconut milk wafted up to him—he realized just how hungry he actually was.

Kaso asked the detective again if he was absolutely certain. He was, so Kaso agreed to stay. It was a delicious meal and the two brothers were thankful for every bite. But more than the rich, enticing flavors embedded in the food, they enjoyed the detective. *This is a kind, good man*, Kaso concluded, and the rest of his unease started to fade.

They talked for quite a while about what it was like growing up in Region 3, how they came to be orphans, and how thankful they were to have found a place in one of the few good orphanages in their region. The detective listened and seemed quite interested in their story, but Kaso was thankful that he didn't press them with any questions about their father. He did, however, take great interest in how they'd come to be at the Festival, so Kaso shared his reasons, being careful not to say anything specific about Quint or the others.

Once they'd finished their meal, and after Anteen had served them each a mug of hot taro milk tea and a complimentary bowl of three chocolate-flavored almonds, the detective stood up and said, "Thank you for keeping me company. As much as I'd like to spend more time with you, I must get moving. There are a few things that need to be done before I head over to the Ceremony."

Kaso looked up to the nearby red stone communication tower and saw a single beam of Cyan light shining up into the sky. *It'll be Blue soon. I didn't realize how much time had passed.*

"Don't lose hope," the detective continued. "It really is a shame they changed the rules so abruptly—allowing foreign orphans to test was something I admired about this region—but I encourage you to keep looking for a sponsor. There are many good people in Region 2."

"Thank you." Kaso bowed his head. "You've shown me that."

A big smile spread across the detective's face. "I'm glad to have been able to do something to cheer your spirits. Don't give up, Kaso. And I probably shouldn't say something like this while wearing my uniform, but . . . well, your brother was right to say, 'Tav is real and acts in the islands today.'"

This took Kaso by surprise. *Oh! So he did overhear us earlier. Does he know about the stolen globes? Was all this just his way of trying to get information out of us?* Kaso's uneasiness returned. *No, stop. This detective has shown us great kindness, and it was genuine.*

Kaso breathed deeply and allowed his hard, self-protective shell to soften. *This is a good man. He's not trying to trick or trap us.* His uneasiness faded.

"Master Detective," Coby asked, "do you believe Tav is really real?" Instead of answering, the detective took out his strange-looking baton. Coby tensed and quickly said, "I'm sorry, Master, please don't—"

"Young Coby, you've done nothing wrong, so you have nothing to fear from me," the detective said and touched his forefinger to his chest. In an instant his IIRP uniform disappeared. There was a brief glimmer of his threadbare, and then he was dressed in plain, ordinary clothes. He then pulled his baton apart and extended it out until it was a long stick. "It's a weapon and a blind person's cane. Pretty mega, right?"

He looks nothing like a detective. Now I know why they hired him, Kaso determined. *Who'd expect a blind person to be a detective for the IIRP?*

"The words you said to your brother struck me when I heard them," he said. "My mother used to say the same thing to me—the exact same phrase. It gave me a lot of hope when I was young, but I don't know what I actually think about it anymore. I've experienced so much that seems to contradict that idea, yet I still want it to be true.

"I suspect that's why I love meeting people who still do believe it and do their best to live like it's true. I think it gives me hope for the future of our islands," he said. "So, Coby, go and live your life in a way that can help a blind detective see that Tav really is real. Okay?"

Coby jumped up and exclaimed, "Okay!"

Kaso watched as the detective walked away—tapping his stick in front of him as he went—and was filled with great hope. He was no closer to finding a sponsor, yet somehow he knew deep in his gut that everything was going to work out. *It was no accident that we met this man.*

"What's wrong?" Coby asked as they left the table. "You look like you're thinking about something."

"I am," Kaso answered.

"What is it? Didn't you like the detective?"

"I liked him very much," Kaso said, and he let out a deep, contented sigh. "I'm thinking that I don't need to worry about finding a sponsor anymore. Everything is going to work out okay."

"You really think so?"

"Yes," Kaso said. "Now, let's go find Quint."

Coby was delighted. "Oh good! So we're going to use the globe he got you?"

"No."

"But you just said . . . I don't understand." Coby's shoulders drooped.

Kaso smiled. "We're going to find Quint so I can do what I should have done in the first place—destroy that image of me in the globe."

"But why?" Coby asked. "If you do that, you won't be able to use it."

"Exactly."

Coby looked down at his toes and his voice trembled slightly as he said, "So . . . you're giving up?"

"No, Coby. I'm trusting that what Auntie said is true. I'm trusting that Tav is real and will help us. I can't tell you exactly how that's going to happen, but all that storminess I've been feeling is gone. It's like I'm swimming under a calm, graceful Cyan sea and floating around me as far as I can see are stars, all lit up. For us."

Coby was silent for a long time before he looked up at his brother. Then, with a big smile, he said, "Cyan stars?! Wow! I knew it! I knew it!"

"You knew what?"

"Tav wants my big brother to become a magician."

"He does?"

"Of course. You wait and see. Someone's going to sponsor you, and then you'll get a Color tonight. Probably two Colors! Violet and Cyan! Then it won't be long before you'll become a magician. It's all going to happen."

"I don't know about all that." Kaso paused, took in a deep

breath, and exhaled as he said, "But I do know we're going to be okay."

"Yeah?" Coby asked. "You're not just saying that? You really, really mean it, right?"

"Yes, Coby, I do," Kaso said. He couldn't really explain it, but a peace filled his soul like nothing he'd ever felt before. There was a strong and unwavering certainty in him now, and he was fully confident that whatever was in store for them next, it would be—above all else—good.

END OF VOLUME ONE

The story of *The Magician's Workshop*
continues in Volume Two

In which:

It's revealed who will be marked by a Color and who will be found void.
Layauna is attacked at Nosy's and later discovers a Whoosh secret.
Weston is transformed into the fast-as-lightning Red Racer.
Luge continues his life unaffected by all this nonsense.
Quint prepares Kaso for a perilous predicament.
Jaremon comes to a painful realization.
Kalaya's blue wallaroo dances.
Kai and Talia say goodbye.

Available now.

www.oceea.com

Region 2

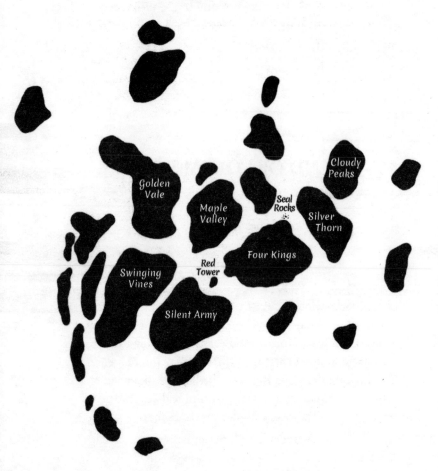

Golden
Vale

Maple
Valley

Cloudy
Peaks

Seal
Rocks

Silver
Thorn

Four Kings

Red
Tower

Swinging
Vines

Silent Army